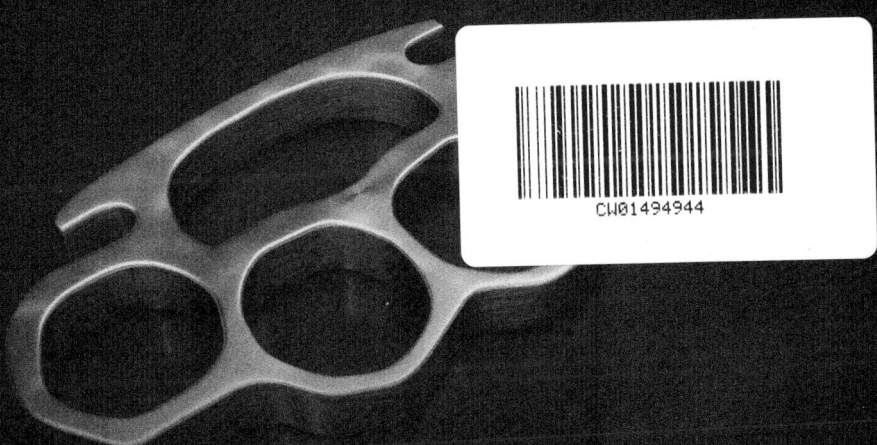

SKIRT

RUTHLESS KINGS MC
BOOK FIVE

K.L. SAVAGE

ISBN: 978-1-95200-11-4
LIBRARY OF CONGRESS CONTROL: 2020912405

PHOTOGRAPHY BY WANDER AGUIAR PHOTOGRAPHY
COVER MODEL:JOSH MARIO JOHN
COVER DESIGN: LORI JACKSON DESIGN
EDITING: MASQUE OF THE RED PEN
FORMATTING: CHAMPAGNE BOOK DESIGN

FIRST EDITION PRINT 2020

To jean wearing people,

Get the skirt.
Wear the skirt.
You're a fucking hottie.

And to Lori Jackson,

Here is to our first cover and many more to come. You
envisioned the grit and made it come to life.
Your Skirt's first and last. And to Skirt and me, that means
everything.
Thank you ♥

SKIRT

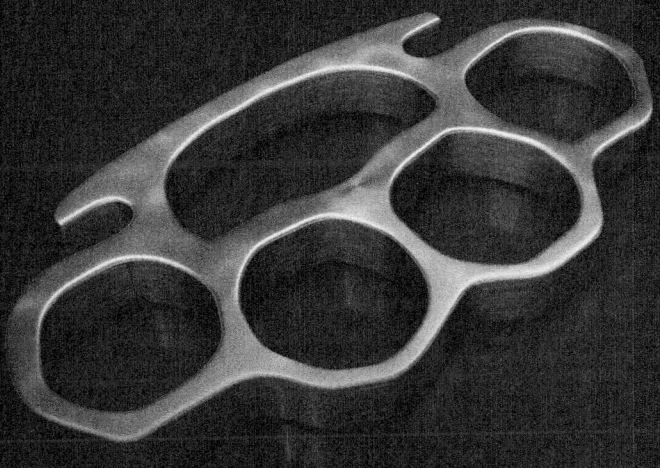

PROLOGUE

Skirl

Five Years ago

PAIN IS INEVITABLE IN LIFE. THERE'S NO DOUBT IT'S MEANT TO be felt every second of every day in some way, in some capacity; whether it's for a fleeting second, or a fucking lifetime. The kicker is I've never really felt real pain before, not until last week. I've had it easy growing up. I've never been in trouble. I've never been arrested. I've never talked back to my ma because I knew better. I saw her take a wooden spoon to me brother's arse more than once for giving her lip.

I learned to never disrespect her.

Me, Ma, and Da came to America when I was a wee boy, not but knee high, but there was one family member who didn't come with us. My brother, Conor. He stayed behind in Scotland because he was in his prime in MMA and UFC. He was a champion, undefeated, and one of the biggest men in the ring.

We were so proud of Conor, but life went on in America. We visited Conor every summer, and I grew up wanting to be just like him. He was ten years older than me, my role model, my idol.

Since growing up so far away from Conor, I had to find my own way without him, but the road I wanted to take darkened.

I don't know where to go now.

The thing he loved the most was the thing that killed him.

The road might be rough, but the reward at the end is worth every tear.

"It wasn't worth every tear," I say to the tombstone as I sit on the freshly broken dirt covering my brother's casket that is settled six-feet underground. I'm wearing a tie too tight for the thick of my neck, and I fucking hate wearing this goddamn kilt. Things are traditional here, in Scotland, and when someone dies, we have to get out the kilts and bagpipes, and it's pure fucking torture.

Conor fought in his kilt, lived and breathed wearing the damn thing, and he died in it too.

After today, I'll never wear the damn skirt again.

I read the quote on the engraved stone again, the one that my brother said before a fight and after, and then I toss some dirt at it. "It wasn't worth this, Conor. It isn't worth seeing Ma cry and Da just as blank as a damn sheet. He's been expressionless. We don't know what to do without ye." I blink away the burning sensations in my eyes and look away from the stone, the only thing that's left of my brother. The only damn thing. The man was twenty-eight, and the only thing he has left is a rock slab.

It's fucking bullshit if you ask me.

"What am I supposed to do without ye, Conor? Huh? What the hell were ye thinking going up against the damn Irish? Ye know they don't fight fair." I knock my fist to my head, the same place O'Roark hit my brother, the one hit that killed Conor before his body hit the floor of the ring. "Ye were the best; why couldn't ye just accept it? Ye had to fight him, and I'll never forgive ye for it. I lost a brother. My only brother because ye wanted to be selfish. Couldn't ye, for once, think of someone other than yerself?" I stare at the stone, waiting for him to answer me. "My brother is buried a half a world away, and if ye aren't here alive, what's the point of me ever coming back?"

"Rohan?" Ma's voice has me turning to look over my shoulder. The last of the relatives have left, and the only people at the family plot in the cemetery are me, Ma, and Da. "We are leaving. Come on, let's go."

I shake my head. "Go on without me. I'm not ready to go." Thunder rolls above me, and the once blue sky is being encroached with black swirls of rain clouds. Maybe it's a way of Conor telling me he's pissed off.

Yeah? Me too, asshole.

"It's not good to stay here. We need to leave, Rohan," Da raises his voice over the loud boom of thunder that vibrates the air. The bagpipes finally stop too, and I can breathe a little easier. I know I should love them because they are a part of my heritage, but I can't stand the damn things.

"I'll find a way back to Conor's. I'm not ready to leave him just yet," I say over the rain that starts to pelt against the ground.

Ma, God love her, she's stomping her way toward me, and I can't tell if it's tears or rain against her cheeks. Her feet hit the ground causing the water, that's quickly gathering in puddles, to splash around her ankles. Ma's black leather flat shoes are getting ruined with mud. That doesn't seem to be on her mind at the moment as she marches toward me.

Her red hair seems to be flaming with how pissed she is, and when she finally stands in front of me, she raises her hand and backhands me across the face.

It's the first time in my whole life Ma has hit me.

My brows furrow together after my head snaps to the right from the force. The tiny woman packs a wallop. I shouldn't be surprised since we come from a family of fighters, but I am. I lift my hand to my cheek as it starts to burn. Lightning cracks across the sky, and as I turn around to look at me ma again, wind blows causing her hair to dance in long twirls. She looks like a witch, and the storm is her power. Ma's anger is brewing, and I'm at the receiving end of it.

"Get off yer arse and get in the car, Rohan! I don't want to be here another second, ye hear me? Not one more second. Ye brother is dead! Dead. Do ye understand? Sitting on the damn dirt, on his grave, it ain't gonna bring him back. Get in the car."

"No," I say again. I don't care if the water drowns me on top of Conor's grave. I'm not moving a damn inch. I'm not ready to say my final goodbyes yet.

She rears her hand back and slaps me again. With the water drenching my cheek, it only makes the sting that much worse. "Yer stupid. Ye have always been the dumber one. I wish it would have been ye! I wish ye would have died instead of Conor. What good are ye? Tell me, what good are ye to me? I hate ye, boyo. I hate ye. I wish ye were in that grave because I wouldn't miss ye nearly as much as I miss my Conor right now." Ma doesn't hesitate to give me blow after blow with her words.

They are worse than any hit I've ever received, including the two slaps I just got from her.

"Conor was more of a man than ye'll ever be, Rohan. I'd give anything for ye two to change spots."

"Ari, that's enough," Da finally unglues himself from beside the car and runs to Ma. When she lifts her hand again, he catches her wrist before she sends another wail against my cheek.

I can take it. Her words, while they hurt, I know she's just experiencing the pain of losing a son. If she wants to take her sadness out on me, she can. I won't stop her. "Da, it's alright. Let her work through it."

Her mournful eyes narrow at me, the jackhammer of depression jabbing me in the chest as she decides to hate me instead of love me. "There's nothing to work through." Her eyes morph into lagoons as tears fill them to the brink. "I hate ye, Rohan. I want me boy back. I want Conor."

I stand from the grave, my shoes digging into the mud along with my hands as I push myself into a standing position, but Ma shoves my chest. Conor's tombstone catches me as I stumble back, and I almost tumble over it.

"I don't wanna see ye back here again; do ye here me?" Ma yells through the veil of rain.

"Ari, don't. Yer gonna regret this," Da urges her to calm down and think about her decision to cast me away.

"The only thing I regret right now is Conor being dead and Rohan being alive, and Rohan, I will never forgive ye for that. I never want to see ye again." Ma is soaking wet; hell, we all are. She spins on her expensive shoe, and water fans around her, splashing against me stomach. It's a hopeless feeling then, but when it comes from Ma giving me her back, soaking me in resentment, it's detrimental.

Ma's black outfit disappears into the rain when she gets to the car and climbs into the passenger seat. Now all she's waiting for is Da.

"She doesn't mean it, son," Da says, doing his best to cover for her, but no matter what he says, nothing can fix the damage that's been done. "We do miss Conor, but we don't love ye less. Ye have to know that."

"Don't worry about it, Da. I'll see ye around. Okay?"

He leans in and pulls me into a tight hug, patting me on the back. "Ye can always come to me. Ye Ma, she's a stubborn woman, depressed right now, but ye have me. I love ye. I can't lose ye too. Alright?"

Emotion clogs my throat, and right as I clear it, thunder booms above so Da doesn't hear it. I want to believe it's Conor having my back, but I don't believe in that sort of thing. Once someone is dead, they are dead, and if people want to believe their loved ones stay around in the afterlife and it brings them comfort, then that's great.

I want to believe the dead are *dead*; no spirits, no nothing—just peace.

It isn't death that is hard. It's living because finding peace in life seems nearly impossible.

"Ye, Da. I got it. I love ye. Go tend to Ma. She needs ye right now. I'll be fine."

"Where ye gonna go? It's raining pools, son."

"Don't worry about me. I'm fine. I'll figure it out." I sit on Conor's headstone and cross my arms. Da gives me one last hug and lets go, leaving me alone with Conor's memory. That's all graves are, just memories being relived on repeat until the loved one, like me, finds light in the darkness somewhere.

The engine of the car purrs as it comes to life. Conor

just bought them a new Mercedes Benz two weeks ago, and they treat that car, well, better than did me right now. I watch the red taillights fade as they drive away, and I stand here, drenched. "Well, Conor. That proves it, ye were always the golden boy. I love ye anyway." Lightning cracks, sending veins along the clouds. "Where the hell do I go now, Conor? Ma seems like she hates me. I can't go to yer place." I know I have to, though. My stuff is there, and I have a right to take some of Conor's stuff with me to the States. I have no idea where I'll go when I go back to America, but I'm not staying here in Scotland.

I push off the headstone and cross my arms over my chest. It takes everything in me not to turn around and sit on the mound of dirt again, but no amount of missing him will bring him back. Death isn't that kind, and love has its limits.

My kilt is heavy from the rain, and I can't wait to take it off. I don't know how Conor wore it during a fight, even if it is kind of freeing in all the right places.

No, I still hate it.

Or… I could wear one every day in Conor's memory. Let go of the jeans and see what the fuss is about. Maybe I'll learn to love the kilt. "Ye've lost yer mind, Rohan," I snort at myself and shiver as the cold starts to sink in. I'm losing it if I'm actually thinking about wearing a kilt. Conor is just on my mind, that's all.

It's a long walk back to Conor's cottage. I pass the cliffs that overlook the ocean, and the low-hanging Scots Pine trees and the willow branches sway violently from the wind. The waves crash against the shore, the sea livid with strength and force. I can't smell the salt like usual since the rain is drowning it out. I miss it.

My socks squelch when I come to a stop under an oak tree as I stare at the cozy white cottage nestled against the forest. I can see why Conor loved it here. It's quaint and quiet. My teeth are chattering, but at least the canopy of the tree provides me some cover. I stare into the window into the kitchen where Ma is crying as she holds Conor's coffee mug against her chest, and Da is holding her tight. He turns her away from the kitchen, turning off the light, only to turn on another in the hallway.

They are going to bed.

I slide down against the tree, waiting until the light is off so I can climb through my brother's window. Ma falls asleep quick, so when the light is off, I get up and take a deep breath before running into the rain again.

Shite, little bullets of water hurt when it's coming down this hard. When I get to his window, I smile when I see how worn it is from my hands opening it throughout the many summers over the years. We never walked through the door. "Good times, Conor. Good fucking times." Once, Conor slammed his fist right through the glass for no reason at all. He cut up his right hand, the one that gave a mean right hook. He didn't care.

Damn it, I miss him.

I ease the window open and pause when it scratches against the wood. I cringe and wait for the hallway light to come on, but it stays off. I exhale a relieved breath and open it the rest of the way and slide inside. Water drips onto the floor, and I make a mental note to clean it up before I leave.

Rain pours in sideways and it floods the floor. It's a damn hurricane out there. I close the window and turn on the lamp beside me. A rush of emotions floods my chest, and when the tears come, I can't hold them back. I'm surrounded by Conor.

His bed is unmade, clothes are on the floor, and his fighting gear is hanging on a hook. I take off my boots and socks and pad my way over. I run my finger over the black gloves and then notice a picture of us on his nightstand. His first win in the cage.

"Fuck ye for dying, Conor. Fuck ye," I say to the empty room that smells like him. It isn't fair. Opening his closest door, I grab one of his suitcases and shove the gloves inside, the picture of us, and then I throw all of his damn kilts in there too with his shirts. We are the same size, so I'm going to wear them.

I slip on the puddle of water, and my hands reach out in time to grab onto the back of the computer chair. I steady myself and try to brush the tears out of my eyes, along with the water dripping down my face from my hair. I need to dry off. I can't see shite. I undress, the clothes plopping with a wet smack on the floor. I steal some gym shorts and a plain white shirt from Conor's drawers. Next, I run into the bathroom and snake a towel from the rod, pausing when I see the cap off the damn toothpaste and the clothes around the laundry hamper.

He always was a slob.

I never thought I'd get to view the 'last times' my brother had and it's … sodden. I can't handle it. I dry off my face, including the damn tears, and dry off my hair, then I mop up my mess on the floor. I'm scooting along the floor, sliding by the computer desk again when I see an envelope sticking out under the desk calendar. I tug it and see my name written on the front in my brother's handwriting.

"Oh, ye asshole. Of course, ye have parting words." I rip the envelope open and look toward the bedroom door, listening to make sure no one is awake. Unfolding the paper, I read:

Rohan,

I knew ye'd find this. Ye've always snooped in me room. I read somewhere that I needed to have me affairs in order. I didn't want lawyers involved. That's a bunch of useless shite. Every cent to me name is underneath the loose floorboard we used as kids. It's yers. Do me a favor. Go to Vegas. Win big. Live yer damn life for yerself, for once, and I'll be there.

I'm sorry I lost. I love ye.

-Conor

If this is the reward at the end of the road, it still isn't worth every tear.

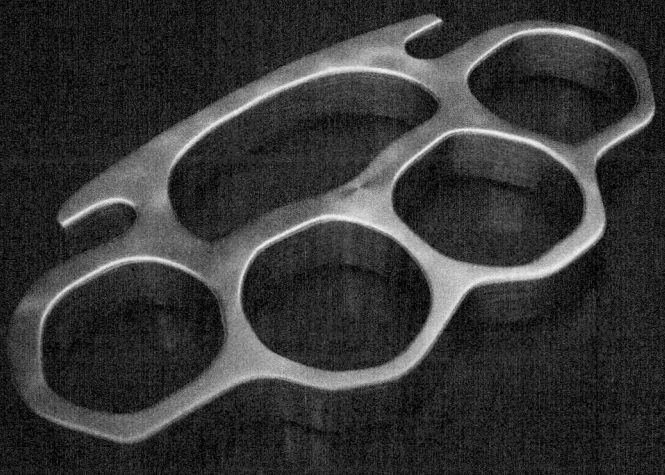

CHAPTER ONE

Skirt

Present Day

OH, *FUCK YES, APPLE PIE.*

I love it when Sarah makes apple pie. She refuses to tell me her secret ingredient, but I'll figure it out one of these days. I refuse not to figure it out, especially when she makes me my own pie.

"Damn it, Skirt. You either need to wear pants or learn to wear fucking underwear. Your white ass with red hair blinds me," Slingshot averts his eyes and plops down in one of the kitchen chairs, rubbing his eyes awake. It's nearly noon, but Slingshot has been pulling long hours at Kings' Club lately. He's allowed to be tired.

I straighten and hold the circular pan to my chest and peel

back the aluminum foil. "Whatever, Slingshot. Ye like it. Ye love it. Ye want some more of it," I singsong. That Tim McGraw song has been stuck in my head for days. No matter how much I listen to it, I can't get enough of it.

"Please stop. No country music." He cradles his head in his hands, then peeks through his fingers at me and cocks his head. "Hey, Skirt?"

I toss the foil in the trash and take a clean fork from the drawer and dig in the pie. "Aye, Slingshot?"

"Is that a new skirt?"

I give him a twirl and lift my leg in the air like I'm some hottie getting kissed. "It is. Thanks for noticing." I give him a slight curtsy. The guys like to give me shit for the kilts. Half the time I wear them because I like giving them shit and the other part of me actually warmed up to the idea of wearing a kilt. My brother, Conor, was right. The kilts are freeing.

And I've always not worn underwear; I like my dick being able to breathe.

Slingshot rolls his eyes and laughs. "Can I have a piece of pie?"

"Fuck off. Get ye own!" I hug my pie closer and turn around, giving him my back, then scoop another bite in my mouth. Apple, cinnamon, sugar, vanilla, and something else. It's heaven.

"Please? I'm starving. I won't ask again. And why is it that your accent isn't as strong anymore, only when your mad? I kinda miss you bellowing your Scottishness everywhere."

"First off, I don't bellow." I cut him a piece of pie and place it on a small plate, then pour him a big cup of coffee. "Second, I moved from Scotland to America when I was a wee boy. Ye know that, Slingshot. Now, it's just there sometimes. It's no big deal."

"You're not trying to hide it, are you?"

Slingshot hit a little too close to home. I've done my best to put Scotland behind me. I'm not trying to hide my accent, but I don't want to flaunt it either. Being in America so long has diminished it naturally, so that helps.

"No, I'm not. The longer I'm around ye fucks, the weaker my accent becomes. It's called acclimating to your surroundings."

"Acclimating? Big word for a dumbass," Slingshot teases.

As he dives his fork in to get a chunk of pie, I snatch the plate away from him. "Ain't no man call me a dumbass and gets *me* pie."

"Aw, Skirt. Come on. I'm sorry. You know I was just kidding," he says, licking his lips as he stares at the pie like it's his salvation. He's practically salivating for it.

"Do I know? That's not very nice, Slingshot. I'm sharing my apple pie, the pie Sarah poured blood, sweat, and tears into, then you insult me?"

"I hardly put blood, sweat, and tears in it." Sarah enters the kitchen with a jollity smile on her face. Her hair is a mess, and she wipes her lips just as Reaper follows behind her with a glaze to his eyes telling me he just got lucky.

"Morning, Prez," I greet. Slingshot reaches for the pie, and I lift it out of his reach, giving him a look that tells him not to even bother.

"Skirt," he pouts.

Slingshot isn't the kind of man to pout, so I'm enjoying this a little too much.

"Prez, he won't give me my pie!"

"It was my pie first!" I defend myself, keeping the pie out of reach of Slingshot's greedy hands.

Reaper groans and lays his head on Sarah's shoulder, wrapping his arms around her waist. "Seriously, guys. Can't you figure this out on your own? It's pie, not a fucking check for a million dollars."

"Might as well be. That pie is worth a million," Slingshot sulks and slumps in the chair, crossing his arms over his bare chest.

"Fight me for it." I give him a shit-eating grin, knowing he's never going to fight me. No one would. Recently, I've had to use my fighting skills for the club, and everyone has seen the beast that lurks beneath.

Reaper snatches the plate out of my hand that holds Slingshot's pie and slides it across the table to him. "We don't have time for this kind of bullshit today. Skirt, I need you and Poodle to make a local run for me. Okay? You're getting a duffle bag full of money from the Circus, Circus."

"Why the hell are we going to that dump?" I ask, shoving a bite of apple pie into my mouth at the same time as Slingshot. We stare at each other as we eat, unblinking. "You chew like a cow," I tell him.

"You are a cow," he says back.

"You act as if it's an insult."

"Will you two shut the hell up? Eat the damn pie. You're giving me a headache with your bickering."

I listen to the Prez, not wanting to press his buttons. He's been on edge lately ever since Sarah started IVF treatments. They have been trying their hardest to have a baby, and now they are at the last resort before it seems to be hopeless. The treatments are rough on Sarah; emotionally, she's always all over the place.

I hunch over the table, my arms bracketing the pie and my

fists clench, ready to punch anyone in the face who tries to take this pie from me. I don't bother asking the other question on my mind. Why the hell am I getting paired with Poodle? He's my best friend, but I'm still mad at him for not being honest with me about his life, who he was, the kid he had, the girl he loved that died, and the fact he was—is a killer. He knows everything about me.

My brother's death, my skill for fighting, the reason I haven't been home since five years ago—everything. He obviously doesn't view our friendship the same way as I did. It hurts. He was my first friend when I found the club. I confided in him.

I won't question Prez on his reasoning to pair us together. Poodle and I work well when it comes to club business; that hasn't changed, but our friendship has. I'm carrying a chip on my shoulder. I'm holding a grudge. It isn't right; I know that. I haven't been able to count on people since my brother died, and I expect my MC brothers to be those people, especially Poodle. All these years with him, I feel like I don't know him at all.

"Because the owner is paying us to be the security detail for the tournament he's hosting there in a few weeks."

I nearly choke on my damn pie. "Tournament? I'm sorry, what? Circus, Circus is the place you go if you want a viral infection, Prez. Place is a dump."

"Not for long. Once people see the Ruthless Kings are involved, people will start going there more. More people, more money, more money, renovations for Circus, Circus. Good business? Better name for the MC with the Vegas locals. That's what matters. So if new clientele comes along wanting to do business with the Ruthless Kings, business that could be good for the club, we're going to fucking do it, got it?"

My cheeks flame a bit from the slight scolding he's giving

me from my questions. "Aye, Prez. Got it." My stomach turns when I think about going to Circus, Circus, the place where I've been fighting to make some extra money and to get the anger out of me. It's legal-*ish*.

The club knows I'm good at fighting, but they don't know I do it professionally. I want to keep it that way. It will bring attention to the club and what we do. The last thing we need is people looking in too close to who we are.

In the ring, I'm Rohan.

At the MC, I'm Skirt.

Two different people, two different lives, two different reasons for living.

Fuck, I really don't want to go to Circus, Circus. If I see Maximo, he's going to ask me to fight this weekend. I make him money, but Maximo, while he puts on a show for the hotel and casino, he isn't a good man. He has his hands in many illegal things, and I know if I bring that trouble home to the clubhouse, Reaper will hand me my ass. Poodle has scars from defying Reaper, so does Tool, a damn heart carved in his chest. I sure as hell do not want that to be me.

I'm not supposed to be doing anything the club doesn't know about. My brothers are always supposed to be involved, but it's just fighting, so what's the harm in doing something for myself?

I polish off the pan of pie, licking my fork clean, and Sarah grabs the empty plate from me. "I would have done that, Sarah. You don't have to clean up after me," I say. She's been doing that a lot lately, cleaning up after the men like a momma bear. Reaper's worried about her. Sarah hasn't been the same ever since she miscarried, and now with struggling with getting pregnant, she's gotten depressed.

Reaper is going to take her on a trip to see Boomer soon. Apparently, he has been in contact with the pyromaniac, and Boomer is just as concerned. Reaper wants to get her away from Vegas for a vacation, hoping it will get her back on track mentally.

"It's not a problem, Skirt. I enjoy doing it." Sarah bends down and gives me a quick kiss on the cheek, and I feel like a schoolboy all over again.

"Shucks," I say, rubbing my heated cheek. I'm a bit bashful around women. Always have been, always will be. I have a secret that I haven't told anyone. It's embarrassing, and I don't like to talk about it, but I've never been with a woman. I've messed around, blow jobs, hand jobs, making out, eating pussy—I've done all that.

I've never wanted to fuck a cut-slut, never wanted to fuck a woman I've met at a bar; never been that kind of man. I see the guys do it with the whores around here all the time, and it doesn't appeal to me. I guess I'm a bit of a romantic when it comes to sex. I can't be like Pirate or Slingshot or Bullseye, where they pass around the girls all night.

I want someone who is mine, not everyone else's. I'm weird like that, I guess. If any of the guys ever found out I was a virgin, I'd never hear the end of it. Badass bikers who don't blink at carnage, who kill in a blink of an eye, who have no mercy—we are the kind of men that fuck.

"You're so cute, Skirt," Sarah says, kissing my cheek again. I blush harder; no doubt the skin of my cheeks match the hair on my head. "Look at you blush."

"Stop kissing the man. Only kiss me." Reaper snags Sarah around the waist and pulls her tight to his side, laying a protective hand on her hip. "Those lips are mine, doll. Don't you forget it."

Like she could. She has Reaper's name tattooed on her collarbone, a wedding ring, and an ol' lady patch. There isn't much else he can do to claim her as his, and every man in the club knows it. Respects it.

Sarah rolls her eyes and sits on his lap. "You know my lips are only for you."

Reaper whispers something in her ear, and Sarah giggles. Slingshot takes that as his cue to leave, as do I. Once Reaper and Sarah get in their little bubble, there is no yanking them out of it unless someone is hurt, or unless Reaper is pissed off at everyone for annoying him.

Which is more often than not.

"I'm going to find Poodle, and we will be on our way."

"Keep me updated, Skirt. Any problems, you call me immediately."

"Aye, Prez." I nod and go in search of Poodle. The closer I get to his room, the more I hear little yaps of the Pi-doodles Lady gave birth to a few weeks ago. I knock on the door, and Ellie swings it wide open. Her blonde hair is cut shorter, to her chin, and she has a big smile on her face showing a dimple in her cheek. She's a pretty gal. Poodle will have his hands full with her when she is of age, especially with the guys around here.

"Dad is in the other room," Ellie informs me at the end of a laugh when one of the puppies rams into my leg.

"Right. I keep forgetting that you switched rooms. Sorry, Ellie."

"It's okay." Ellie looks down and points to my boot where a little fluffball is growling, tugging at my boot string. "I think he likes you."

The pup is short, stocky, white all over with a tan pouf of

hair on top of its head. I can't tell if it's so cute it's ugly, or if it's so ugly it's cute.

"He's the only one that hasn't found a home."

"Really? Why?"

"He looks different than the rest," Ellie says, and damn if that doesn't break my heart.

"I'll take him," I say without hesitation. I pick him up, and he licks my nose. All I can smell is puppy breath. I can't stand the idea of this pup feeling like no one wants him. He seems like pure chaos.

Hmmm. Chaos. That seems like a pretty good name.

"Didn't know you were looking for a puppy," Poodle notices from behind me.

"I wasn't. He needs a home. I have a house and a yard for him. I'll pay when we get back from our run. Reaper wants us to go to Circus, Circus."

"That dump? Why?"

"Money. A job. Just snatching a drop and leaving." I hand Ellie the little pup, and he growls, wiggles around, and tries to bite her finger. "Aye, none of that, Chaos." I use my commanding voice, deep and threatening. Chaos stops wiggling and then pees, right on the floor as Ellie holds him up by two hands. "You little shite," I growl. I swear, he laughs. If a dog could fucking laugh, this little arsehole does. "I'll deal with you later. You got piss on me boots! No one pisses on me boots!" I turn on my piss-soaked boot and march through the main room with Poodle right behind me.

Pirate is on the couch, drinking his sorrows away. I've always wanted to know what happened to the poor bastard for him to be like he is. He always looks so lost, vacant, like he's drowning his body in rum to feel whole again.

I step over the empty bottle on the floor and make my way to the front door and swing it open. The air is cool since fall is approaching, but it's still dry, and the sun is hot.

"After maybe we can get a beer and talk," Poodle offers as we get on our bikes. He's been reaching out like that for a few days now.

"Maybe," I reply. I hook the black bucket helmet under my chin and crank my Harley. The engine grumbles loud, drowning out Poodle's next words, and I pull away. Dust and rocks kick up in a cloud behind me, and I know he is pissed. I'll need to meet Poodle halfway soon, or there will be nothing of our friendship left.

Braveheart opens the gate and waves at me. Tim traded in his glasses for contacts, and he looks like a whole new man. He even put a tiny bit of muscle on his bones recently so he doesn't look like he'll blow away in the wind.

When the gate creaks open enough, I hit the throttle and speed down the dirt road. Reaper finally got all the potholes fixed after a few of us bitched enough about having to fix our bikes every few months from the suspension coils giving out. Poodle catches up beside me, but I don't look at him.

This isn't about friendship right now. It's about work.

When we get to the end of the road, I take a right toward the Vegas strip. Poodle and I ride side to side, speeding down the road with our bikes roaring through the air like angry beasts. The wind slices through our cuts causing the leather to flap. Poodle's hair is swaying behind him, shining like new polished oak. The man cares more for his hair than he does his bike; that I can bet my life on.

We are going around sixty-miles-an-hour when something up ahead rolls from the dead bushes along the side of the road.

The closer we get a figure comes to view, and when he or she falls, they crumble in the middle of the lane I'm in.

"Shit!" I panic. I can't turn left because Poodle is in the way. I can't go straight or I'll run over whoever is in the road. I yank the handlebars right at the last second, and my bike flies into the desert. I struggle as the bike sways, struggling to control the machine. The bike wins on the last effort as I try to straighten my front wheel out, but the front tire hits a rock, and I fly over the handlebars and land on a cactus. "Motherfucker!" I scream when I feel the needles pierce my arse. I roll over from the small plant, barely able to catch my breath; not just from the air leaving my lungs, but the damn cactus stuck to my backside.

The sand is hot under my palm, and my vision swims from the disorientation of hitting the ground so hard. "Fuck," I curse when I see my bike. The entire front end is bent. Who the hell just falls in the middle of the road? Whoever it was, they owe me repairs on my bike. I hold my ribs and somehow stand. I balance most of my weight on my good leg and limp since the pricks of the cactus pull my skin on my right butt cheek. I'll never hear the end of this. Doc is going to have a field day.

"Skirt! You okay?" Poodle hops off his bike and jumps over the brush on the side of the road.

"Who the hell was in the road?" I should have them pluck the needles from my arse. That will teach them not to get in the way of bikers. I grunt in pain as I trudge through the desert plants on the road, and don't ya know, they're all fucking sharp and sticking me.

"Don't know," Poodle says. "I wanted to check on you first."

"I have needles in me arse, Poodle. How the fuck do you think I'm doing?" I snap as I fall to my knees on the road. My

21

hand grabs the shoulder of the person, and I flip them over onto their back. I gasp.

"Holy shit!"

It's the prettiest woman I've ever seen. She's black and blue all over. Looks like she got her ass handed to. Her hair is filthy. I can't tell what color it is. Blood is caked in it. She has cuts on her chest and arms.

She doesn't look like she's breathing. I lay my ear against her chest and sigh in relief when I hear her heartbeat. It's strong.

Da-dum. Da-dum. Da-dum.

"Call Reaper!" I order Poodle, and he pivots on his heel, pulling his phone from his pocket.

"Who did this to you?" I ask her, knowing she isn't going to answer me. Her bottom lips is busted open, and her cheek has a deep cut on it too.

"Guys are on their way," Poodle states and squats next to me. "Who do you think she is?"

"Don't know," I answer honestly, but my brain is screaming one thing.

Whoever she is, she's mine.

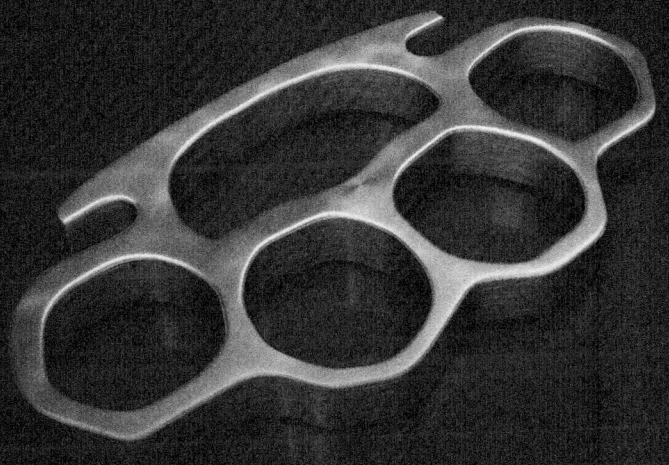

CHAPTER TWO

Skirt

"SHE HASN'T WOKEN UP YET?" I ASK, LAYING ON MY stomach in Doc's treatment room in the basement. It's nice, better than most emergency rooms I've been in, which is over a few dozen if I include the times I needed stitches in Scotland. The basement walls and floors are stainless steel walls and floors, with a dozen beds, heart monitors, ventilation machines, and whatever else a hospital needs.

Down here in the cold darkness is also the playroom, but it isn't as sexual as it sounds. A lot of blood gets spilled in that room.

"You have to give her time, Skirt. We just got you guys down here."

He doesn't remind me that it took four guys to carry me since I could hardly walk. My arse was burning so bad from the damn cactus needles. My cheeks are starting to tingle, and I'm afraid I'll lose my balls. It's worst-case scenario, but I'm having terrible thoughts of the pricks being poisoned. What if I get a rash? What if it makes my balls fall off? It *won't happen*.

But *could* it happen?

Yeah, that's what I'm worried about.

"Skirt landed on a cactus! Doc has to pluck the needles out of his ass!" I hear Knives yell out to the entire clubhouse, and a stampede of boots sound above on the floor.

"I'm going to kill him," I hiss through tight teeth, debating if I want to use Knives' own ninja stars to shut him up.

Doc chuckles and lifts up my kilt. His face turns from funny, concerned, then pained, which doesn't help my panic. "What is it? Is my ass rotting? Falling off?"

"It's the whitest ass I've ever seen."

"Oh, fuck ye, Doc." I flip him off, and he cackles like a mad scientist. His laughter bounces off the walls of the room as the rest of the members of the MC parade down the stairs. This is going to be a nightmare.

"That doesn't hurt. I've had knife wounds bigger than that," Tongue says, popping his lips as he lifts my kilt to check the damage. "Not too bad at all. I can pry these out real fast. Flick of the wrist with the knife."

"Ye aren't getting near my arse with a fucking blade. There are important things down there. And ye get all twisty, turny, and excited with yer blade."

"Just saying," Tongue drawls.

"My ninja stars make bigger holes than that. Stop being a baby," Knives decides to join in, clicking his tongue as he inspects my rear.

"Fuck off, the lot of ye. I have a hundred needles in my arse!"

SKIRT

"A few dozen, maybe," Doc corrects me.

I fold my arms under my chin and plop my head down. "It feels like a hundred," I grumble. I turn my head to see the girl we picked up off the road as if she were roadkill. Doc has her hooked up to a bunch of monitors and an IV in her arm that's hooked up to fluids. Whatever happened to her, I'm going to go out on a limb and say it wasn't good. She looks so small in the bed, so broken. What if we weren't riding our bikes; what would have happened to her? I don't even want to think about it.

"Ow." I reach back and slap the tweezers out of Bullseye's hands. "Only Doc is allowed to pluck things out of my arse."

"I have steady hands, Skirt. You've seen me with darts. Who better than to pluck needles out of your ass than me?" Bullseye asks, and what scares me is that he's serious.

"The doctor," I say as if he's stupid. "Ye know, the one with the fucking medical degree. I don't trust ye, any of ye down there."

"We aren't going to pluck the hairs off your balls." Tool chuckles.

"Ruined my surprise." Tongue's laugh is a mix of dark and light. I can't tell if he's serious.

"Doc? Where the hell are you? Get these things out of my arse before these dumbasses hold me down and pluck them out themselves."

Metal clinks behind me, and since I can't really see, another round of nightmares enter my head. What, he has a torture device? *No, he's a doctor. He took an oath. I'm fine.*

"Okay, guys. This isn't a pony show. Go on, leave." Doc takes charge and tells them to get on with their damn lives, shooing them away like the pesky vermin that they are.

"Fine."

"Didn't wanna be down here anyway."

"I never get to do anything."

"This is a bunch of horseshit."

"I need to sharpen my knives anyhow."

All of them bitch and moan, dragging their sorry asses up the steps one by one. Yeah, like I've ruined their life or something. What about me? They aren't the one with needles in their ass. The basement door slams a bit harder than usual, and I shake my head from their tantrum. "They act like they never seen a guy fall on a cactus before," I mumble.

"Well, to be fair, I've never plucked cactus needles out of a guy from falling on a cactus before," Doc says, just as he plucks one of the things out of my ass.

I flinch and nearly roll away from him. "Damn, Doc. Can't ye numb me up or something?"

"Are you going to be that big of a bitch about this?" He steps beside me so I can turn my head to see him. He's wearing his cut, which he never does, over his pretty boy polo shirt. He has purple latex gloves on and a face mask, but it's the long silver tweezers that get my attention and have me swallowing. I never, in my life, have seen tweezers that size. Is that necessary? Are those a scare tactic?

It's working.

"You fight. You literally beat the shit out of whoever Reaper asks you to, and you can't handle getting a few needles plucked out of your ass?"

"Well, when ye put it that way…" I say and shove my arse up in the air. "Go to town, Doc." He walks away and flips up my kilt, and I turn my head in embarrassment. This is not how I wanted to start my day. After this is all over, I'm going to go get me a big pint of ale. I deserve it.

I clench my teeth as he yanks every piece of cactus out of me, and I try to focus on anything, everything that isn't the burning sensation in my lower half. I fixate on the girl in the bed beside me and map her delicate features with my eyes. Even under the cuts and bruises, I can tell she's beautiful. Her hair looks like it would be a strawberry blonde if it weren't for all the blood and dirt caked in it.

"Is she going to be alright?" I ask Doc after a few minutes of silence. I wonder if I got to her in time.

"She'll be fine. She's exhausted. Dehydrated. I don't know how long she's been out there. She needs to gain some weight, but with rest, she'll make a full recovery."

"That's good to hear. I wonder what her story is."

"Well, if it brought her here to us, it can't be that good. It never is."

I know that's right. Anything that comes through our door brings bloodshed. We fight for what we care about, what we protect, and we will do it for anyone who stays under our roof. I hope that isn't the case for her, but if it is, I'll fight for her. She'll be the most important thing I'll bring my fists up for. I bet she's more woman than any other woman I've ever met. I bet she's a fighter; her bruises speak for themselves.

"Alright, you're all done. I'm going to prescribe you some antibiotic cream. You'll need to rub it on your ass twice a day—on clean skin. Don't go rubbing it in after sweating your ass off on your bike."

"I won't be sitting on my bike for a while. Front end is completely smashed."

"That sucks. Good thing you missed her, though. If you would have hit her with your bike, I don't know if she would have survived it."

"Yeah, good thing I took that cactus up the arse, right?" I snort, trying to ease the heaviness in the room. Death is never easy to talk about, even when you're so used to seeing it.

"You took it like a man too," Doc says, spreading cream over my sore cheeks.

Emasculating, I tell ya. Emasculating.

Then to make it worse, he puts bandages over each cheek. I thud my head against the exam table. *This. Can. Not. Be. Happening.*

"Alright, you're all set, Skirt. You can go on about your day now." Doc snaps off his gloves and tosses them in the trash next to the bed.

I gather the small pillow underneath me shove it under my chin and stare at the nameless woman beside me. "I think I'll stay here, Doc. If she wakes up soon, I don't want her to be alone."

"I think that's a great idea. She'll be scared when she wakes up. It's new place, somewhere she hasn't been. She'll need a kind face."

"I'm a kind face?" I ask him in surprise. My knuckles are scarred, my nose is a bit crooked from being hit too many times. I've got tattoos all over my body. If anything, I don't look as kind as Doc does. It would be best if he stood at the foot of her bed when she wakes up. Polo shirt, blue eyes, and messy light brown hair, she'll feel like she's in heaven. If she sees me looking at her, she'll see a man with red hair and a kilt and probably run screaming. "You know, it's better if you stay, Doc."

"Nah, don't be ridiculous. You're a nice guy, Skirt. You're nicer than half the men upstairs. What if Tongue was down here? Knives? Even Bullseye, they are scary motherfuckers. You're scary, but you aren't as scary. You're her best bet. Plus, she'll see you in bed, nursing your butt wounds, and she'll need a good laugh."

"Great. I love being the *butt* of someone's joke." I can't help it. I snicker from my own joke. I'm such a funny bastard.

Doc chuckles and flips down my kilt. I breathe a bit easier knowing my hairy ass isn't exposed to the world. Poor woman, if she woke up and saw that, she'd wish she was on the side of the road again. The guys aren't wrong, my arse is white and a tad bit hairy. Last thing I want to do is scare her.

"Why don't you get some rest? It will be a few hours before she wakes up."

"I need to go on that run for Reaper. Fuck, we never made it to Circus, Circus."

"Poodle and Bullseye are on their way for that. Reaper is aware. Just relax." Doc taps my ass with his hand, and I wince, then turn my head to give him a dirty look. "I had to."

"You're just like them." I squeeze the pillow tighter and mumble incoherent nothings under my breath.

Doc throws his head back in laughter as he walks away and turns the light to a low glow. He doesn't say anything else as he climbs the steps and I get settled, trying to get comfortable on my stomach, which is impossible since I'm a back sleeper.

This fucking sucks.

Then I think about Maximo at Circus, Circus and decide that maybe a cactus up the ass wasn't the worst thing that could have happened. I avoided having to deal with him. He's a shady guy, and every day that passes he becomes a little more questionable. He wants me to fight in an illegal ring he started. He wasn't involved in the ring the Ruthless Kings took down a few months back with Tool.

Maximo saw dollar signs in his eyes when he saw the news

about the fighting and prostitution. He's a shitbag, but he'd never abuse and traffic women. I guess there are bad criminals, then worse criminals. No way in hell do I want to be a part of that. Reaper will kick my ass, kick me out of the club, or kill me.

Probably torture me, then kill me if I think about it.

I shiver at the thought. No, I need to stay focused. Maximo can offer me as much money as God has, but I won't take it. My morals are too high.

I hope.

The monitor at the other end of the room starts to beep quicker and quicker. I press my palms against the bed and lift myself up to see what's going on. "Oh, shite," I say when I see that it's Moretti. His body is trembling, and the heart rate monitor is going spastic. I slide out of bed, heart pounding with a bit of fear since I have no idea what I'm doing, and limp my way over. "Doc!" I yell for him, but my voice just reverberates back to me since the walls are metal. "Doc! Doc! You need to get down here!" I scream and drag my left leg since it throbs more for some reason, while I struggle to Moretti. I'm sweating up a storm. Beads of salty liquid puddle on my forehead and drip down to my eyes, stinging them. I wipe the sweat away with my forearms, and I see his mouth foaming. His eyes are rolled so far back I only see the whites. He looks void, blind, inhuman, and it chills me to my core.

This is not easy to see. He clearly needs help, and I have no idea what to do. "Fuck, fuck, fuck," I curse, then run my fingers through my hair, contemplating my next move.

"You have to turn him to his side." A weak, tired, yet harmonic voice says behind me.

I look over my shoulder to see the brightest green eyes I've ever seen staring back at me through bruised orbital sockets. Her voice is hoarse as if it has gone through a meat grinder. "Hurry," she said, snapping me out of my hypnosis. "You need to get him on his side and swipe the fluid from his mouth so he doesn't choke; hold his head still. All we can do is wait." She holds her side and takes a deep breath, then shuts her eyes when a fresh wave of pain hits.

I try to open his mouth, but his teeth are clenched shut. Foam sprays from between his teeth, and I move out of the way before it hits me, then I flip him on his side. "I can't get his mouth open," I tell her, grunting as I fight Moretti with every jerk of his body. It's like trying to manhandle an alligator.

I've never wrestled a gator, but I'm going to assume it's like this.

"Just going to have to hope he doesn't bite his tongue off," she says as she lays down. Her eyes flutter shut again, and I want to tell her to open them because I've never done this before. What if I hurt him? What if I mess up?

"Where the hell is Doc?" I rattle under an anxiety-ridden breath. The seizure is going on forever. Every jerk of his body, every drip of spit gathering on the bed, my heart races.

"I don't know who that is," she rasps. "What happened? What day is it?"

"I don't have time to tell you right now. I'm kind of busy."

"Could have already told me instead of saying that," she says with attitude. I don't expect a woman with a smart mouth in her condition. I look in her direction. She's laying calmly in the bed, eyes closed, and it seems like she went back to sleep.

Moretti's heart rate starts to slow, and the spasms in his body start to fade. Finally, after what seemed like an eternity, but was only a few minutes, I release my hold on him.

"Scoop out his mouth," the peanut gallery chips in.

It's a good thing I like peanuts.

I grab a glove and snap it on, open his mouth, and scoop out all of the foam and bile from his throat. He didn't bite his tongue, so that's a good sign. I gag when I take the glove off and throw it on the trash. Blood, I can do. Pain, I can do. Scooping shit out of someone's mouth? I can barely do that. It's a limit. And I just surpassed it.

"I think he's okay now." My chest rises and falls from exertion. My arse begins to throb when the adrenaline starts to crash, and that's when I remember I just got needles plucked out of me. I rub my forehead against my shoulder and remember I have my fucking cell phone on me. Christ, I can be such an airhead sometimes.

I type Doc a quick message.

"Get the fuck down here. Moretti just had a seizure."

My cheeks bubble as I blow out a breath when I hear boots pound along the floor. "Porch, main room, kitchen," I say as I follow where Doc is walking, and then the basement door opens. "Basement."

"Oh, you're good. What gave that away?"

I narrow my eyes at the new pain in my arse, laying stock still as if she's trying to catch a quick snooze. The bruises and cuts are just a front, but she's just a five-foot-one body packed with damn attitude, and I bet the other guy she fought looks worse than she does.

Doc slides down the rail on the staircase and jumps down to the floor. He doesn't bother with me or the woman; he runs straight to Moretti. He slides the pale yellow curtain closed to give him and the mobster some privacy. I'm not sure how much longer Moretti's body can handle this. He's healing on the outside, but the inside? It's like he is getting worse. If it were me, which I'm glad it's not, but if it was, I'd want someone to put me out of my misery.

I shuffle over to my bed, but before I sit, I freeze, thinking better of it. Nope. Better not do that. I push my hands against the mattress, holding the weight of my body as I pull my legs up and then lay on my stomach. "Oh yeah, that's the damn stuff right there." I sink into the mattress, and the blankets are nice and warm.

"What happened to you?"

Her eyes are the color of evergreen. They say the eyes are the windows to the soul. If that's the case, she's a forest waiting to be explored, so much beauty and so much mystery. I can wager if someone, anyone, tries to figure her out, they'll get lost in the many directions that lay inside of her, forever trying to find their way to her heart.

I bet many men have failed on that quest.

I don't plan to fail.

"Where am I?" Her eyes widen a bit more and the familiar monitor starts to beep. "Who are you? Where am I? What happened?" She snaps out of her haze, and reality comes crashing down. Her bottom lip trembles.

Oh, shite. I'm horrible when women cry. Lagoons form in their eyes, and I'm helpless.

Doc slides the curtain from Moretti's bed. He has a grim expression on his face. I've seen that look before. He's running out of hope for Moretti. Doc approaches her bed and pulls a small black flashlight out of his pocket and peers into her eyes. She jerks away from him, then slaps his hand away.

"Who the hell are you?" she cries to him. "Don't touch me. Don't fucking touch me!" she screams and slaps Doc's chest. "Get away from me. Get off me!" The woman won't stop shouting, and her pleas to leave her alone break my heart. She's obviously been fighting for far too long.

"Hey, look at me," I say as Doc gets ahold of her wrist. She lands those green eyes on me, and I'm a goner. A tear falls from the puddles filling her eyes, and I watch as it slowly flows down her cheek, causing a wet shiny path. "Yer okay here. That's our doctor. We call him Doc. Yer okay," I repeat, hoping my words calm her.

"Skirt here found you on the side of the road." Doc nudges his chin in my direction while holding her wrists. "He got in an accident to avoid hitting you."

"You should have left me there," she sobs and yanks her wrists away from Doc's grip. "You should have left me."

"We will never leave a woman in harm's way. What's your name?" Doc asks as he places his stethoscope in his ears and listens to her heart.

"Dawson West. My friends call me Dawn." She gives Doc and I a once-over with her eyes, lingering on me for a bit longer than normal. "I guess you can call me that since you saved me," she says. Dawn wipes her eyes on her arm, but it's no use; the tears are replaced again. "I'm sorry you got hurt because of me. I tend to do that to people," she whispers, tangling her fingers together. Then she cups her face with her hands and shakes her head. "My son. I need to get out of here. I need to get my son. He has him! He has him! He isn't safe there, please. Let me go. I need to find him. I need to get to Aidan before he hurts him." The words get slower and slower until her eyes start to droop.

I roll off the bed when I see Doc putting something in her IV. "What are ye doing? She was just waking up."

"She needs more rest. She's hysterical. She can't think like that."

"That wasn't yer decision to make. She was asking about her son," I sneer at him. For the first time in my life, I'm questioning his ability to be a good doctor.

"I'm her doctor. It's my decision. It sure as hell isn't yours. Go back to bed, and when you have a medical degree, that's when you can question me."

He's right, but still, I don't have to like it. I push her hair out of her face, feeling more connected with her than I have anyone. Where do I know her from? She's familiar, but I can't put my finger on where I could have seen her.

My eyes fall to her lips, and I grin when I remember how sassy they get. They are big, plump, almost too big for her face, but they aren't injected with that fake shit. No, they look soft, like pillows that I want to lay my mouth across for comfort. I bet they taste like sweet berries, and with that attitude of hers, I bet she'd leave me with a sour taste in my mouth that I'd want more of.

Yeah, she's got a set of lips on her, that's for sure.

And I want them.

CHAPTER THREE

Dawn

YOU THINK YOU CAN WALK ALL OVER ME? THEN LET'S SEE HOW YOU do walking home from the desert. Maybe when you're half dead and walking through the door, you'll know better. Your ass does what I say; it isn't the other way around. You're such a stupid bitch thinking you can tame me. I tame you! You hear me? I own you, and Aidan too.

I sit up with a violent gasp and cough. My chest hurts. It feels like someone hammered nails into the thick bone of my sternum. Cohen did punch me in the chest before he tossed me out of the van; that's probably why it hurts. I hold my hand to the side of my head as everything starts to swim. I can't focus on anything around me. It's dark, cold, but I remember glimpses of unknown faces, and I know I'm safe.

It's strange. I don't know why I feel safe, but my gut is

telling me I'm okay here. Not that it matters. I need to leave. I need to get my son. Aidan is my everything, and Cohen always uses Aidan against me so I stay in line. It's the only reason I'm still with him. Cohen will never let me leave unless it's through death. I'm stuck in his grasp forever.

He controls me no matter where I am, including this room I find myself in.

What is this place? How long have I been here?

I glance to my left to see if the man with the accent is still here, but the bed is empty, and the sheets are crumpled. I flip the lamp on the nightstand to be sure I'm alone. When the bulb flicks on, I lift my arm to block the sudden burst of light. Damn, it's bright. I blink a few times, and different colored spots float in my vision. That's when I notice the IV in my arm. The needle is pierced in the soft space of my elbow in the vein. I follow the tube to a bag hanging on a metal stand.

Where the hell am I? I'm not in a hospital. It's too quiet for that. Plus, the room is different than any hospital I've ever been in. The walls and floors are made of stainless steel, I think, since the light reflects off it. There's a room to the left that has a barricaded door, which only makes me curious, but since I don't know where I am, I won't get snoopy just yet. For all I know, these people are going to keep me prisoner just like Cohen does.

There is a plus to being here; the linens are so soft.

The blankets are soft under my hands, and I bring the cotton to my cheek and rub my face against it. Cohen only lets me sleep with scratchy wool blankets. And the bed is soft. I haven't slept on a bed in years. Cohen makes me sleep on the floor.

I lay the blanket over my lap and continue to study my

surroundings. There's medical equipment, but there are book-shelves stacked with books, and between each bed is a rock-ing chair with a cute-patterned rug beneath it. My eyes follow each bed, and every single one is empty except the bed at the end.

That was the man who had the seizure, if I remember correctly. Or was that a dream? Everything is so hazy. I wonder what happened to him. Seizures aren't easy. Aidan has them and every time he has one, my heart breaks, and I feel so help-less. It's emotionally and mentally debilitating for me, but it wreaks havoc on Aidan. He will sleep for hours after one. He's only four. His little body crumples in my arms with every jerk and spasm the seizure causes. Aidan cries because he doesn't understand what's happening to him and why. Aidan knows it's something he has to deal with, and now he is in the hands of Cohen, that monster.

He thinks Aidan is a freak and I know that man won't help him. I need to get to him. Aidan won't survive long in the hands of a beast like Cohen.

The floorboards above me creak and groan as someone walks above me. *Boom. Boom. Boom.* The boots pulverize the hardwood like a meat hammer. Whoever is walking up there, I bet they can smush me like an ant.

"I need to get out of here," I say, my voice echoing back to me in the lonely room. I press my thumb against the needle in my arm and take a deep breath as I pull it out. I toss it on the ground and throw the warm, cozy blankets off me.

Okay, *maybe* I'll take one blanket. They don't need them, right? I take the soft blue cotton off the top, take the ends and fold it together, then tuck it under my arm. Aidan will love a blanket that is soft, as long as Cohen doesn't steal it.

I hate that man with every breath I take. I met Cohen O'Roarke in Vegas five years ago after he moved here from Ireland. He's a beast in the cage. No one has been able to beat him. I watched him fight, and when we locked eyes through the hexagon shapes of the fence, I thought I had found the person I was going to spend the rest of my life with. He made me swoon. Cohen was a gentleman, always made me laugh, cared about me when we had sex, and was handsome? *Whew.* The man was so good looking with his bright blond hair and blue eyes. I even loved to hear his Irish accent when he spoke.

Now, I hate everything about him.

Something changed.

Like all relationships, passion was lost, and we fell into a routine. He turned hateful. His accent was like toxin, and it made my body shiver with repulsion every time I heard it. Cohen started yelling, mentally and verbally abusing me.

Then, that wasn't enough.

He kicked me, punched, and shoved me. He thrived off hurting me just like he hurts opponents in the ring. Every time he saw a bruise on me, it was his own personal victory.

All of that happened within months of meeting him, and then we broke up. I thought that was the end of it.

Until I found out I was pregnant.

And Cohen was not the father.

We got back together soon after that. I know. I'm an idiot, but at the time, Cohen was all I had.

No one knows about Aidan not being Cohen's. It will be my secret until the day I die. They just thought he was born early and if Cohen ever finds out that he's raising a kid that isn't his, he'll kill Aidan. I'll protect my son until my last breath, and if lying is what I have to do to save us, then I'll die a liar.

Fast forward until now, my beautiful Aidan is four and the only father he has ever known hates him. Cohen is a mean, hateful drunk and with every fight in the cage, I pray to whatever god that his opponent kills Cohen.

Wishing for death on someone isn't kind, but I'm okay with that. If it earns me a front row seat on the ride to Hell, so be it. It can't be much different than my life now. I welcome the change.

With my son in mind, I know I need to get out of here and get to him. What if he has a seizure while I'm gone? He only has a few days of his medicine left, and it's so expensive. Cohen already said he wasn't going to buy the pills for Aidan anymore.

I don't know what I'll do, but Aidan needs his medicine and I'll do anything within my power to take care of my boy. Lie, cheat, steal, kill—Aidan will live.

I slump against the beam against the wall when fatigue hits me out of nowhere. My entire body feels like I was thrown out of a van.

Oh, wait… I was.

The steps are high and intimidating as they escalate further into the unknown shadows. Only a faint glow of light from the crack at the bottom of the basement casts along the steps. I take a minute to catch my breath.

Inhale.

Exhale.

Why is life so hard? It isn't supposed to be this way. Life isn't meant to be a constant struggle or an exhausting journey through quicksand to try to overpower you. There are hard times, I'm not naïve to that, but when does good balance the bad? Is that the way the universe works? Where's the goddamn good? Where's the break?

I roll against the wall and push myself off, closing my eyes when the pain throbs on my left side. My fingers grab the hem of my shirt and lift. "No wonder," I say under my breath when I see a big black bruise spreading over my ribcage. I tug my torn, dirty shirt back down, and take the first step up the staircase.

"Fuck." I slump against the wall as the pain possessing my body becomes too much already. Aidan. I have to get to Aidan. The bottom of my foot finds the wall, and I push off. My foot slips on the slick staircase, and my hand flies out to catch myself before my body hits the hard surface. I bite back the cry of pain as my ribs burn with agony. My nostrils flare and bile rises up my throat, but I swallow it down.

Nothing perseveres more than a mother fighting to be reunited with her son.

I lean against the wall for support and take aching slow steps by lifting each leg until I'm at the door. I'm sweating, my stomach is turning, and my mouth is watering. Any second now, I'm going to puke. Closing my eyes, I bring up Aidan's face in my mind and focus. His bright green eyes staring at me with love and warmth. His memory, his need for someone to protect him is enough for me to reach for the door handle and turn it. I take my time opening the door. I peek my head through and survey the room.

I'm alone.

I'm staring at a kitchen with yellow curtains and updated appliances. The dining table has seen better days. It's worn with carvings and scratches, the stain of the wood is faded in certain spots, and the left corner is jagged from being broken off. I look left and right, but most of the noise is coming from the front of the house. Soft rock music is playing low, and the clank of balls tells me someone must be playing pool.

Which also tells me not to go in that direction. I slip out the door and flatten my palm against the grainy wood, then push it shut. I close my eyes when it clicks. My pulse spikes with a rush of adrenaline as the possibility of being caught crosses my mind. I don't wait to find out.

I slip to the left and take the sharp turn down the hall. There's a door at the end, and light shines through the window in the center. It's stained glass with reds, blues, and greens. Sunlight shines through, and a kaleidoscope of colors glitter along the floor. I haven't seen something like that in a very long time. I didn't know people still cared about the simplistic beauty of stained glass.

Granted, even from here, I can see the skull artfully designed in the middle. If the goal is beautiful and intimidating, they have achieved it.

There are photos scattered along the wall, ranging from old black and white to new age color. I love pictures, and I want nothing more than to stop and look at them, but there's no time. Aidan needs me.

I need him.

A bubble of tangled emotion tightens my chest the more distance I close between me and the door. I reach my hand out, tighten my palm around the metal knob, and swing it open. I don't bother closing it because freedom is an inch away.

There's one small step between me and the ground, so I jump, ignoring the pain all over my bruised body.

There's only one thing left to do.

Run.

I limp faster and faster, and I ignore the pain in my thigh completely, the deep ache in the core of my bone, but it's nothing compared to the pain of losing my son if I don't get to him.

The wind whips through my hair and the rumble in the sky has me tilting my head back to look up. The clouds are rolling with shades of gray and black. It's about to pour.

Bright side, the desert needs rain.

Downside, I'm about to get soaked which will make my journey colder and longer.

Dirt swirls around my feet from my shoes kicking up dust. Rows of bikes fill my vision, and I nearly break my neck looking at them and the building I ran from. They are all different shapes and sizes, miles of shining chrome and long exhaust pipes parked along the front of the porch.

What the hell is this place? There's nothing to tell me who or what they are, just a skull sign that stares at me with its hollow eyes uprooting the fear I try to keep buried inside. My eyes burn with too much familiarity from the dark voids staring at me.

My eyes are so focused on the bikes and the skull, I don't keep an eye out on what is in front of me, and I slam against something hard that has my head ringing and my body falling to the ground. I groan, holding my arms across my stomach as my ribcage screams at me for pushing myself too hard.

Fuck, that hurt.

I gag, the amount of anguish is unbearable, and I roll over to my hands and knees, spewing up yellow bile, the acid burning my throat and leaving a bitter taste in my mouth, which only makes me gag more.

Wiping my mouth, a black blur catches my attention out of the corner of my eye, and what I see sucks all the hope out of me, the air evaporating from my lungs. "No." I follow the gate as far as the eye can see. I push myself up until I'm standing on my unstable, trembling legs. The gate looks like it goes on for eternity in either direction. "No!" I shout and follow the iron bars in desperate search for a way out.

The further I walk, an unsettling reality falls over me like a veil. I'm in a fortress. There isn't a way out unless they let me out. I'm getting dizzy with all the circling I'm doing. There are other buildings that look like homes, a garage, and whatever the hell this main building is that has a saloon appearance. Below the skull is a sign that says 'Unwelcome.'

Fitting.

I don't feel welcome at all. Mission accomplished.

The door to the main house opens, and a few men file out. All of their outfits are the same. Black jeans, boots, some are wearing chains, but all are wearing these leather vests. What the fuck is this place?

All eyes are on me, and their laughter dies down while a man at the end with shaggy hair and a psychotic look to his face takes a swig of beer. I press my back against the gate to get away from them, the bars digging into my back, reminding me of how trapped I am.

I'm a mouse, and they are definitely the cats.

No, fuck that.

They are lions and they have their predatory eyes set on me. If I run, they will give chase. Cohen, I can handle. His abuse is just from one man, but all of these mean looking bikers? I'll die quicker here than I will with Cohen. I've heard horrible things about bikers. What if they pass me around?

Oh, god. I'm feeling sicker by the second.

"Let me through. Get yer arse out of the way, Bullseye." The crowd of intimidation parts for a man with red hair wearing a green kilt.

It's the man I saw laying in the bed earlier. He was real. He jumps down the stairs, and I turn left to bolt when he holds up his hands. "Aye, now. Wait. Just hold on a minute. No one here is going to hurt ye, okay?" he says in an accent that's similar to Cohen's but different. Scottish, maybe?

With every long stride he takes, his black boots get too close for comfort. I notice how gorgeous he is. He has red hair and a beard to match. He has his hair half up, half down. He's wearing a black shirt that is tight across his body and the kilt, while different than anything I've ever seen before, looks damn good on him. He has tattoos up and down his arms and a silver sword hanging off his hip. I'm not sure what that is about, but I don't want to find out.

"Please, I won't tell anyone I was here. Let me go. I need to get to my son."

"Dawn, we will get ye where ye need to be. I swear it, no one here is going to hurt you."

The men in front of me are telling me something much different. Plus, what he's saying, I've heard before.

I hate liars.

CHAPTER FOUR

Skirl

O H, SHITE. SHE LOOKS LIKE SHE'S ABOUT TO RUN. I HOPE SHE doesn't. I hate running in my kilt, especially when I'm wearing the sword. It's just for show. I guess I could learn to wield it, use the sword instead of my fists, but it's a family heirloom and whenever my brother is heavy on my mind, I clip the sword to my belt.

It was his first, since he was the oldest.

It has ruby gems on it with two chains dangling from the handle to the sheath. It's expensive, not something to ruin with blood. My fists do just as much damage anyway.

"Ye don't believe me. That's okay. What do I need to do to prove it to ye?"

"Where am I? How did it get here?"

"Ye don't remember?" I ask her with concern. This will be

the second time we have told her. "We found ye in the desert. I almost hit ye with my bike. We brought ye here instead of the hospital because we didn't know yer situation." I take a step closer, and she moves down the fence, so I pause. I lay my palm against my chest. "I'm Skirt. Yer at the Ruthless Kings MC clubhouse. Yer on our property. We aren't going to hurt ye."

"I don't believe you," she says. Her words are a powerful blow to my chest. She doesn't trust easily, that much is apparent. "Stay away from me. Don't come closer." Her fingers wrap around the bars of the gate and squeeze tight. Her eyes betray the fear her body is putting off in waves. Those green orbs hold a monster, and they are daring me to take another step.

I've always liked a good dare.

"Trust is earned. I get that," I say. My hands are still up, showing that I'm not reaching for my weapon and she's safe, just like I promised. The rocks crunch under my foot as I move closer.

Her jaw squeezes tight and the muscle jumps, reminding me of when Sarah doesn't get her way with Reaper.

"Open the gate and let me out. Let me get to my son."

"I can't let that happen." I'm finally in front of her, and now that I see her out in the natural light, everything about her calls to me. She's fucking gorgeous. She does have strawberry blonde hair and the eyes the color of that cactus that destroyed my ass.

Bright green but fucking deadly.

"Then you're not who I need to be speaking with, are you?" she sneers just as she throws her fist in the air, punching my jaw with a mean right hook.

Hells fucking bells, the woman packs a damn punch.

"Oh, shit! Skirt is getting is ass kicked!"

"Get 'em little lady!"

"Aw, hell. This is better than sharpening my knife any day," Tongue says.

I wipe my lip off with my thumb and see a bead of blood on my fingertip. I haven't had someone draw blood from me in a very long time, and the fighter in me pushes against my skin, begging to get free. I crack my neck and when I lay my eyes on her again, her chin is jutted out and her shoulders are thrust back. "That wasn't necessary, Lips. I'm not here to hurt you." I lick my lips, the taste of iron exploding as blood lingers in my mouth.

"It's not necessary to keep me here, yet here we are. And my name is Dawn. Not Lips."

"Oh, Lassie, yer name is Lips with that smart mouth ye got there."

She clicks her tongue and sends the same right hook through the air, but this time I catch it, and spin her arm around, pinning it behind her back. She arches, and her arse presses against my pelvis, rubbing against my semi-hard cock. Christ, I've never had a woman fight me like this, and it's turning me on.

"Calm down, Lips. I'm only here to help ye. I swear it," I whisper against the side of her ear, inhaling the dried sweat against her skin. Fuck, her sweat smells sweet. If I really wanted to scare her, I'd flatten my tongue against her neck and taste her flesh, which I'm not going to do.

That's weird.

Doesn't mean I can't think about it.

"I've heard that before." Her foot smashes down on mine as hard as she can and then her elbow slams into my gut, then she bends her arm quick and her fist lands right above my cock, stealing the air out of my body.

"Fuck me," I moan through a held, painful breath. My grip

loosens on her wrist, and she yanks out of my hold to drive her knee straight into my balls. "Oh, shite." My hands cup my bruised orbs, my pair of good fellas, and I fall to my knees. "Low blow." I fall to my side, and the guys are hollering in laughter, stomping their feet against the porch.

The loud pound of their boots sound like the thunder in the sky, and my sack throbs in rhythm. I never lose a fight, but this woman brought me down in a matter of seconds. I think I'm in love. It's the hottest thing I've ever experienced. I want her to take me down again, only in the bedroom, where she can really fuck me up.

The pain in my balls must be cutting off the oxygen to my brain because no man could want that.

A shadow falls over me, and I open one eye to see her dirty hair fall around her shoulders as she stares down at me. Her hands on her hips, her plump lips are pressed together, as if she's annoyed by me.

Me!

It's unheard of.

"Take me to your leader."

A bubble of laughter escapes me. It's loud and obnoxious and carries through the vast desert, but I can't stop it. She sounds like an alien since she has no idea what title Reaper is known for. I flop to my back, holding one hand on my balls, and the other on my stomach as tears gather in my eyes from how hard I'm laughing.

My arse twinges with pain, but I don't even care.

"Don't laugh at me. I want to talk to him. Now! Or I'll… I'll…"

"Ye'll what, Lips?" I flop to my side and lay one hand on the ground to push myself up onto my legs. "Kick me in the balls?

Well, ye've done that. It hurt, by the way." I dust off my kilt and sigh. Damn, that was a good laugh.

She narrows her eyes at me, the green-eyed monster coming to life, and she stomps toward the row of motorcycles, which are all parked in the same direction, leaning on their kickstands. It's a beautiful picture. The symmetry doesn't happen like that all the time.

"Woah, woah, woah!"

"Not the bikes!"

"I'll give you a knife. Just don't touch her. I just got her painted!"

The guys shout in protest, hoping to stop her, scared that she'll kick the first bike and start a domino effect. Fuck. And of course, the one she's standing at is Reaper's. She lifts her leg and cocks her head at me, daring me not to take her to Reaper.

Fucking dares, always more trouble than what they are really worth.

"Take me to whoever is in charge!"

"Okay. I can do that. No need to go overboard with damaging the bikes. Those are expensive fixes. Person ye want to talk to is Reaper. He's in his office. Where'd ye learn to fight like that?" I ask, rubbing my jaw as it throbs.

"None of your damn business."

"Yer attitude won't get ye far here, Lips. I'm nicer than a lot of the men here, and ye'll do well to stay in line."

She plants her foot and marches over to me, pointing a finger, then pushing it against my chest. "I don't give a damn what you think about my attitude. I've had it listening to men telling me I need to stay in line. Fuck your line; you hear me? I'm never walking it again. So shove your warning up your Scottish ass and take me to the person I need to talk to."

I'm glad I'm wearing a kilt because I'm so fucking hot I bet I could weld two pieces of metal together. "Not many people get the Scottish thing at first." I lean in and glance to the porch where the guys are leaning their arms against the porch rail, watching me and Dawn as if they are a bunch of damn gossip girls. I lower my voice so they can't hear me. "And ye must be thinking about my arse for ye to bring it up like that. Ye tell me when and where, Lips, and when that happens, feel free to kiss it."

That has her throwing that rogue fist through the air, and I catch it, then reach down and grab her other hand. I bring both of her wrists between us and pin them against her chest. "That's becoming a habit, Lips."

"Looks like you bring out the worst in me," she sneers, her eyes locking to my lips.

My eyes dart all over her face, impressed by this woman in front of me. She's strong, fierce, but I know she's scared. It's why she feels like she has to fight for herself. Throwing punches can be exhausting, but there has to be a better reason than snap judgment, or any energy for a real fight will be drained.

"That's too bad because I think ye bring out the best in me," I say. I've never felt more alive than I do right now. My skin is buzzing, my lips are trembling to kiss hers, and my heart is racing faster than a thoroughbred. "Come on, follow me. I'll take ye to our leader." I snicker. She's so naïve about this sort of life, and I find it refreshing. I stretch out my arm. "Ladies first."

"I don't know where I'm going," she says, swallowing nervously as she looks up to the men on the porch. I can imagine it is intimidating for her to see all these bikers, but they won't ever hurt a woman. They will give their life to make sure a woman lives. It's the Ruthless way of life. It's law.

"I'll make sure to tell ye," I say.

The torn pieces of her shirt blow in the breeze, and I see bits of her smooth white flesh along her hipbone. Strands of her matted hair flicker over her shoulder, reminding me of a flame dancing along the wick of a candle. Sure, the strawberry blonde locks are covered in filth, but shucks, she looks good fucking filthy.

"Okay." Her hand holds her side as she takes the first step, and her knee buckles from beneath her. Her arm catches along the rail, but I can see the pain along the lines in her face.

I lunge forward and swing her into a tight hold. She's staring up at me with her bright eyes; the whites of her right eye is tinged red from the black eye, and her lashes curl up to touch her brows. Fucking beautiful. "Look at that." My boots slam against the steps, and my MC brothers part to give us space to enter the front door. "I've done swept ye off yer feet. Before ye know it, yer going to love me."

Dawn's arms wrap around my neck, and she rolls her eyes at my statement. "Love? Love doesn't exist, Scottish."

"I can't wait to prove ye wrong, Lips." I bring my foot up and kick the door open since it isn't shut all the way.

"You're a pain." Dawn stares ahead, not meeting my eyes, but instead, she sees a few cut-sluts hanging around, one draped all over Pirate's drunk ass, kissing on his neck. "No standards, huh? This is how it is here?" she asks, and Candy breaks her lips from Pirate's neck, and flicks Dawn off. "No thanks, sweetheart. I don't want whatever you got."

I rub my lips together to keep from laughing, and Candy lunges for Dawn, but not before Dawn chops her in the throat. Candy stumbles back and wraps her hands around her neck, gasping for air.

Hell yeah, this woman is a badass, and her fearless personality is turning me on more and more with every second that ticks by.

Even Pirate looks like that sobered him up a bit. He stares at Dawn like a dog eyeing a piece of beef. I give Pirate a sneer and hold Dawn closer to my chest, tighter, like I'm afraid some other man is going to come and take her away from me, from my arms. I'll fight to prove I'm worthy.

I might not have the experience a lot of guys have here in the club, but I can be what she needs. Shucks, thinking about us having sex makes me nervous. Maybe I should fuck a cut-slut or two to make sure I know what I'm doing. The thought of getting with Candy doesn't sit right with me, though.

I'm not waiting for marriage or anything. I'm not religious. It's nothing like that. I've had the opportunity to fuck plenty of times, but something told me to wait for someone better. Well, I see why it's so important to listen to your gut now.

I found the someone better.

Now, I just got to make her see I'm better than what she's used to, what's she settled for, because I know the love I can give isn't a settlement.

It's an aspiration.

She wants castles in Spain?

I'll build her towers until they reach the goddamn sky. The heaven she will come to love will be the one I create.

"That's what you get for thinking you can come at me without consequence," Dawn says to Candy. The fake blonde with big tits is still choking, eyes watering, but she still allows Pirate to feel her up, so she is obviously fine.

"Bitch," Candy gasps.

Shucks, the heaven I want to create for her she has already

created for me. I've never really seen any of the women here put the cut-sluts in place. I'm not sure if Dawn is feeling defensive because she doesn't know anyone here or she frowns upon the club whores; I don't really know. Her hackles are high being in a strange place. She's worried about her son and whoever did this to her.

And all I want to do is take her to our heaven, the place I've created and imagined in my mind since the moment I laid eyes on her.

Fuck, I'm such a damn sap.

Whatever. I don't give a fuck. Tool and Reaper are pussy whipped too. I dare them to give me shit.

"Nice kitchen," she says, looking around the industrial-size room. "And basement. If you're a serial killer," she mumbles.

"Don't say serial killer too loud." I glance over my shoulder to make sure Poodle isn't around. "We have one in SKA."

"SKA?"

"Serial Killer Anonymous. He's in rehab with our leader." I can't hold back the snicker again. *Leader.* I snort.

"To stop killing!" she squeaks and tries to roll out of my hold, but I grip her tight. "What the hell kind of place is this?" She kicks and wiggles, doing her best to get away from me, but it's just turning me on.

"He killed really bad people if that makes any difference."

She purses her lips and stops wiggling as she thinks about if what I said is right or wrong. I want to steal those lips in a fiery kiss to see if her passion runs as hot as her anger.

"How bad?"

"The worst of the worst. The world won't miss them."

"Why is he in … SKA?" Her voice gets higher with every letter from the uncertainty of if she said the acronym right.

"To stop killing." My shoulder hits the wall as I take another left down the hall, and I grunt from the damn thing being
in the way. Stupid wall.

"But if he is killing really bad people, why stop?"

The question has my steps faltering, and I nearly drop her
on the ground, but I lean right to catch myself along the line
of pictures hanging there. My shoulder hits the glass and one
breaks, and a web of cracks show along the surface.

"Ye don't care?"

"Horrible people should have a horrible death. That's my
opinion," she says in a cold, distant voice as she stares at the
stained glass in the middle of the door at the end of the hall.
It's storming outside now, and the rain gathers along the skull
on the different colored glass and drips down the eye sockets,
giving the mirage of tears.

Everyone knows skulls don't fucking cry.

I get moving again, staring at the side of her face with so
many questions that I know she won't answer right now. What
the hell has this woman seen and been through to believe such a
thing? It isn't easy to numb a heart, but once it is, hell, it's nearly
impossible to thaw. Dawn's is frozen solid.

If there is hope for me to be with her, I either have to become numb too or melt the ice she's encased herself in.

Time for me to get a fucking blow torch because this arse
doesn't do well in the cold.

"Prez!" I shout through his closed door and knock.

*"Fuck, that's it, doll. Just like that. You suck my cock so fucking
good. Jesus Christ."*

I take a step back when I realize what's going on in his
office. I blush, my hot blood pooling in my cheeks. "He's a …
he's busy. It will just be a second—minute. Probably a minute

or two, considering how long it's … a … been going on." I clear my throat and stare at a picture on the wall I've seen a hundred fucking times. And then I start walking.

Her hand grips my arm. "No, stay."

"But … he's. I mean … he's—" I set her on the floor and reach up to scratch the back of my head. I hate feeling awkward about shit like this. I shouldn't. I've gotten my dick sucked before.

"I know," she says. "It's hot, right? Just listen," she whispers, placing her index finger against her lips, telling me to be quiet.

"I can't listen to my Prez getting a damn blow job."

"You're still standing here, so it looks like you are to me."

Those lips! I just want to silence them with mine, so she stops revving up my fucking lust with her hot mouth.

"I'm going to come, doll. Take every drop like I know you can."

Dawn turns her eyes on me, and her pupils are dilated. Does she like hearing people fuck? No, no way. She's too … angry for that. She has to be screwing with me.

"That's hot. How he talks to her. I've never had a man talk to me like that before."

Mental note. *Check.*

"Ye haven't been with the right men," I say with wee bit more confidence than I have a right to.

"Apparently," she says as the door opens, and Sarah stands there in a mess of blonde hair and swollen lips.

Reaper is going to punish me for listening. I know he is. My life as I know it is over. Women always get a man in trouble. I'm so fucked. This is what I get for listening to Dawn.

"How long have you been standing there?" Reaper zips his pants, and Sarah rights her red summer dress.

"Not long. Just now," I lie. I fucking lie to my Prez. If he finds out, I'm a dead Scotsman.

"Why are you blushing?" Sarah asks, a knowing mischievous twinkle in her eye.

"I told him he was handsome," Dawn says from beside me, and I wonder if she means it or if she is saving face.

Shucks.

Saving face, probably. Who would want a pale ginger who wears a kilt that people think is a skirt half the time.

"You're the woman Skirt found on the side of the road. I'm assuming you have business to discuss."

"I do. I want to leave. I need to get to my son. He isn't safe."

Reaper let's out a breath, and Sarah spins around, stands on her tiptoes, and gives him a kiss on the cheek. "I'll let you get to it, Jesse."

"Love you, doll."

"Love you too, Jesse."

Reaper watches Sarah walk down the hall until she's out of sight. He'd reap a million souls if it meant giving Sarah a baby. To have a love like that, well, in my eyes, that's bliss.

CHAPTER FIVE

Dawn

I'M USED TO SEEING BIG MEN, BUT NOTHING LIKE THIS. EVERY
single man in this clubhouse is huge. And the guy who
calls himself Reaper? Or Prez? I don't know what the titles
mean, but he's massive, and he scares the hell out of me. He
has shaggy hair, tattoos, and one along his collarbone that says,
'Long Live The King.' I'm going to go out on a limb here and
assume he is the king of kings in this lovely establishment they
call a home.

And yeah, men in charge scare me.

I can deal with the loose girls here. I can deal with the guys
too. I've been slapped more than once by Cohen from my smart
mouth getting away from me when I'm tired of holding things
in.

"Step into my office." Reaper opens the door wide. I peek

in to make sure it's clear and nothing is about to come down from above the door and chop my head off or something for being an outsider. "I ain't going to bite, Dawson."

"Dawn," I dare to correct him. These bikers, while they scare the hell out of me, they did save me, which means I owe them more than friendship. I owe them my life.

"Dawn," he says instead. "Skirt, go inform Doc—"

"No!" I panic and reach for Skirt's hand, and I grab onto it like the lifeline it is. He's the first man I saw when I woke up, he's the man I punched in the face because I was scared and he didn't hit me back; he's the man who carried me because my body was weak. "No, please." I swallow the spit gathering in my mouth to coat my dry throat. "Can he stay? He's ... he's the only one I'm not afraid of," I admit, and Skirt's hand tightens around mine. I know my bravado was big earlier, but I'm on high alert being here.

Reaper has crow's feet around his eyes, from either smiling or squinting. I'm going to go with squinting. He doesn't seem like the kind of guy to smile. Either way, the crow's feet soften when I tell him the truth, and he nods. "Of course. Skirt, come in," Reaper says.

I tug on Skirt's arm, and he stumbles over the threshold, giving Reaper a chance to shut the door. I don't want to tell him that his office smells like cum either. He probably knows, and he's probably proud of it. I'd bet he knows Skirt and I listened in on him getting his cock sucked. I can't believe I told Skirt it was hot listening to a guy getting off. I've never been so bold before. Skirt makes me nervous, so I said what I thought he'd want to hear, but then he blushed like a damn virgin. I wonder if I overstepped.

Then again, a man like Skirt has to be used to getting his

cock blown with all the women around here dressed in nothing but their skin.

"Take a seat," Reaper says, but it sounds more like an order.

And if there is one thing I know how to do, it's to do what I'm told. I sit right away, and Skirt stands behind me. I crane my head to the side and look up at him. He has a thick red beard that looks well-groomed and his red lashes fan over the tops of his cheeks as he stares down at me. "Sit. You heard the man," I say.

"I'm going to have to stand." Skirt brings his fist up to his mouth and coughs.

Reaper chuckles and laces his fingers behind his head. "And why is that?" He leans back in the chair and plops his boots on the desk to get comfortable, then his eyes pinch as he stares at the black leather. He unhooks his hands from behind his head, licks his thumb, and polishes a spot on the tip of his boot.

"Uh, no reason. I just feel like standing." Skirt's cheeks turn a pretty shade of pink, and for a badass biker, he sure does get bashful. I think it's cute. He has this charm that I can't put my finger on and these good looks that remind my soul what it's like to lust after someone again. I really like the kilt too.

Two words: easy access.

"Skirt here had to avoid hitting you when you passed out in the road, and he swerved off the road. His bike crashed into a rock and he flew over the handlebars and landed on a cactus." Reaper starts laughing halfway through his explanation, and I can understand why it's funny. I want to laugh, but he got hurt because of me, and that isn't humorous at all.

"Skirt, I'm so sorry. I never wanted that to happen."

"It's okay, Lips. The needles didn't hurt that bad coming out."

"Whatever. You wanted numbing cream." Reaper throws Skirt under the bus.

"Ye have needles close to yer ball sack and ye let me know how ye want to handle it." Skirt crosses his arms over his chest, pouting. "And my arse is sore, okay? It's just a little tender. A hundred cactus spikes will do that to someone."

"I'm so sorry." I reach around and lay my hand on his ass cheek and gasp when I realize what I just did. I thought I was reaching for his arm to comfort him, but I went in right for the rump. I yank my hand back and fiddle with my nails as I wring my hands together on my lap. "Um, sorry," I say. He has a firm butt, one that I wouldn't mind getting a handful of if it were mine.

"Let's get to the issue at hand. You aren't in any state to go anywhere, Dawn. No offense, you look like shit and you can barely walk."

"You don't understand." I look to Reaper, then down at my hands, and then up to Skirt nervously. "I need to get to my son. He's in the hands of a very dangerous man. You have to let me go. He has seizures. He needs me."

"That's how you knew to tell me what to do."

"Yeah," I reply sadly to Skirt. "Unfortunately."

"This man," Reaper starts. "He do this to you?" Reaper's finger traces an invisible line down my body. "And don't lie to me, Dawn. I hate liars."

"He does. Don't lie," Skirt warns and then gives me a small shake of his head. I'm trying to get a good look at his eyes, but I can't see the color. I'm trying to think back to when I saw him outside, but I was so consumed with fear and rage that I didn't really pay attention to him.

His lip is busted because of me, probably his balls too.

"Dawn?" Reaper snaps his fingers, and the kind expression he had on his face is gone, replaced with annoyance.

I flinch out of habit, waiting for the blow to come. I prepare myself by squeezing my eyes shut and tensing my body.

"Oh, Dawn."

I recognize that tone. It's pity.

"I ain't going to hit you, Dawn. Ever. That's not my cup of tea, and any man here who ever lays a hand on a woman is dealt with."

Dealt with.

No need to fill in the blanks there.

"My son's name is Aidan. He is epileptic. I'm the only one he can depend on. He is in danger, not just because of his medical condition, but the man who has him. My boyfriend—ex-boyfriend—thinks he is the father."

"Sounds like you say he isn't," Reaper puts two and two together.

I'm not ashamed about getting pregnant from a brief fling, but I wonder what Skirt thinks about me now. I don't look at him. I shouldn't care what he thinks, but I do. I don't want him to care that I've slept with multiple people.

"What's this guy's name so we can track down your son?" Reaper asks, getting out a pen and paper.

"You're going to get him for me? Really?" Tears sting my eyes as I sit forward on the edge of my seat. I want to launch myself across the table and hug this big, scary biker man.

"You need to rest, Dawn. I'm serious about that. Plus, this sounds like a Ruthless job. Name," he repeats again, and a tiny speck of fear drops in my stomach since he doesn't seem like the kind of guy who likes to repeat himself.

"Cohen O'Roarke," I say, prying my tongue from the roof of my mouth.

"What the fuck did ye just say?" Skirt seethes and is

suddenly in front of me, caging me in with his arms. His hands grip the arms of the chair, and as he leans in, I lean back. His hot breath caresses my cheek, and the brush of the heavy puffs feels dangerous, promising harm if I don't obey.

The pure hatred in Skirt's eyes has me trembling.

"Skirt!" Reaper bellows to get Skirt away from me. "Back down."

"I need to know. Did ye just say Cohen O'Roarke? The Irish fighter? Is that who ye said?" His voice is calm, but it isn't light and kind; it's deep with rage. My heart is soaking up his anger and transforming it into terror. A tear slips down my cheek as I wait for the inevitable.

A knee to the face.

A kick in the ribs.

A violent face fuck that leaves me in tears and gagging.

"You're scaring her, Skirt! Look at her. She's shaking." Reaper grips Skirt by the collar and yanks him backward with so much strength, Skirt slams against the wall. The plain white drywall cracks and dents from Skirt's shoulder, showing just how fragile everything is around these men. "I said get the fuck back!" Reaper screams until his voice breaks.

"I'm sorry," Skirt says, gripping the sides of his hair. He rolls his body, his back flattens against the wall, and he slides down it until he's sitting on the ground, head between his knees. "Ye couldn't have said that name." The denial can't be missed, but I know the truth. I'm O'Roarke's property. Cohen will burn down this city to find me, and he won't find me out of love.

I'm a possession and that's all I'll ever be. "I've been with him for a few years now." I wipe the tears off my cheek with my palms. "He's a horrible man. I haven't been able to get away. He's dangerous. You have to believe me." I snag Reaper's wrist, and my fingers don't even meet around it. My lashes bead with liquid, and every time I blink, a few more droplets fall from my eyes.

"I see the proof. There's no need to have to beg me, Dawn."

Skirt stands and runs his fingers through his hair, then he scrubs them over his face. He gives me his back, the muscles tight with stress as he lifts his arms up and over his head. Skirt lays his hand on the wall and exhales a long breath. His head hangs between his massive shoulders, then he spreads his arms out to his sides, showing the impressive wingspan.

"Skirt, why does that name sound familiar?"

"Because, Prez, that's the man who killed my brother all those years ago." Skirt turns around, and when I see his eyes, I see the bright burning blue orbs, scalding like the hottest part of a flame. He's furious. "I've been fighting all my life to get ready for the day I take that man down once and for all."

My fingers wrap around the armrest of the chair as Skirt's words sink into me. The world can't be this small. How can I go from one pissed-off fighter to the next? Cohen killed Skirt's brother? This is all too much. My son is with a killer. "Oh God." I press my palms against my forehead and start to rock to try to calm myself down, but the more I move, the more emotional I become. "This can't be happening. I'm so sorry, Skirt. I had no idea. I—Aidan. I need to get to Aidan!" I want to vomit again, but I'll just dry heave if I do. I haven't eaten anything.

Skirt blocks the doorway and stretches each arm out to stop me from going anywhere. "Ye can't go," his Adam's apple bobs. "I can't let you go back to that monster."

"That monster has my son!" I shove Skirt's chest with all

the might I have, but he barely moves. "Get out of my way, Skirt."

"No, Lips. I can't. I have to protect ye, and I can't do that while yer fighting a man who's never lost a fight in his life."

"I've always wondered why you fight," Reaper chimes in as he leans against the desk and crosses each ankle over the other. "Makes sense. You're damn good at it too. Can't believe you've been holding out on me all these years."

"I only fight to get better at throwing punches. Once I hit the man I need to, I'll hang up my gloves."

"You mean, your brass knuckles." Reaper lights a cigarette and blows out the thick cloud of smoke. "Don't tell Sarah about this, Skirt, she thinks I quit. If she finds out, I'll scar a heart in your chest forever."

"Yes, Prez," Skirt says automatically as if he has said it a hundred times, but he never takes his eyes off me. The icy irises have me shivering, teeth chattering, as if it's winter, and I'm standing in the middle of a snowstorm.

Torment meets torment, and I find myself falling into the shattered pieces of his heart. Instead of bleeding from the sharp shards, a piece of my own jigsaw soul fits perfectly against his. If I spend any more time with Skirt, somehow, someway, our fucked-up parts will meld a mechanical heart that will learn to beat again—together.

And that scares me because for all I know, only my side will pump the blood needed to sustain us, while his is dead set on revenge.

"Skirt, please." Another tear falls and I lay my palms against his chest. "I need to get Aidan. He's the only thing good I have in this world. He's four. He doesn't understand how bad Cohen is yet."

"We will get your son, Dawn. You don't have to worry about that. Do you know where Cohen is staying? Can you give us details?"

"I'm going to go get the kid," Skirt says, grinding his teeth together.

"No, the fuck you're not. You're going to stay right here with Dawn. I don't need you going in pissed and forgetting there's a four-year-old boy who needs rescued."

"I won't forget that!"

"Yeah? Tell me you wouldn't kill Cohen right in front of Aidan's eyes without thinking. Tell me," Reaper urges, flicking the ashes of his cigarette on the ground. The way the burnt tobacco floats to the floor reminds me of snow. It's oddly beautiful and just as dangerous. Cigarettes cause cancer, but snow can freeze people to death.

It's what happened to my parents.

"Yeah, that's what I thought." Reaper kicks off the desk, walks around the side, and opens a drawer. A gold ashtray is revealed, and he rubs the end of the ember against the metal to put out the cigarette. "I won't repeat myself; I fucking hate doing that. I'll gather Poodle. He's got an itch to scratch."

"Poodle? A dog? You're going to send a dog after my son?" I holler, ready to throw my fists again. Not that they will do any damage, but I'll try.

Reaper chuckles. and the smoke still lingering in his lungs is forced out of his nostrils. "No, Poodle is member. Good guy."

I have a feeling there's something he isn't telling me. I spin on my heel, away from Skirt blocking the door, and charge toward Reaper, my index finger pointed. My chin wobbles and sure, I always cry when it comes to my kid, but right now, I'm furious. I'm a mother on a mission, and I will go to any and all lengths to get Aidan in my arms.

If that means I have to take down every man in this building to walk out these doors, I will.

"You better not be lying to me, Reaper." I stare at him in the eyes that remind me of something lifeless; they're so deep and dark, like a well. A tear drops down my cheek for added effect, and the hardness along the edges of his mouth go soft. He can see my agony. He has no idea how much it hurts to not have my kid with me. It's like a piece of my heart can't beat, and I'm struggling to live, but I'll live for Aidan. He doesn't look away. He understands the point I'm trying to make.

"That's my son. I need him here. If you are lying, I will kill you. I don't know how"—a big tear falls down my cheek—"but I will." I won't. I don't think I have it in me to kill a man, but I'll go to any length to protect my son.

"Threat received, noted, and won't be forgotten. I'll tell you this..." He cracks his neck then his sausage-like fingers. "I don't take kindly to threats, but I'll let you go with this one because of everything that's going on. Make no mistake, we are the really good bad guys, Dawn. You might have switched one hell for another, but the devil is a little nicer on this side of town. I'll give you three chances like everyone else here. Don't threaten me again. Get out. I need to track Cohen. Send Badge in here, Skirt, so I can update him on our next target." Reaper pushes us out of his office and slams the door in our faces.

"What happens after three chances?" I stare at the fogged glass on his office door as if it will swirl and become clear to show me the answers to life.

Mirror, mirror on the wall, who is the biggest fool of all?
I am.

"He rips your heart from your chest and watches it struggle to beat in his palm."

"Something tells me you aren't joking," I say, rubbing my hand over my heart as it steadily beats.

"That's nothing to joke about."

It just clicked how the men get their names, and I don't like it one bit.

Once I have my son, I'm getting the hell out of dodge. Vegas can burn in the eternity of the hell that keeps it alive for all I care.

I'm done with dangerous men, no matter how captivated I am by Skirt. Men aren't worth the misery that comes with them.

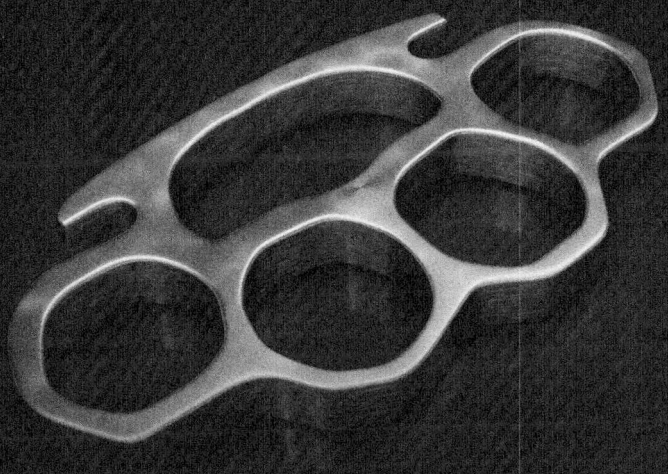

CHAPTER SIX

Skirl

JAB, JAB, HOOK. JAB, JAB, UPPERCUT, HOOK. JAB, JAB, FUCKING JAB. Sweat pours off me in gallons as I hit the Everlast bag in front of me in the gym Reaper had me build as an extension. I have my shirt off, gloves on, and I let out all of my frustrations. All these years, all this time, and Cohen O'Roarke is back in my life. Out of all the fucking ways to get to him, I have to get to him through Dawn.

Dawn. So fucking beautiful. Strong. Sassy. A mouth I want to silence with a kiss. Son-of-a-bitch, she's going to be the fucking death of me. This isn't how it's supposed to be. She's been around the bad life for far too long for me to pull her into mine, into the club's. If she finds out that I'm just another O'Roarke, fighting until I see blood, she'll hate me.

She is better off hating me than loving me, anyhow. Hatred

is stronger than love. Sure, many things are built out of love, but hatred, that's the one emotion that towers over the rest. It looms over fucking houses, marriages, kids, and whatever else people like to pretend they are building based on love.

Until one fucking thing slides out of place. Money problems, partner cheats, sickness, and that ugly bitch *hatred* roars her head and takes over.

Hatred is the only power in this world that is strong enough to drown out love. It's the only thing that truly lingers after loves fades. I've lived it… Fuck, I'm still living it.

Dawn deserves peace, a good life for her and her boy, and I'll make sure they get it. She'll never see me again, just how it should be. I don't need my head fucked up by some las anyway. My cock might be harder than it ever has been, but I can't get it up for any of the cut-sluts. It's time for me to get my head out of my arse and just fuck. Maybe I'll get Candy. Pirate seems to like her best. I hear she sucks cock real fucking good. And I need that right now.

The anger burns my muscles; the frustration, the memories of Conor, and the pent-up aggression is nearly bursting at the seams. I can't take it anymore. I'm not myself. I won't ever be myself again. I should have taken care of Cohen years ago. Maybe this abuse wouldn't have happened to Dawn. She wouldn't be here bruised to hell and back. She wouldn't be tempting me with those bright green eyes. She'd be safe from me, from my fists.

A fighter is just an abuser, after all. What if I'm just like Cohen? What if I hurt her?

The thought has me hitting the bag harder. The material of the gloves smack against the heavyweight bag. I make it sway, dodge, keep my feet planted against the floor, and keep light on my toes.

Jab, jab, hook. Jab, Jab, uppercut.

I exhale with every hit, punching the bag harder with every beat that passes. I intentionally miss the next hit, soaring past the swinging bag so I can keep my reflexes quick.

"Hit the bag any harder and you'll punch a hole through it."

I jab the bag one last time before turning around, seeing Poodle leaning up against the doorway, cut on, hair brushed and fluffy like it always is, looking just like his damn dog. Shit, the dog. Chaos.

I forgot all about him. I'm sure Ellie is taking good care of him for me.

"Fuck off, Poodle. I ain't in the mood for anymore shite today."

"Accent is heavy today," he notices, uncrossing his ankles as he pushes off the wall to walk toward me. "Something on your mind?"

I scoff, chuckling sarcastically as I hit the bag again. "Fuck off, Poodle. Don't act like ye know a damn thing about me."

"Come on, Skirt. I've been trying for weeks to talk to you. You have something on your mind. I want to be your friend—"

"Me friend? Me fucking friend? Are ye kiddin' me with that bullshite right now?" He's right. My accent always comes out a lot thicker when I'm mad. I can't help it. Right now, I want to kill and Poodle. With the tension between us, he'll be my target if he doesn't get the hell out of my way. "Yer out of yer damn mind if ye think we are friends right now. Ye know everything about me, Poodle. Why don't ye take a guess at what is bothering me? Hell, I couldn't begin to decipher what is on yer mind. Fuck off, Poodle. I'm not in the mood." I square up, ready to hit the bag again. I want to spend a few more hours hitting the bag. I need to feel the ache in my bones, my muscles; I want to be tired. I want this anger buzzing in my system to set me free.

"Grow the fuck up, Skirt. Talk to me. We aren't kids anymore. Man up, turn around, and fucking talk to me."

The bag in front of me rocks left to right, right to left, and for about an hour now I've been imagining it's Cohen; right now, I'm imagining it's my best friend.

My ex-best friend.

I turn my head until I only see the wall to my right since Poodle is standing behind me. "What the fuck did ye just say?"

"I think you heard me, Skirt. You hard in the ears now? Or just in the head?"

I turn around slowly, my chest heaving, my body boiling, my fist aching to plummet him. "Ye have a death wish, James?" I call him by his given name, letting him know where we stand now.

"Not as much as you do, *Rohan*."

We circle each other, just like fighters do in the ring. The only thing Poodle has on me is that he hasn't been hitting a bag for an hour. My chest heaves, and my muscles burn, twitching. "Ye realize I'm trained in fighting or did ye forget?"

"I didn't forget." He cracks his neck and then pulls up his fucking hair.

"Yeah, wouldn't want to get yer pretty mane messed up, would we?" I run my hand down my hair and bat my lashes. "A real bitch fucks with his hair," I sneer, then spit on the floor next to his boots.

"A real man fights with his fists, not fucking brass knuckles." Poodle fakes a left hook and hits me with a right.

Shite, it makes my ears ring. I shake my head and wiggle my jaw back and forth. There's a familiar burning sensation spreading along my jawline. "Not bad," I say, impressed, and lick the inner part of my cheek where the blood is gathering. "For a poodle."

His lip curls with anger, but he doesn't charge me again. He's smart when it comes to fighting. I had no idea. I spit again, getting the damn iron out of my mouth.

I don't swing my fists; instead, I swing my leg to the side and knock him off his feet. Poodle hits the mat with a hard thud, and his hair comes out of its tie, so I grab ahold of it like bitch reins. "Is that what Melissa does when yer fucking her? Holding on to yer hair to control ye? Cause that's what this shit is for!" I rear his head back and smash it against the mat, watching speckles of red flow from his mouth.

He wraps his legs around my waist and rears his head back, busting my nose. It's enough for the hold I have on his hair to loosen, and he rolls out from under me, smashing his palm against my nose. A river of blood flows down my face as I holler in pain.

"To have been trained by the best fighter in Scotland, you're real shit," Poodle taunts, landing a blow in my stomach.

I double over, groaning when puke rises up my throat. It's a vulnerable position to be in. A fighter never bends over like this because it leaves room for—

A sick crunch sounds when his knee connects with my face, and I stagger back, the world caving in around me as my head spins.

All I taste is blood.

I fall to my knees, tired, exhausted—the fight leaving me. I leave myself open for him to finish me off, but he falls to his knees in front of me. He grips the back of my neck and lays his forehead against mine. "You're a fucking dumbass if you think you can go in a ring and fight one of the greatest fighters who ever lived thinking with your emotions, Skirt. I don't know shit about fighting, and I just took you down. I know how you fight. You're a killer. I've seen it. If you can't win against little old me, how the fuck can you beat Cohen?"

I pull from his grasp, not ready to be brother-brother with him just yet. I wipe my nose on my arm, streaking blood along my freckled, tattooed skin. "Fuck ye! I'd just been beating on a bag for an hour. I'm tired." It's a sorry ass excuse.

"Yeah? How's that going to go when you're seven rounds in the ring?"

"That's different," I hiss and pound my fist to my chest, the gloves soft and forgiving the blow.

"How?" Poodle flips his hair over his shoulder, looking like he belongs in a Head and Shoulders commercial.

"Because I won't be fighting someone I thought I could trust." I wipe my lip again. "Or I won't be fighting someone who thought he couldn't trust me."

Poodle's shoulders sag, and he tosses up his hair again in a messy girly bun. "It wasn't about that, Skirt. It wasn't about not trusting you. I trust you with my life. I still do."

"You know how important it is to me for my brother to fucking confide in me!" I yell, blood and spit flying. "Then ye went and proved I couldn't be trusted. I couldn't be confided it. I wouldn't have told anyone about yer psychopathic killing ways. I would have joined ye, Poodle. I would have helped ye, without question. And then—just fucking forget it. Ye don't understand." Shite, I feel like I'm breaking up with a long-term girlfriend or something with how me and Poodle are talking.

He was my brother after my own flesh and blood died, though. Poodle was the first person I recognized as someone who wouldn't fill Conor's space or replace it, but he came real fucking close. He doesn't understand how much his friendship meant to me or how much I needed it to keep me grounded. Poodle was the only one who understood me.

And now?

I've never felt more alone.

I'm starting to wonder if my ma was right. It should be me in the ground instead of Conor. No one can confide in me. Not like Conor. That died when he did.

"You don't think I wanted to talk to you? Do you know how lost I was? How dark I felt? I was afraid to tell you."

"Why?"

"Because I thought I'd lose you as my friend, but it looks like I did anyway."

"If you two are done having your fucking pillow talk, Prez is calling Church," Bullseye's voice cuts through the heart to heart Poodle and I are having, and I'm glad for the interruption.

My eyes meet Poodle's, then I place my hand on my hips and stare at the wall. "We are done here anyway," I say and march toward the exit, leaving Poodle behind me.

I'm not even sure what I'm mad about anymore. All I know is that I'm furious. It's consuming. I can't stop it. I'm mad at everyone. Everything. I know I can turn around right now and count on Poodle, but my pride stops me. I want nothing to do with anyone. My bare, sweaty shoulder slams against Bullseye, and I don't bother saying sorry.

"Better watch who you're running into, Skirt."

I grunt in return and make my way through the gym, prowling to Church, my footsteps pounding across the hallow polished floors. I yank the door open, and it slams against the wall, the metal rattling my brain. I rip my gloves off with my teeth and throw them on the floor as I walk down the hall that leads to the kitchen.

This place has grown so much since I got here. There are homes that I've built by my hands, something I didn't even know I enjoyed doing until I tried. My hands always need to be busy; that much I've learned.

When I kick the door open from the hall to the kitchen, Sarah and Melissa are there, and they gasp when they see how Poodle kicked my arse. I don't care. Prez calls for Church, I'm there busted nose and all.

"Lassies," I tip my imaginary hat to them, and their eyes roam my body. They seem shocked that someone got the upper hand on me, but there's only one person alive who will ever be able to do that, and he has girly fucking hair.

"Skirt," they say with a tone that's garbled with disbelief.

The basement door taunts me, reminding me of the time I spent next to the Dawn as she laid there sleeping. Just the memory of her has my heart doing those fucking flips that I don't have time for. I try to rub the pains out with my fist, but it's no use. The damn gal has sunk her claws into my heart, and if I spend any more time with her, she's going to yank it from my chest.

Something about her calls deep to me, the reminder of what home feels like. Not here, but Scotland. Dawn reminds me of the waves crashing against the cliffs, the scent that hangs in the air after it rains, and the way the skies open up after a storm. She's the day I walked through the rain from my brother's funeral.

Dawn washes away the agony, but I can't be without pain. It's what drives me. Washing myself in her rain won't cleanse me, it won't baptize me—it'll ruin me.

I stop outside the door of Church and get my bearings to-gether. A few guys are still in the main room, drinking beers, and Tank, the big fucking teddy bear, is talking it up with Becks, the club's massage therapist. I don't know if other clubs have one of those, but they should. There's nothing like getting a rub down after a run. Muscles are tight, stressed to the max, and then Becks cracks her fingers and rubs hot oil all over your body; fuck, it feels good.

My eyes fall on Candy, sucking Pirate's cock. I can hear the slurping from here. He just sits there, eyes pointed to the ceil-ing, bottle of rum in his hand, and a dead expression in his eyes. Pirate doesn't even look like he's enjoying the blow job. Candy is moaning like a real bitch putting on a good show, shoving her hands between her legs to get herself off, but Pirate just pours rum into his mouth. The liquid drips down his chin and chest, wetting his shirt. Jesus, what a sad fucking sight.

"I called for Church! Get your asses in here!" Reaper shouts as he enters the room, pushing me in there with him.

Poodle comes in a second later, knuckles red and bruised from kicking my ass. "What the hell happened to you two?" Reaper asks as he takes the seat at the head of the table, taking the gavel in hand. The one made of human bone.

"Poodle kicked my arse," I say, not wanting to lie to my Prez.

Reaper's eyebrows hit his hairline with shock as he runs his fingers through his beard. "That so?"

"Once in a lifetime sort of thing, Prez."

"You two bury the hatchet?" he asks.

"No," I say quick.

"That's too bad because we have a problem, and I need you two to kiss and make up." Reaper's eyes scan across the room, glancing at every brother in the room, and my sweaty arms land on the table. I hate that look. It's the look that says he's about to burn Vegas to the ground. "Close the door," he says to no one as he stares out the window, but Pirate comes in, zipping up his pants, and kicks the door shut.

"Can't find the kid," Reaper says.

My stomach drops to my fucking feet, and I stand so fast, the chair slams against the wall as beads of sweat from my earlier work out falls from my hair and onto the table. "What the fuck do ye mean, Prez?"

"I mean, we cased Cohen's place, his gym, everywhere. The kid is missing and so is Cohen."

CHAPTER SEVEN

Dawn

"DAWN."

The sound of my name has me turning my head. Skirt is standing in the doorway of a room they call 'Church'; whatever that means. I'm going to take a wild guess it has nothing to do with prayer and everything to do with what people pray against. He isn't wearing a shirt. Skirt's skin is wet, glistening with sweat, and his chest heaves from exertion, and he has dried blood trailing down his nose and lips.

"What happened to you?" I stand up from the couch and run over to him, laying my palms on his chest. His body is warm, sticky. He smells of blood, sweat, pain, and torment. My eyes roam his body. He has abs under all the tattoos and carved hips meant to be held onto as he fucks a woman. His pecs are defined, swollen with muscle, and he has a dusting of red hair along his chest that makes thousands of goose bumps rise on my body. I've shivered from fear, with pain, but I've never shivered from pleasure, never by a simple touch.

His nostrils flare, and one of his rugged hands that has a black and white tattoo of a devil screaming across the top lands on mine, holding my palm against him. The air between us charges with this unseen force, this energy that I've never felt before. My body is being called to him, and I move a step closer, unable to fight it any longer.

I've been fighting the urge to fall into his arms ever since I laid my eyes on him. I thought he was a dream. He's the walking, talking, real-life version of my perfect man, plucked out of my fantasies to make my reality sweet at last.

"Dawn," he repeats my name, and I love how it sounds with his accent. Skirt lays his forehead against mine, and my breath catches from his lips being so close. The blood doesn't even bother me. "Lips, we need to talk about Aidan."

Hope springs to my chest, and I pull away, but I keep my hand on his pec and feel the wild heartbeat beneath my palm. "You found him!" I say with glee, but when disappointment fills his eyes, the creases between his eyes furrowing, dread falls into the pit of my stomach. I yank my hand away, missing Skirt's heat when my hand turns cold. "Please, tell me you found him, Skirt. Please," I beg as tears fill my eyes. My hands cup my mouth the longer he stays quiet.

His silence speaks volumes, and it's deafening.

"No!" I scream at the top of my lungs and double over. "No, please," I sob so hard I gag. I can't seem to get enough air into my lungs. The world tilts, and nothing makes sense. Aidan has to be with Cohen. He has to be. I don't know where else my boy could be. Every ounce of strength I've had to fight to survive Cohen drains from my body, and my knees give out from under me.

"I got ye, Lips." Skirt catches me, wrapping me in the safety of his arms, the strength he uses to fight.

I can feel everyone's eyes on me. I don't care. My heart is breaking. No one knows how this feels. It's like my heart is being ripped out of my chest and stomped on. My hands dig into Skirt's arms, and I lay my cheek on his chest, inhaling the musky scent of his skin. It's oddly relaxing, but it isn't enough to stop the onslaught of tears.

"You can't find him," I mumble with moist lips against his chest, the salty liquid from my tears spilling onto my tongue.

"No, they can't find Cohen either," he replies, rubbing his hand down the spine of my back. His chin settles on top of my head as I cry. We're standing there, in the middle of the doorway, a dozen eyes on us, and he doesn't care. He lets me hash out the pain.

I untangle myself out of his arms and step away from him. I look over his shoulder to see Reaper staring at me, pity in his eyes, and I cock my head at him, then point my finger. "I thought you said you'd find my son. You didn't. All of you are the same!" I shout. "Just more men making promises you can't keep. I'll find him myself. I'll find my son. He's probably not even at the top of your priority list. You probably need to go find some drugs or whatever the fuck an MC does; maybe just sit around and get your cocks sucked," I spit and shove a finger into Skirt's chest.

"No man has ever held up a promise to me." I take another step away and bolt to the front door. I have no idea where I'm going, but my path will lead me somewhere. Aidan needs me.

I have to think about Cohen, the steps he takes, the places he goes. I have to think like a lying, conniving snake.

It's the only way I'll ever be able to find Aidan.

As I open the door and let the sun in, a pair of arms wrap around me, stopping me from leaving. I see the familiar devil on the top of the hand, and I know it's Skirt. I kick and scream, punch and shout, "Let me go! Let me fucking go!" I wiggle, putting as much force as I can into my body, bowing my back, but Skirt's hold is too tight.

"Ye aren't going anywhere all pissed off. Ye won't get any-thing done that way." His mouth is against my ear, and he whis-pers, "Calm down, Lips. I swear, I'll find ye son if that's the last thing I ever do on this earth, but ye got to give me a chance."

My body sags against him, the fight once again draining me from as I fall limp in his arms. Suddenly, I'm swung in the air, and Skirt holds my head against his chest, blocking my eyes from everyone staring at me as I silently weep into his chest. I feel like such a burden. My soul is heavy. Without Aidan, I don't think I'll ever learn how to breathe again.

I'm not sure where Skirt is taking me, but I'm going to trust him. I have no one else here I can trust. I may as well try my luck with the nicest guy of the group that calls themselves ruthless. Not Ruthless enough to find my son, though.

We seem to walk forever. His boots pound against the floor, and then a door opens, and the sun heats my skin; the warmth feels good, comforting, but not as comforting as Skirt's embrace. He isn't supposed to have this effect on me. No man can have this kind of hold over a woman so quick. I've made that mistake once, and I can't afford the lack of judgment again.

The familiar feeling of rising with every step jars me, and that's how I know Skirt is going up a set of steps. An awning of shade blocks the sun, stopping the scorch of light from burning my skin in such a short distance from the clubhouse to wherever we are going.

A long creak squeaks as Skirt opens another door. The air dries the sheen of sweat on my flesh, and something soft is under me in the next second. I wipe my eyes and look around. I'm in a cabin sitting on a black leather sofa. Logs make up the home instead of plain drywall. No pictures hang, nothing personal.

There's a TV on the wall, big and wide, set on a glass stand. There's a wooden coffee table that has yet to be stained, and I wonder if Skirt made it. It looks handmade, but people can buy things like that left and right these days. I sniffle, wiping my cheeks again when Skirt lays a blanket over me.

"Thank you," I say in a small, weak voice.

"Aye," he answers and tucks the blanket around my body. He's close, and my eyes catch his as something quickly passes between us, but then he pulls away and clears his throat. "I'm going to pour myself a drink. Ye want one?"

"Yeah. What do you have?"

"Just whiskey, babe. It's all a man needs," he says.

There's a mini bar on the far side of the wall, and the shelves are full of different whiskeys. He gathers two scotch glasses from under the bar and adds a square chunk of ice into each. I watch as he scans the shelves, deciding which whiskey will do for the day when he finally plucks one off the shelf and pours until each glass is nearly full.

Christ. I can't drink all that. I'll be drunk.

That sounds good right about now, anyway.

Skirt carries the glasses in his hand and sets them on the coffee table, then plops on the couch next to me. He stretches his defined arm over the back of the couch and sips the amber whiskey down his throat. His skin is pale, but with the freckles and tattoos, it seems darker than what it really is.

He sighs in contentment and leans his head back against the couch, closing his eyes. I reach for my drink and take a large swallow.

Bad choice. Horrible choice. It burns. My eyes are watering for another reason now. I can barely gulp it down my throat before I'm coughing. My nose is burning, and I want to gag. This shit is disgusting.

"Shite, Lips! Ye can't drink it like that. This stuff will grow hair on ye chest." Skirt pats my back as he stares at me, a slight twinge of a smile on his lips.

"I know. I can feel the hairs spurting from my skin." I cough so hard I think I'm about to lose a lung. Forgetting it's whiskey in my hand, I take another sip to clear my throat, but all the harsh liquor does is burn my airway. "Shit, I forgot."

"Ye crazy. How can ye forget?" He takes the drink from me and sets it on the coffee table. "Yer something else, ain't ye?" he asks, his sky blue eyes lock onto mine, and his thumb wipes my cheek. He seems to do that a lot. Always wiping my tears away. He's the only man that ever has.

Besides my son.

"Aidan," I say with a brokenness I've never heard from myself.

"I know," Skirt says. "I'm fucking sorry, but I'm telling ye right now…" His hands lay on either side of my face, his touch so gentle my bruises can't even feel him "I'm going to find him. I'll make it my personal mission. Okay? He won't take Aidan away from ye like he did my brother."

I know he means Cohen. It sounds like he doesn't even like saying his name. I don't blame him. Cohen brings death and destruction wherever he goes, and Skirt has experienced it firsthand just like I have.

We're connected that way. I've never connected with anyone so effortlessly before.

"You can't promise that," I say, looking away from the intense gaze.

"I can promise that. I know ye aren't used to men holding up their end of the bargain, but I'm not most men. I'll fight, okay? I'm used to fighting."

"Me too," I whisper, reaching for the glass of whiskey again and wrap my fingers around it. I bring it to my lips and take a few deep swallows. This turmoil is rushing inside me, an intricate web of pain and worry.

I'm doing my best to keep my emotion in check, but not knowing where my son is, is going to make me become unhinged. My hands are quaking, and the ice is clattering against the sides of the glass as I bring it to my mouth. It's disgusting, but I guzzle it down, just like an empty tank needing gasoline to get me to where I need to go.

And hopefully this whiskey makes my eyes close and takes me to a world where my son is in my arms again.

Another sob breaks free, and the whiskey spews from the glass onto my face. Skirt takes the drink from me, it's almost empty, but the tears just won't fucking stop. "I can't ... I can't control it," I say, thinking of Aidan's sweet face, crying out for me, needing me. It tears me apart. If I wouldn't have pissed off Cohen, I would be with Aidan right now.

"Don't cry, Lips. Ye making me feel helpless; I don't know how to make this better."

"What if ... what if he's dead, Skirt?"

"Nay, ye can't think like that, Dawn. Ye can't. Come here,"

he says, laying his hand on the back of my head as he pulls me against him again. "Ye'd feel it." His hand falls over my chest, right where my heart thumps, and he pats it. "Ye'd feel it right here if he were really gone. I knew. When my brother died. I knew he was never coming out of that ring again." Skirt's hands fall to my side, the strong fingers digging into the dip of my waist, and his nose brushes down my cheek. He exhales hot air, and the scent of whiskey never smelled so good before.

I'm not scared of how he looks at me or even how he's seeing me right now. With Cohen, if I cried, he'd give me another reason to cry about it. Skirt isn't like that. He's kind; I can sense it. He's good in a world of bad, and that says a lot since there is a lot of bad out there.

I lick my lips as his eyes flicker to my mouth, and I hold my breath. I stopped crying a few second ago, but a wayward tear falls out of the corner of my eye. "I hate seeing ye cry," he admits, brushing his beard against my cheek and in doing so, he cleans away the tear.

His soft pants tickle the shell of my ear as he debates something inside himself. His hands fist my shirt. "I hate it so fucking much." He tilts my head back and doesn't think about it for another second; he steals my mouth in a brazen kiss that takes my breath away, along with my ability to think.

Skirt's mouth on mine takes away all my worries. He transcends me to another place in time, a place where nothing and no one can harm me. The softness of his lips are a contradiction with how rough he kisses. His tongue dives between my lips and licks over mine. He groans alongside my whimper when I realize how different the bourbon tastes coming from his mouth.

He leans me back and settles between my legs. The hot

steel of his cock presses against the apex of my thighs, and my body surges with arousal, something I haven't felt in years. My fingers claw at his back, wanting more of him; knowing I shouldn't want him, but I can't stop it.

My nipples are tight, and his hands are around my waist instead of plucking the tight beads like I want him to.

"Fuck!" he yells, ripping his mouth away from mine. He pushes off the couch, leaving me breathless and dizzy. "Fuck, I'm sorry. I shouldn't have done that. I just took advantage of ye. Yer all sad and shit, and I just couldn't stand to see ye cry. Ye fucking my eyes with ye lips. Fuck!" He paces and pulls at his hair. He looks like a fighter prowling the cage, waiting for his opponent to strike. The dried blood on his face doesn't help matters any. He looks reckless, carnal, ready to kill, but when he sets those dangerous eyes on me, fear is the last thing I feel from him.

He *wants* me.

"Damn it!" he yells, grabs his cock to readjust it, then stomps away from me, slamming the door to the bathroom.

I hear the water of the shower turn on, and I'm left with my mind reeling. What the hell just happened? My lips tingle from our kiss, and my mind is numb. I can hardly string a complete thought together. I never felt anything like that when I kissed Cohen. This was different.

It can't happen again.

My focus has to be on finding my son and getting out of Vegas. No matter how tempting Skirt is with his bad boy looks and his possessive charm, falling for another fighter won't get me anywhere good in life. My son deserves the best, and being with a man who enjoys hitting flesh? It's too much for me to handle.

What kind of mother am I to give into temptation and kiss Skirt when Aidan is missing? I cover my face with my hands and turn over to my side, letting the darkness wash over me as a welcoming cloak. I deserve the misery I feel right now. Thinking with lust instead of my brain isn't going to get my son back.

Whatever is building between me and the sexy Scotsman, cannot happen. He's a fighter. I'm a mother. The two don't go hand in hand. Fighters fight for greed. Mothers fight for love. Last time I checked, greed and love only forms hate.

I've experienced enough hate to last a lifetime.

Skirt's different, the voice in the back of my head pipes up out of nowhere.

I don't care how different he is. No amount of difference can change the fact that he's in a dangerous MC, has women walking around half-naked ready to suck cock, and he throws his fist for a living. None of that screams that this is a safe environment for Aidan.

It's settled.

When Aidan is back in my arms, we're putting our fighting ways behind us.

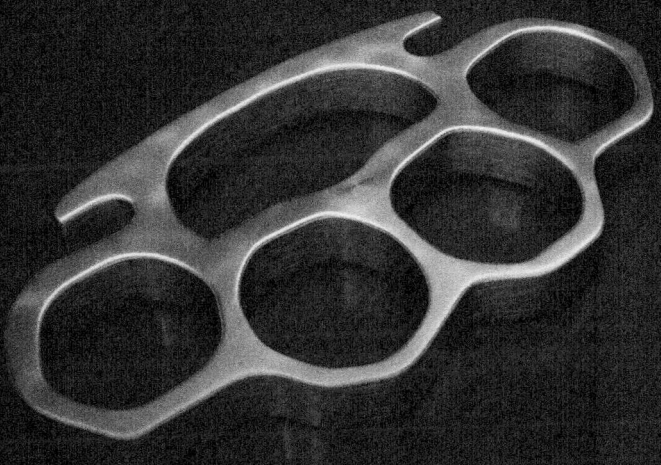

CHAPTER EIGHT

Skirt

MY COCK IS HARD AS A ROCK, AND MY BALLS ARE PULLED TIGHT to my body thinking about her lips against mine. Fuck, I've never had a kiss like that in my life. I've never felt so much desire that if I didn't stick my cock inside her and feel her heat, I'd explode right out of my skin. It's that feeling I've been waiting for.

So long now, I thought something was just fucking wrong with me because I never wanted to fuck, but now it all makes sense. It's Lips I've been waiting for, and fuck if those lips didn't taste as good as I thought they would.

I groan as I wrap my palm around my cock and stroke myself. I lean my head against the tile, letting the rush of water fall down my body, heating my skin along with the lust in my veins.

The drain gurgles as light pink water rushes down the pipe,

the dried blood finally coming off my body. I pay no mind to it. I watch my cock slide in and out of my palm, wishing it was Dawn's fucking tight cunt I was sliding into.

For the first time.

I slam my fist against the wall as I imagine how her pussy feels all wet and soft, like fucking velvet squeezing me as I fuck her. "Fuck me…" I reach down and pinch the space between my arsehole and balls. My taint is fucking sensitive. I've had a lot of time to explore what gets me off and what doesn't, and the rougher I am with myself, the quicker I come.

What if Dawn likes that too? What if she likes being slammed against the wall, hand wrapped around her throat, and my cock driving into her sheath without protection? If I asked her to fight against me, would she?

"Fuck, I'm a sick bastard." I don't have a rape fantasy or anything. It's hard to explain. I want her to shove my chest, slap me in the face, and ask me to fuck her harder.

I hiss when I twist my sack and fuck my cock simultaneously. The water rushes over my face as I lean back, picturing her hot mouth sucking each swollen orb between her lips before she licks my taint. Fuck, I want to. I want to come all over her face, paint it fucking white with my seed, then wipe my fingers through it and make her swallow every single drop.

My fist hits the side of the shower as I come. I jerk myself through my orgasm, wanting that sensitivity to stop me from touching myself, but I keep going. I always do. "Dawn," her name falls from my lips in a soft whine. Thick jets leave my cock as I point my shaft where the drain is, so I don't have to clean up.

By the time I'm done, my cock is still rock hard, and I only feel more on edge. Not even a fight will help this feeling.

SKIRT

No matter how much I want Dawn, no matter how much I want to prove to myself that I can show her love, I'm starting to realize that maybe I can't. She deserves better than a guy like me, a fighter, a better life than I can give her with the club. Not everyone can handle it, and with what she has been through with Cohen, she shouldn't have to. She needs to be happy without any pain in her life.

I need a cut-slut. That's what I need.

I turn off the water and dry off with a towel, my cock tenting the damn thing. I just had the longest, most intense orgasm of my life, and the fucker wants more. All because of Dawn. It's her fault I'm suddenly like this. Her big fucking green eyes, strawberry blonde hair, her cock-sucking lips that have the perfect shape to them.

She'll wreck me, and I'll let her.

I'm good at giving people what they need from me, but I never get what I need in return.

She has to stay away from me.

Steam swirls out into the living room as I open the bathroom door, almost blocking my view of the lone figure on the couch. She's asleep. Good. She needs the rest. With my hand gripping the side of the towel, I enter my bedroom, I designed it with me in mind. High ceilings, big bed, and walk-in closet. I whip off my towel and toss it on the floor, then walk to my closet butt fucking naked, my cock swinging as I go.

I have two rows of kilts.

And I find myself not reaching for one. It's the first time in years, but I need something else today. I need to be someone else today, so I reach for the only pair of jeans I own. They are black, worn, old as fucking dirt with the knees torn. I put them on, leave my hair in a wet mess, and slide on my cut.

My reflection catches my eye and I hardly recognize myself. No wonder my brother hated jeans. My balls can't breathe. I comb my beard out and walk out of my room, grab the bottle of whiskey, and take one last look at the woman who has dug up emotions I thought were buried; emotions I never thought I'd feel again.

I run out the door, lock it behind me, and take a deep breath of the dusty Vegas air. Fuck, it's so much better out here than it is in there. It's stuffy, with awkward sexual tension, and I need to get my head on straight. My boots scuff along the dirt, and I bring the bottle of whiskey to my lips, smiling when I think about Dawn taking a big swig of it.

She can't handle whiskey, but she sure did try.

No, fuck. I can't be thinking of her. She deserves better than me, and I'm not going to give up my revenge so she can sleep tight at night. Fuck that. No woman is going to come in and change my plan. Not one fucking woman.

Before I know it, I'm passing the bikes and climbing up the steps to the front door. When I walk through, all heads turn to me. Every single mouth is open. Except Pirate. He's drinking and he starts laughing, pointing his finger at me. "Holy Shit. The Skirt has went and found himself a pair of pants."

"You feeling okay, Skirt?" Reaper asks from the bar, taking a swig of beer.

"I'm fine," I grunt. I'm here for one thing and one thing only. To get off and hopefully I can feel better about my decision to leave Dawn alone. I scan the room for any cut-slut who gets my attention, but none of them are ringing my fucking bell like Dawn does. They don't even compare.

"I don't think I've ever seen you in pants," Tongue says while he looks at the TV, ankles crossed over his knee while

Candy tries to get his attention by rubbing her tits on his face. He isn't interested. I'm not either. Fake tits have always been a turn-off for me.

"Well, welcome to the fucking show. I should charge ye assholes for staring at me like this." It's not a big deal. They're just fucking pants. There is no significance. People need to leave it alone and drop it.

"I like the show," Jasmine, one of the sluts, purrs as she nestles her body against mine. She isn't bad. She has long dark hair, brown eyes, and a set of tits on her that would make Pamela Anderson jealous. She'll do.

"Ye want to show me how much ye like it?" I ask, backing her up until she hits the pool table. Her legs wrap around my waist, and she lets out a breathy laugh as she rocks her pussy against my cock.

I'm soft now.

No, no, no, I need this. I fucking need this. I can't have Dawn. She needs more than me. I'm not enough.

"You know I do, baby. What do you want?"

"I want ye to shut up and wrap that mouth around my cock." Her fingernails run down my chest, and her hand gropes my cock through my jeans.

"So big." Jasmine rubs me with her palm and, don't get me wrong, it feels fucking great, but it doesn't feel nearly as good as kissing Dawn.

"Don't go complimenting me, Jasmine. We all know ye'd suck any cock here regardless of the size."

She puts her lips to my ear and licks the shell of it. "I have sucked all the cocks here, Skirt. All but yours. You aren't an easy man to persuade."

"When I want ye, I'll come to ye. I'm here, aren't I?" My

mind is buzzing from shooting back the glass of scotch. I don't feel like myself. My gut is telling me to stop what I'm doing, that this isn't me, but I'm tired of being me. I'm tired of fighting myself.

"Skirt, I want to talk to you," Reaper says from behind me.

"Can't it wait? I'm kind of busy, Prez." I pick Jasmine up by her ass and notice the weight difference between her and Dawn. Jasmine is heavier, which isn't a bad thing, but she doesn't feel right.

It's all wrong, and Prez knows it.

I head toward the fuck rooms where the guys go with the cut-sluts if they want privacy. It's nothing special. Just a few rooms with a bare mattress and condoms. Don't need anything else, especially when it's just a quick fuck.

"See me after," Reaper sighs, the sound of disappointment clear.

I don't care. Everyone's expectations of me are too goddamn high. My expectations of me are too goddamn high. I push open the curtain, kick a door open, and throw Jasmine on the bed. I don't waste any time. I unzip my pants and fish out my cock.

"Crawl to me," I say.

"Oh, kinky." She giggles.

It ain't fucking kinky. It's normal. "Don't speak." Her voice grinds my nerves. It's too fake, all moan with a pornographic edge all the time. She tries too hard. When she finally gets in front of me, I stare down and watch her tongue lick the base of my cock to the crown, then sucks the brim between her lips.

I grunt and tilt my head back, waiting for that simmer of lust. Hell, I'll take a fraction of it if it means I come down this whore's throat. I look down at Jasmine, and her dark hair morphs to that strawberry blonde and her brown eyes turn a bright shade of green; soon it's Dawn's lips I'm imagining, and she's the one sucking me down the back of her throat.

"Fuck!" I rip my cock out of Jasmine's mouth, tuck myself in, which isn't difficult since I'm not all the way hard, zip up, and slam the door behind me. Dawn has fucking ruined me, and I barely know a damn thing about her.

The hallway is dark for a split second before I'm walking through the curtain again.

"Knew that wouldn't happen," Reaper says, slapping his hand on my shoulder. "Unless it did, and that's the quickest—"

"No, it didn't fucking happen. I'm not a quick shot." Hell, I hope I'm not. I don't know.

Reaper steers me in the direction of Church and shuts the door. I hate being in a room alone with the Prez. Usually, people get punished, and I'm not trying to have him carve anything into my chest.

"I want you and Tongue to go to Circus, Circus. There's another bag of money to get picked up."

Shite. I really don't want to go there. I can't say no to the Prez, though. "Can I ask what the money is for?"

"Just security," Reaper says.

I narrow my eyes at him and tilt my head. Security my arse. I don't get to ask questions, though. I don't have a position of authority. I'm just another member. "Aye, I'll grab the crazy fuck and get on."

"Actually, take Knives. I want Tongue to do something else for me."

I walk out of the room and try to locate Knives. He's sitting in the corner, practicing throwing his ninja stars at a can that is settled on top of Braveheart's head. Poor bloke looks like he's about to piss himself.

"Knives, we're heading out. Come on."

I must have distracted him because Knives doesn't throw it perfect. The star hangs to the left.

"Ow! Fuck you, Knives!" Braveheart groans as he cups his ear. He brings his hand away, and I wince when I see blood in his palm and his ear split in half. Right down the fucking middle. "My ear!"

"Doc!" I shout and grab Knives by the cut. "Sorry, lad. We got to get going. Club business. Have Doc stitch ye up."

"It isn't even that bad!" Knives tries to defend himself. "He's being a pussy."

"Aye, but not everyone likes sharp objects being thrown at them, Knives."

"He shouldn't have offered."

"Did he?"

"Yes." Knives swings his leg over his bike and cranks it. "Okay, no."

I bark out a laugh and start my engine, the loaner bike Tool is letting me use until I can find a replacement for mine. The rumbling vibrates between my legs, the sound nearly making me hard, and I peel out of the parking lot and press the button for the gate. I forgot to put on a shirt. Oh, well. Circus, Circus isn't exactly the best establishment anyway. Free nipples and shit. That's my opinion.

We're roaring down the open lonely road, blazing toward the strip. I lay my hand on my knee and wish I wore my kilt. The jeans are too damn tight. How did I used to wear these all the time? My balls hate me right now.

I look out onto the beautiful desert horizon and notice all the cactuses pointing to the sky, and I feel betrayed. A low throb builds in my arse, reminding me how many of those damn needles got me.

I think about Dawn and all the what-ifs and could bes. If I give up fighting, I can be the man she needs, but I don't know if I'll ever be able to. It's an outlet for my pent-up anger. What if I don't have it, and I take it out on her? Give her bruises? I'm starting not to trust myself, and I had no idea how much I didn't until she spoke Cohen's name.

Casinos and bars illuminate the strip and causes an aurora of lights to glow against the darkening sky as the sun sets. Kings' Club is somewhere in there. Maye I'll stop by there tonight to hear Tool's ol' lady sing a tune, and then I'll grab a drink. I need to get my head lost in something, because right now it's lost in everything.

We turn down the strip and Circus, Circus is there on the right. I don't know what people see in this place. It's a shit hole, and it has a creepy fucking clown smiling down at me from the sign. It's nose lights up red and for second, I think about the movie IT. Pennywise is about to fucking eat me.

I roll into a parking spot and turn off the engine, staring at the entrance of the casino. I know Maximo is there and when he sees me, he's going to ask me to fight, and I'm not going to be able to say no. Not today.

I've been out of the game too long, doing dirty business for the club. It's time I jump in the fighting scene again. Who cares if it's a little on the illegal side?

"You okay?" Knives asks.

"Yeah, I'm fine." I hop off my bike, and a few guests give me and Knives the evil eye.

Knives never takes his eyes off them as he pulls out one of his ninja stars to clean in between his teeth. "Boo!" He fake jumps toward the old couple and they gasp, then run inside to save their lives.

"Aw, that's just mean."

"I don't care."

We gather a few looks like we always do, but I ignore them. There's no need to get in a fight right now. In and out. This is a quick job. When the doors slide open, the thick veil of smoke mutes the lights on all the slot machines. Maximo is standing right in the middle of the floor, duffle bag is his hand.

He is tall, Italian, always wears black, and when it comes down to money, he doesn't care what he has to take to get it. He places his drink on the serving tray as one of the cocktail waitresses passes by, turning his deviant smile my way.

It's the kind of smile that tells me he just found another way to make cash.

"Skirt, long time no see," he greets, holding out the bag for us to take. "I'm grateful for the Ruthless Kings offering me protection. Reaper is a good President."

Knives lifts a brow at me, wondering how I know this guy.

"Aye," I utter and reach for the bag, but Maximo holds on to it. Knives senses tension, and he pulls out his star, ready to slam it between the Italian's eyes. We stare at each other, not saying a word, and I wait for the demon lurking inside his soul to come out and take mine. I know that's what he wants.

He chuckles, then releases the bag, putting a cigarette between his lips. He lights it. An orange ember glows in the haze of fog as he inhales, then blows the smoke into my face. "I'll be seeing you around, *Rohan*."

"Rohan?" Knives jerks the bag from my hands and gives me a dirty look before giving me his back.

I'm so fucked.

CHAPTER NINE

Dawn

I'M SITTING ON THE PORCH IN A WHITE ROCKING CHAIR, STARING AT the desert sunset, watching the sky turn a bright shade of red. It's the only place I can find peace here. Skirt's cabin smells too much like him, and the clubhouse has too much noise going on and too many women pawing at the guys. I have no idea why they do that to themselves, but that won't be me. I won't allow Skirt to turn me into one of his whores, another notch on a bedpost. I want more for myself.

A guy named Tank and Braveheart are out in the front yard, building a bonfire for later. It reminds me how the world keeps spinning even if my world has come to a complete stop.

It's been three days since Skirt told me they can't find Aidan. It's been three days since the kiss that changed my life. It's been three days since I've even seen Skirt.

"You alright?" Pirate sits in the chair next to me, bottle of rum in his hand. "Want some?" He offers me the bottle.

"No, thank you."

"Your kid is lost, huh?" he asks, rocking in the char. The man has a haunted look in his eyes, the kind that replay a bad memory over and over. His face is gaunt, and his hair is dirty. He's stopped caring about himself.

"Something like that," I say, shaking my leg from the slam of anxiety that hits me when I think about Aidan being with Cohen.

"Fucking sucks when you can't find the people you love," he says.

"Did that happen to you? Is that why you drink so much?"

"No one fucking asked you!" he yells at me and stands on his feet, swaying. "Don't fucking talk to me like you're trying to get to know me. You don't know me." He takes a swig of rum and points his finger in my face. "I ain't none of your business. You're just another whore. Another fucking slut for me to sink my dick in to. You're nothing!"

His words, while harsh, don't bother me. He's lashing out. The whites of his eyes are red from lack of sleep, and his lips are chapped from dehydration. Pirate is slowly killing himself.

Out of nowhere, Pirate is tackled to the ground, and I hop up on the chair to get out of the way. The rum bottle falls down the steps, shattering on the ground.

"What the fuck did you just say?" Skirt straddles Pirate's chest and punches his face. "She isn't a whore. Ye owe her an apology! Tell her," Skirt shakes him, and Pirate turns over and pukes up the rum. "God, yer a sorry bastard, Pirate. Ye need help."

"Don't tell me what I need," Pirate spits out the remainder

of liquid in his mouth and stares down at the bottle of broken rum on the ground. "Look what you did! Look. No." Pirate crawls out of Skirt's hold and fumbles down the steps until he gets to the puddle of rum. He lifts up the broken glass and licks it, then tosses it back on the ground. "No! I need it. I need this." He lays flat and starts to lick the rum from the dirt, eating red clay instead of rum.

"Jesus Christ, Pirate. What's happened to ye?"

"I got it," Doc comes out of the house next with a syringe in his hand and squats near Pirate. Doc puts his arm around Pirate's shoulder as Pirate licks another piece of glass. His tongue is bleeding, he's cut his fingertips, but all the drunk can see is alcohol. Doc plunges the needle into Pirate's neck, and there's shock in his eyes for a second before he slumps over. Doc catches him before he face plants into the broken glass.

Doc carries Pirate away, probably to the basement, and I know this is the lowest point in Pirate's life by how the guys are staring at him.

"Are ye okay?" Skirt stands in front of me, and his hand cups my biceps.

My eyes flick to meet his, and my hand reaches up to touch the black eye. "What happened?"

"Nothing that's more important than ye. I'm sorry Pirate went off like that. He hasn't been himself lately."

"It's okay. I understand fighting your demons."

"Yeah, ye do, don't ye?" Skirt takes another step forward, and I lean back, forgetting that I'm still standing on the chair, and I fall, losing my footing completely.

Skirt is fast, catching me before I hit the ground. The rugged handsome features on his face pinch as he smiles, shaking his head as he lifts me up and sets me on my feet. "Always needing to be carried, aren't ye?" He roams my body for the first time since coming onto the porch, and his eyes harden when he sees what I'm wearing.

Short shorts and Sarah's black tank top that doesn't really fit. My boobs are too big. It's more like a crop top on me. He stares at my bare stomach, and his square jaw tightens as a strand of hair falls from his ponytail. His fists clench at his sides, and right as I think he's about to take my mouth again, he turns around, slams his fist against the door and dents it as he vanishes.

"You have him all fucked up," Reaper states from the other rocking chair across the porch. "Skirt's always been a bit light-hearted, a fighter, a bit serious some days, but I've never had to worry about him before."

I ignore Reaper's words and storm in after Skirt. I'm not about to be blamed for someone else's problems. I won't be blamed for a man's actions ever again. It isn't my fault. I watch Skirt go into the rooms that the other guys go in when they take a slut, and my anger blows through the roof.

I'm done dancing around him. I kick open the door to see Bullseye getting his cock sucked, and I hurry and shut the door before he can see me. My face heats, and my pussy throbs from seeing the intimate act. I shake my head and kick open the next door and Skirt is there, by the window.

Alone.

His arms are up on the windowsill, stretching his muscles that have me tightening in all the right and wrong places. He's a tortured soul, a man clawing his way from the trenches of whatever hole he's made in his head.

"Skirt."

His shoulders tense when he hears my voice, but he doesn't

turn around to look at me. He stares out the window. "Ye don't need to be in here. This isn't the place for a lass like ye," he says.

"You don't get to tell me where my place is. I decide that. Not you."

"Ye maddening woman!" he shouts at me, and I jump. He spins around and charges at me, and I back up until I'm against the door, and his hands hit the wall on either side of my head. "I'm a fighter," he hisses through gritted teeth as his eyes rake over my face and stop at my mouth. "I'm not the kind of guy ye need. And seeing ye, all the fucking time, dressed in these tight little shorts, it drives me mad. Do ye like doing that? Driving me crazy?" He circles his finger next to his head. "Cause ye are."

"I didn't know," I gulp. "I haven't seen you."

He tilts his head left and right, inching his way closer to my lips. "I know. I've been watching ye. I can't get enough of looking at ye. Those fucking lips, this hair, the moment I saw ye laying in the road I knew ye'd fuck me up in ways I wasn't ready for." His chest heaves, and he opens the door for me to leave. "Go. I'm meeting Olivia in here."

"Olivia? Another slut coming in here to suck your dick?"

He looks shocked that I know that.

"Jasmine is running around telling everyone how she got to suck your dick." I lift my hands and shake my head, biting away the anger twitching my tongue. "Whatever. Have her suck your cock. I don't care." I take a step out the door, ready to call it quits on this fucked up clubhouse and hire a private detective to find my son, when Skirt grabs me by the back of the neck and yanks me back into the room.

He slams the door, locks it, and pushes my body against the wall with his. His weight holds me down and my breasts rub against the wall, my nipples tightening.

My ass is aligned with his pelvis and I can feel how hard he is for me. "What I want, you can't give me. Not right now," he growls into my ear. "This can't happen."

I know that. I have too much on my mind that's more important than falling for a bad boy biker who is also a fighter. The days get longer without my son and having no new update. That leaves me thinking about Skirt.

A bed bangs against the wall from the bedroom next to us where Bullseye is. I gasp, thinking about him fucking the girl he had in his room.

"Ye like that, don't ye? Ye hear Bullseye fucking that slut?"

I nod, barley able to move my head since my ear is pressed against the wall. I can hear everything going on in the next room.

"*Bullseye, fuck me harder. Yes! You're so thick.*"

By complete accident, I saw his cock, and I'd have to agree with the woman.

"*Shut up and just take it,*" *Bullseye orders, and the hard slap of his balls hitting her ass is erotic.*

Skirt rocks against my ass, and every instinct is telling me to stop, to run, that there are too many red flags waving in the air in the clubhouse, but I can't seem to get my voice to work. I'm safe here. A deeper part of me knows that, and I think that's why my feet are glued to the ground.

He spins me around and lifts my leg around his waist, his nose touching mine, as we breathe in each other's ragged breaths. The wall next to us continues a steady beat, and the woman wails her passion, causing my nipples to bead and poke against my shirt. I've never been so turned on in my life.

Even the one-night stand that got me pregnant with Aidan was nothing like this. Whatever I feel for Skirt is on another level, one too difficult to understand and too high to jump off of to run away.

Skirt's fire is the same as mine; a twin flame born out of the same heat and ferocity. It's dangerous. Eventually, there's a melting point.

Which one of us will it affect first?

"Dawn," my antagonist gravels my name low in his throat, sounding like broken glass.

He's a fighter, but he doesn't have to fight me.

I melt first. Fuck it all. Fuck everything. I throw my arms around his neck and smash my lips against his and take control. The rough coarse hairs of his beard scratch along my lips and around my mouth. I feel raw, exposed, and I want more. His kiss burns just as much as his touch does, and the more I try to extinguish this passion, the hotter I become.

"Fuck," he hisses, biting my lip and tugging it until there's no more give, and it hurts to the perfect extent.

Just what I needed. Fuck that cock, Candy. Faster.

Bullseye's dirty talk to one of the cut-sluts has me moaning into Skirt's mouth, and my clit throbs for his touch. I rock against him, seeking the friction, seeking something to ease the ache he's causing inside me.

"Ye have no idea what I want from ye," he mumbles against my lips, licking the seam and outlining my mouth. I never thought that would be erotic, but it is. I want him to lick my entire body, set me ablaze.

"Tell me," I beg, whimpering into his mouth as his cock slides over my clit. I haven't dry humped since I was sixteen, and if we keep going like this, I'm going to come.

"No," he says. "I want ye to listen to Bullseye and Candy fucking." He pins my arm above my head and seals his mouth on mine again, rocking until my eyes are rolling back and my groans of pleasure are meshing with Candy's.

His fingers dig in my side, and his kisses his way down my neck, sucking on a spot below my ear. I stretch my neck back, giving him as much access as I can. And then he pulls away from me, leaving me needy and in pain.

He rubs a hand over his mouth, and his cock strains against his kilt, so I know he wants me. "We need to stop. I—ye don't need this. I don't know—"

Before he can finish, I shove him in the chest, and he stumbles back against the window. I grab his cock through his kilt, and he hisses, then I grip his chin in my hand and sneer, "You will not leave me aching. I haven't felt like this in years."

He pushes me off him and wraps his hand around my throat and squeezes. My hands wrap around his wrist as I suck in a lungful of air, then he slams me on the bed. "Ye don't get to decide, Lips." He bends down and kisses me, but I don't kiss him back, which only makes him growl and kiss me harder.

I'm not sure of the dynamic we have going on right now, but it's unlike anything I've ever experienced. He likes the fight, and I like to give it to him. I never got to fight before. I'm always subdued, and I don't like to be.

There's a difference between abuse and consensual rough-ness. With what has happened to me, I didn't think I'd like an-other man touching me like this.

Skirt is letting me fight back where as Cohen, if I fought, made me taste my own blood from hitting me across the face so much.

"Fuck her harder, Bullseye!" Skirt yells to other side of the wall, and the sound of skin slapping stops for a second, be-fore a giggle sounds, then they start back at it again; this time, it's like they are in the same room. They must have gotten off the bed and Bullseye is fucking her against the wall. "Ye like that," Skirt notices, keeping a tight grip on my neck as he cups my pussy. "I can feel how much ye want it." He slides off my shorts, keeping his eyes locked on mine, waiting to see if I protest.

Again, there's a difference between protesting and fighting for more.

When I don't stop him, Skirt's mouth parts when he sees my pink panties. His throat bobs, and for a split second the confidence drains from his eyes. His thumb presses against my clit, sliding the material over the swollen nub, my back bends and his hand loosens around my neck.

"Skirt!" I moan, shouting into the room, being loud on purpose. I want the other room to hear me. It fuels their passion, and the banging against the wall becomes quicker, and the faster they fuck, the quicker Skirt circles my clit. It's been years since I've had an orgasm. Cohen never let me have pleasure.

I was always expected to wait for him on the bed after a fight, ass up face down, and he'd use me. So right now, I'm extra sensitive. The sound of material tearing and a cold burst of air over my bare pussy has me glaring at Skirt, narrowing my eyes. "Those were my favorite pair."

He lifts me by my legs and sets my knees on his shoulders. "I'll buy ye more." On those final words, he feasts on me. He growls into my cunt, tongue fucking my hole and flicking my clit with his fingers at the same time.

"Skirt, yes! I'm going to come. I'm going to come. Yes—" My stomach quivers and spasms. "Yes!" My hands run through his hair, and I grab a fistful and pull as hard as I can. I'm going mad with how good he's making me feel. He yanks up my shirt, pulls my bra down, and smacks my tit with his hand, over and over until my skin is red and my nipple is swollen. "Skirt! Oh, fuck," I cry out when my legs tighten around his neck, and I squirt into his mouth with a powerful orgasm that's been oppressed for far too long. Skirt laps me up eagerly, sucking down every drop.

He pulls away, lips shining with my slick, and his beard has droplets of my cum scattered in the hairs. He kisses his way up my body, dipping his tongue into my navel, and then his hands cup my tits. My right breast is burning from the hard slaps he gave me, and he licks up my body, sucking a nipple into his mouth, then letting it go with a plop.

"So perfect," he says to himself.

"Skirt." My hands grip his hair as reins, and I pull him up to my face, then lick his beard and mouth to taste myself.

"My god, yer going to make me come licking yer cum off me like that." He bends his head to steal a kiss. I snake my arm down and lift up his kilt, then scratch my nails along the inner part of his thigh. He trembles, but as I'm about to wrap my hand around his cock, he stops me, then rolls off.

My legs are parted, my underwear are ripped, my breasts are exposed and one is red from being hit, and he just … stops.

"Skirt—"

"I'm sorry. I'm sorry. It's not ye, it's me. I—" He presses his palms against his forehead and growls. "Fuck!" He hurries out the door and slams it shut behind him.

I don't feel used, so I have no reason to be hurt. If anyone should feel used it's Skirt because I got off. *Oh, man, did I get off.*

I'm coming! I'm coming! Bullseye, oh, Bullseye.

Bullseye grunts and slams his fist against the wall, "Take it, you cum slut."

"Oh god…" I cup my hands over my face as it heats with embarrassment.

What the fuck just happened?

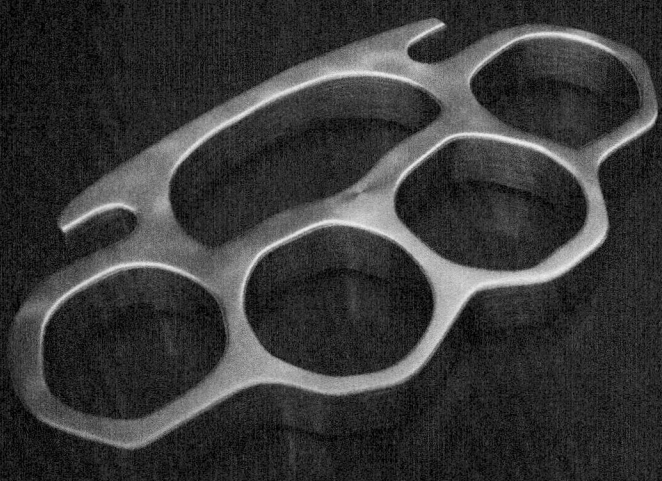

CHAPTER TEN

Skirt

I'M AVOIDING DAWN AT ALL COSTS TODAY.

Whatever happened yesterday cannot happen again. Fuck, as if she couldn't be more perfect, her pussy had to taste like heaven, and she loved to fight me just like I've been fantasizing for myself.

She attempted to grab my cock, and I was already so on edge I knew I'd come right in the palm of her hand, and then I got nervous because—what if she wanted to fuck? I'm a biker, the one thing I should know how to do is fuck, but I don't. So I got nervous. She has a walking, talking, four-year-old proof that she's had sex.

What if I disappoint her? I can't just eat her pretty cunt for the rest of my life.

I mean, I could, no hardship for me…

"Hey, Skirt," Ellie grabs my arm as I'm about to go talk to Reaper. "You still want that puppy?"

Damn it. Forgot all about the damn mut. "Aye, I do." I pull out my wallet hand her a hundred bucks. "Just take care of him for me, okay? I have to go do something. Just a few more days."

"Sure," she says with a gleeful grin on her face. She's going to be a knockout when she's of age, and Poodle knows it. He's already punched a few of the guys in the face for looking too long. I've seen Ellie have eyes for Braveheart too, which will only sign his death warrant. At least they are closer in age. Braveheart is young and in his twenties. Every time Ellie comes into the room, Braveheart runs.

"Thanks, El. I owe you." I give her a quick hug and leave, heading down the hallway to look for Reaper.

I see Tongue sitting at the table, along with Knives, and both look bored out of their minds. Things have been a little quiet since dealing with the strings that came with Melissa coming into Poodle's life.

"Where's Reaper?" I ask them, gripping the back of one of the kitchen chairs. I turn my head to look at Tongue, then Knives. Both of them blow out a breath at the same time. I roll my eyes.

"He's at his house with Sarah, and he's not to be disturbed," Tongue says, throwing up air quotes. "Whatever."

"I'm so bored," Knives groans. "Badge still hasn't found anything on the kid, so we're just sitting ducks."

My heart aches for the boy. He's probably terrified without his Ma, and I know Dawn has been going out of her mind with worry. I hear her at night crying herself to sleep in my spare bedroom. There are times when I'll go and lay next to her, stay awake all night and up all day, just so she knows she isn't alone.

I have to keep avoiding her. She can't know I'm a virgin. No grown man my age is a virgin. I think about Poodle, and why he didn't tell me his secret, and while his is darker than mine, do I have a right to be mad at him when he doesn't know this about me?

I don't have time to think about it. I need cash. Now. And if Reaper isn't available for me to ask for work, then I only have another place to go.

Maximo.

I flip open my phone and type out a message.

Me: *"Any room for an extra fighter?"*

Almost instantly he messages me back.

Maximo: *"Always room for the best, my friend. See you in an hour."*

Shit. I only have an hour? By the time I get there, that barely gives me time to warm up, but if I can fight every opponent, I can win around fifty-grand if I'm undefeated. Maximo treats his fighters good. Every day that passes, fighting for him sounds more appealing, and if Reaper is already in business with him, what's the big deal? I'm not breaking any rules.

Me: *"I'll be there."*

Maximo: *"I know."*

I debate on telling Knives and Tongue so they can come along, but I keep my lips sealed shut. It's better if no one knows where I go.

Over the last few months, Reaper has set up legal, safe fights for me. Ones that raise money for charity and shit, which is great, but I need more. I need blood, grit, a fight without rules. Reaper hasn't brought anyone into the playroom for a little roughening up, so I'm getting an itch just like Tongue and Knives are.

Things are getting slow around here. Slow is good. It means there's no trouble, but with no rival MC, no gangs, or the mafia wanting our heads, sometimes MC life can get dull. Sure, we live hard and die harder, but damn it, where's the damn grit these days? Surely, there's someone out there who wants to take us down.

"Where you going?" Tongue shouts after me.

"Out!" I reply, not giving him an actual answer. I fling open the door and run down the steps to see Reaper sitting on his bike and Sarah between his legs as they talk. His hands are on her ass and when they see me, Reaper juts his chin for me to come closer.

Fuck.

"Where you going?" he asks.

Shit. He knows. That's impossible.

"I need to clear my head. Going for a ride."

"On your way back, can you pick up another bag from Circus, Circus?"

"Another one?" the question slips out of my mouth before I can stop it, and Reaper pats Sarah on the arse, telling her to go inside.

She flicks her blonde hair over her shoulder and gives me a 'what the fuck' look. Yeah, what am I thinking? I keep questioning the Prez, I'm going to have to pay the price.

"Sorry, Prez. I guess I'm just getting worried. It's a lot of money. I don't mean to question you."

"I'm calling Church tonight. You might not be back before then, so I'll go ahead and tell you." He lights a cigarette and puffs it. "Maximo is Moretti's brother. He's giving us sums of money the other casino owed us before it burned down. He wants to come see his brother after all the debts are paid. He knows it isn't looking good and that he might have to take over the family business."

"That's why Moretti's men haven't been here. I bet Maximo called them."

Reaper shrugs. "None of my fucking business. I just want us to get our cut and be done with it. And if we grow a good relationship with the mafia, that's even better. And you're the one going to get the duffle cause I'm putting you in charge of the monies. Pirate can't do it anymore. He's having the title stripped. You've proven yourself. You question me when things need to be questioned. I trust you."

Shit, he's been testing me, and I didn't even know. I hold out my hand and shake Reaper's powerful palm. If he ever finds out I'm fighting for Maximo, maybe giving Ruthless a bad reputation again, I'll have more than my title stripped, but my dignity and possibly my flesh too.

If I win tonight, I'll go straight to Reaper and give him a cut of the winnings and be upfront. I've seen what the man can do when he wants to get his way and, honestly, it scares the hair off my chest.

"Make Church. It isn't a request," Reaper flicks his smoke about five feet away and then pushes off his bike to head inside.

"Fuck me." I blow out a breath once he's gone and breathe in and out. I'm so fucked. Why the hell is Maximo getting involved with us? And he's Moretti's brother? Something doesn't smell right.

As I throw my leg over the seat of my bike and crank it, something moves out of the corner of my eye. I see Dawn, gnawing on her perfect bottom lip. I expect her to stop, but as always, she exceeds my expectations and walks over to me, arms crossed, seeming small and fragile. Nothing like the woman I know, the one with a fighter's heart and a tongue as wicked as the damned.

"I know where you're going."

I rev my engine to drown out her voice.

The light red highlights in her hair capture the sun as they shine a beautiful copper. She glances off into the distance, her lashes curling up as she blinks. She's a goddess. Something so beautiful doesn't need to be ruined by my hands.

That's what I do.

I ruin.

"I've seen the look on Cohen's face before a fight. I've been there before."

"I don't expect ye to go there again, Lips." I can't help myself. I reach out and rub my thumb over the plump pillow of her lip and tug it free from her teeth.

"I'll go there again for you, Skirt. You're different than him." She sighs and places her hands on my face, softer than how she grabbed me last night. Dawn places a soft kiss on my mouth, and it's filled with so much care, so much worry, for me, that I need more of it. I wrap my arms around her and pull her close, enjoying the slow kiss as she pours what she feels for me into my body.

I drink it up with greed, wanting more and more, until I'm fucking drowning in it, and the only way I'm breathing is through her.

Our tongues tease one another, and my hands slide down her back, giving her arse a good squeeze. She brings the kiss to an end and lays her head on my chest. "Come back to me unbroken, Skirt."

"Rohan," I correct her. I want her to know my real name. The name I never hear anymore.

"That suits you. It means red, right?" She strokes her fingers along my beard. "My red warrior," she whispers. "Be safe."

I grab her hand and kiss the inside of her palm before letting her go and reverse my bike out of the parking lot. When I come back from this fight, I'll tell her the truth and why I'm so nervous to be around her, to see if she'll still want me.

I don't look in my side mirror to take one last look at her. I can't, or I'll turn around. I need the release of the fight before I bring it to her. That's my worst fear, that this amazing, beautiful woman is giving me a chance; she's trusting me not to hurt her the way her ex did. I'm so scared I will. My temper, my need to feel people fighting against me, their life struggling in my hands, is a terrible curse.

My bike flies down the road, passing a car every few miles, and the sun is beating down on me until the fair skin on my shoulders is hot. With regret, I flip my blinker on and take a right, then turn into Circus, Circus. There are people everywhere. Women are in short dresses, a few have on matching shirts. Something about a bachelorette weekend, and I assume the one wearing the veil is the bride to be.

Parking it, I kick the stand down and steady my bike before getting off. I can't believe I'm doing this. I'm going behind my Prez's back. My woman knows. My woman reads me better than my brothers, and that says a lot considering she's only known me for a week.

It's been a damn good week.

Shit. I just thought of her as my woman. I pause mid-step with the shock, and then I see Maximo waiting at the door for me. He's dressed in a black shirt, black trouser pants, and his black hair is slicked back. I can see the resemblance between him and Moretti.

I eat up the distance with my heavy boots and hold out my hand. "Maximo," I greet.

"Rohan, you've made me a very happy, very rich man."

"Already?" I ask, wondering how the hell that's possible.

"The brother of a famous UFC champion in my ring? Word gets around. Bets are high. Come." He throws his arm around my shoulder and gives my neck a slight rub. "Ha! This is going to be a great friendship. I am excited! This is good. Real good." Maximo tosses his head back and laughs, keeping his arm around me as if I'm a prize.

The casino looks completely different than it did the other day. The carpet is ripped up and has been replaced with gold tile. Maybe Reaper is right; maybe this guy is okay because apparently the hotel is being renovated.

Maximo and I get on the elevator, and he presses a button that takes us down. He slides a card in, and the yellow light on the panel turns red and then something below the B signaling the basement tells me we're going to a place under that.

Shite. That's not good. That's some secret shit.

"Who am I fighting?"

"Eh, some guy from the East side. You can take him down in no time. I want a quick takedown, no questions, no fucking around. In a few weeks, I'll set you up a big fight. The one that matters to you."

I grip him by the shirt collar and slam him against the side of the elevator and then press the emergency stop button. "How the fuck do ye know what matters to me?"

He flashes a wolfish grin at me, not bothered that I have him pinned against the elevator. His goons behind us pull out their guns, and I feel one on either side of my temples. "Ah, ah, ah, it's fine. Lower your weapons," he orders, and in the next second the metal is gone. "I've done some research on you. Rohan Blackwood, the brother of the famous Conor Blackwood, who died fighting Cohen O'Roarke."

"Don't ye fucking dare act like ye know anything about that." I shove him then let him go, and he straightens out his shirt, smoothing the wrinkles of the expensive black material.

"I can give you the chance to get the revenge you want. You know you can't get that in the real world, Skirt. I can get that for you."

My heart is a raging jackhammer. The urge for blood and vengeance has my ears ringing. When the elevator doors slide open, Skirt is nothing but a myth, and Rohan takes over me, ready to be a legend.

"This is your chance." Maximo guides me forward, and the cage around the hexagon shines. "Win tonight, never lose, and you can take home a nice payment to you and your club. Maybe get your pretty lady something pretty, huh?"

How the fuck does he know about her?

He chuckles in a way that tells me he knows everything. "Win and let the Ruthless and the Moretti name be allies."

I hold out my hand, knowing Maximo sounds too good to be true. When something sounds too good to be true, it usually is, and that's how you know a deal with the devil has been made.

And the only way out, is death.

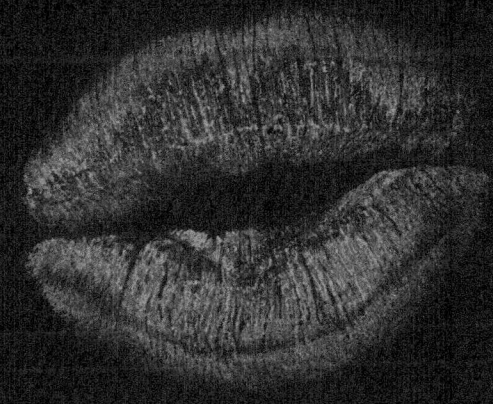

CHAPTER ELEVEN

Dawn

MOMMY!" AIDAN CRIES FOR ME IN THE DARK, BUT I CAN'T find him.

I spin around in circles, searching the abyss of black around me, but I can't see him. "Aidan, baby, where are you? Call out to me. I'm here!" I hold my arms out to reach for anything in my way. It's too dark. I can't see anything! "Aidan, please. Call out for me."

"Mommy, I'm scared."

I shake my head and smile, trying to be brave through the rush of tears on my face. "There's no need to be. I'm here. I have you now. Just come out, Aidan. Come out; let's go home."

I trip over something on the floor, and my shoulder smacks into the ground. I groan just as a light turns on above me and shines on the prone figure on the floor. The body is jerking, spasming, foaming at the mouth.

"Aidan!" I cry and crawl over to him, holding his tiny, fragile body as he battles a seizure. "It's okay. It's okay. I got you. Mommy is here." I pet my hand over his chestnut-colored hair and kiss the top of his head. "It will be over soon."

And then he's gone.

Now, I'm laying in a field. It's green. "Aidan?" I search, but I don't hear him. "Aidan!" my voice echoes through the empty space. Nothing is here. It's just me. All alone.

Until I see something up ahead; it's small. "Aidan?" I whisper to myself as I take a step forward. I'm barefoot. The grass is wet and soft, my toes sink into the mud, and it starts to rain. I run, but I'm not getting anywhere. The figure ahead is out of reach.

I slip and fall into a giant puddle. Mud ruins my white gown. I push myself up, gripping the earth, and worms wiggle and slither all over my hands. I flick them away with a disgusting shout, and that's when I see the headstone.

Crawling on my hands and knees, the headstone is small, square, and made of simple marble. There's a message engraved on the stone. I wipe the water out of my face, only to cake mud on my cheeks and read:

Aidan West.

Mommy let me die.

"No!" I scream at the top of my lungs as my soul is ripped from my body. "Aidan!" My hands dig into the dirt, like a dog digging for a bone, and I scoop the mud out and toss it away, only for the surface of the grave to be replaced. I'm sweating, burning with grief, but no matter how hard I dig, no matter how tight I grip the ground covering my baby, I get nowhere.

A hand shoots up from the grave, wrapping around my wrist, and suddenly the mud disappears, and Aidan's face comes to view.

"You killed me, Mommy."

"No. No! I would never, baby."

"You left me with him."

And then he's gone, and a hand wraps around my throat and throws me in my own grave.

"I'm going to kill you just like I killed that bastard child that wasn't mine." Cohen stands above me with a shovel and begins to bury me alive. Dirt covers my face and gets into my mouth. I can't breathe. The mud clogs my throat, my lungs are being filled with soil, and the harder I fight, the further I sink into the ground.

I open my mouth to scream.

"Woah, hey! I got ye. It's okay."

I'm lifted into a strong pair of comforting arms and I scrub my tongue with my fingers to get the dirt out of my mouth. I can't breathe. *Oh God. Aidan.* I wail and crawl into Skirt's lap, burying my face into his neck as I inhale the musky scent of sweat, leather, smoke, and blood.

"It's okay, Lips. Yer safe. I'm not going to let anything happen to ye."

"He's dead. He's dead. I know it. He's dead. Skirt, oh God. I can't—I can't do this anymore. I need to find him." I lean away from Skirt and place my fist to my chest. "I'm dying every day without him. There's this weight on my chest, and no matter how hard I try, I can't lift it. I'm afraid we aren't ever going to find him."

"We are going to find him. I promise, Dawn. I'm going to bring yer little boy back to ye. Yer here under my protection, the Ruthless Kings protection, and we will never settle for a child missing. I might have a lead."

I lift my eyes from the red spot on his chest—blood—and meet his eyes. His cheek is swollen, and that's the only mark on him that gives away that he's just been in a fight. "What? Really? Tell me. I need to know!"

"The fighting I'm doing. The man says he can get me a fight with Cohen. If I can find Cohen, I'll get Aidan. That I promise ye." His forehead presses against mine, and the feel of him, his comfort, his power, his willingness to put his life on the line to get Aidan, erases the horrible dream I just had. I lay my cheek on his shoulder and rub my fingers down his back.

He's so different than any man I've ever met. Skirt is rough around the edges, but he's soft where it counts. His heart. He might not want to admit it, but I know. Skirt is willing to open up and let anyone he wants inside. He will give his all, even if it means he gets nothing in return.

"Thank you." I kiss along his collarbone, relieved I have an answer of some sorts. It's not much. Skirt might not be able to get a fight with Cohen, but there's a chance. There's hope. Something I didn't have an hour ago.

"Love the feel of yer lips on me," he mutters. "I mean. Yer welcome. I'll always do what I can," he corrects himself, and his body tenses from letting the truth slip.

I peer up at him from his chest, seeing the man beneath the bruises. He's the man who turns on a light when I'm screaming in darkness. "If you love them so much, why did you leave the way you did yesterday?"

"We don't have to talk about that right now," he says, pushing me off his lap so I'm laying on the bed. I miss sitting on his lap with my legs wrapped around him and my cheek against his chest to feel his warrior heart drumming. "Ye just had a bad dream. I wanted to make sure ye were okay. I'm going to shower. I have the blood of ten different men on me." He places his lips on my forehead before rolling off the bed.

He confuses me. Skirt is hot and cold. One minute, I know he wants me, and the next he's fighting me just like he fights the men in the ring. I exhale. Why do I bother trying to get his attention when I didn't even want it to begin with?

He stretches his arms over his head, and my eyes follow the muscles. He has a few scratches, but nothing serious. I bet he is a beast in the cage. When he turns around, his arms fall to his sides, and I see the tears in his knuckles. I scurry onto my knees and reach out for his hand. They're black and blue. "Skirt, what did you do? What happened?"

"The kind of fighting I do, there's no rules. Each person gets a weapon."

I swallow and hover my fingers across the beaten skin. "And what is yours?"

"Brass knuckles. I'm used to it; don't worry about me." His hand slips away from mine as he walks out the door, leaving me alone with the lingering dread of my nightmare and confusion for the redheaded man.

The shower turns on, and I imagine him all wet and nude. Oh, I bet he looks good naked. A man like that can't *not* look good in the buff. I close my eyes and imagine red hair all over his body, legs, ass, and a red bush above his cock.

I've always loved a man with hair. Men always shave these days, and if I want to feel a soft body, I'll touch my own.

"The hell with this," I toss the blanket off the bed and slip my nightgown off until it's around my feet. I step out of it and throw my shoulders back. I'm done pussyfooting around whatever is happening between Skirt and me. It's either he wants me or he doesn't, and by the hard ridge of his cock always pressing between my legs, I'm going with the first option.

I saunter out of the bedroom, the air cool as it breezes across my nipples, making them tight. I swallow my nerves, my belly tightens, and I lay my ear against the door to listen. I hear him moan, then curse, and the ache between my legs grows to the point where I'm reaching down and touching myself, slipping my fingers through my folds.

Steam bleeds from under the door, warming my cold feet. With a deep breath, I grab the handle and turn, swinging the door open to the bathroom.

The bathroom is huge. A chapel-style ceiling, a silver basin for a tub to the left that can sit four people, and a walk-in shower that's made of stone and glass. I can see his body through the fog, a slight outline of his built structure. His head his bent, and his moans parrot off the walls, the acoustics of the room singing me a beautiful song.

"Dawn," my name falls from his lips in passion.

I slink into the stall with him, shutting the door behind me. He hasn't even noticed me yet. His head is still hanging between his shoulders, water is cascading around his strong body in a rush, and his arm is moving fast as he fucks himself.

This is it. There's no turning back now.

I reach out my hand and place it on his shoulder, then glide my palm down the arm that's moving while he touches himself. He tenses, and I wait for him to yell at me, to get the hell out of the bathroom, but he doesn't. Skirt lets me wrap my hand around the hand that's holding his cock, and I help him stroke himself.

"What are ye doing to me?" he asks, and then his body shudders when I grip him tight.

"I'm giving us what we both want," I whisper into his ear, nibbling down his neck. I lick down his spine, drinking the water off his skin. "Do you want me to stop?"

Skirt leans his hands against the wall to brace himself, and he shakes his head, his red hair soaked to his skull. "I never want ye to stop, Lips. I love ye touch. I can't get enough of it."

"Then stop running from me." I unwrap my hand from his shaft and grab his heavy orbs instead, palming them and giving them a slight twist. He arches his back and tenses the muscles in his shoulders. I've yet to see his cock, but by the weight and length of it, he feels big.

I dive deeper and rub the skin under his sack, and he shouts in pleasure. It's the most erotic noise I've ever heard. He spins around, and the move has his cock slipping from my grip. His hands are on my ass, gripping tight, and he lifts me in the air until my back is against the drenched wall, and his cock is aligned with my entrance.

My legs cross behind his back to get leverage, and his palms move from my ass. He caresses my ribcage and then he kneads my mounds, pinching my nipples as he explores me. All I can hear is the water splashing against the floor, and all I feel is the pulse between my legs. I need this. I need to feel him.

I want to feel good. It's been too long since a man has taken his time to get to know my body, and I need this, with Skirt. I know my life will change the moment he enters me.

And I welcome change.

It's better than the shitshow that's become my life.

I have a feeling Skirt is the answer to the sadistic suffering of my soul.

"Is this what ye want?" He squeezes my tits so hard. I whimper when the skin turns white from his grip. "Ye want my cock in this tight cunt? Fucking ye? Pouring my cum inside?"

I shove at his chest, and his hands pin my arms above my head. The water is falling on both of us now, and his sky-blue eyes latch onto me from the sheet of water between us. He has a hunter's stare, the kind that tells me he loves a chase if given the chance. I bring my legs up and kick his body away from mine, but it only buys me a few steps of space. His fingers are still around my wrists and he uses the opportunity to turn me around and presses me against the wall.

Skirt's hand smacks against my ass as he rocks his cock between the crease of my cheeks. "So fucking spirited. I like that. Ye fucking call to me in ways I didn't think were possible." His free hand drifts down my back, and his index finger probs my puckered hole. I gasp when he inserts his finger to the hilt, no lube, no gentle caress—nothing. It burns. His knuckles press against the globes of my ass, and I moan when he curls the digit inside me.

I love unnecessary roughness.

"Ye so fucking tight here. Ye like that, don't ye? Getting fucked in every hole."

"Fuck you," I spit, thrusting myself onto his finger, wanting and needing more.

His other hand buries in my hair and yanks my head back until the water is spewing in my face, and I'm choking on it. "Ye'd like that wouldn't ye? Ye'd like to fuck me." He shoves my head back against the wall. The position gives me the opportunity to turn my head to the left, allowing me to breathe. I gasp, choking from the water, as he spins me around again, pulling his finger from my asshole.

Our eyes meet, my chest heaves, and his stare falls to my mouth. He leans in to give me a kiss, but I rear back and slap him across the face.

I'm not sure what comes over me. I feel alive. I want to do it again.

He freezes, reaches up and rubs a hand on his cheek. He

closes his eyes and lets out a deep groan, and that's when I feel something hot and sticky landing on my stomach. My eyes round when I see thick streams of cum jetting from his fat cock.

Skirt's eyes spring open, and I swear a different man is staring down at me. He pulls my hair and yanks our bodies close, sliding his fingers through his cum dripping down my stomach. He gathers it on his fingers and shoves them into my mouth. "Clean up the mess ye fucking made," he demands, and I eagerly suck the cream off his skin. "Look at ye, hungry for my cum. Such a pretty sight."

I love his praise.

I'll be his fucking chapel if he allows me, and I'll always to do my best to satisfy his needs. I'll be the only religion he will ever need.

He turns off the water and yanks his fingers from my mouth. I'm about to ask what I did wrong, but he lifts me into his arms and carries me out of the shower stall and to his room. My skin turns cold from the sudden change in temperature, and he lifts me higher to suck a nipple into his mouth. My head flies back, and I arch into his rough suction. I want his mark. I want him to do anything and everything he wants to me.

When we get to his room, he throws me in the air onto his bed, wet and all. His cock is erect, arching over his belly button as he struts to me. Skirt knee-walks on the bed, causing the mattress to dip, and my tenacity vanishes as nerves wrack through me. What if he doesn't like me? What if I'm not good in bed?

I honestly don't know. Cohen never let me be active while we had sex.

I swallow when Skirt pushes his way between my legs. He falls over me, caging my head between his arms, and he bends down, kissing me softly. The rough foreplay is over. He's shaking just as I am.

He doesn't ask if I want it—he knows. He guides his cock between my sheath and sinks into my channel as slow as he can. "Oh, fuck. So good. So tight," he says on a held breath.

Whimpering, I claw at his back and pinch my eyes shut as he stretches me. He's way bigger than Cohen. I can hardly handle it.

"Tell me what to do." Skirt immerses his face into my neck and gives me soft kisses along my jugular vein.

"You're doing it," I tell him, moaning when he begins to move.

"No, tell me what ye like. I—I—fuck—yer my first. I want to make ye feel good, Lips. I want to be the best ye've ever had."

To say I'm stunned is an understatement. A man like Skirt, a virgin? It's impossible, but when he pulls back and flashes vulnerability and uncertainty through his eyes, I know he's telling the truth.

"You already are, Rohan." I lift my head up to take his mouth in a kiss.

He deepens it, slashing his tongue between my lips. His confidence increases with every wave of his hips against mine, and soon he's plowing his cock in and out of me like a seasoned pro. He's hitting all the right places, sinking deeper with every stroke.

Skirt reaches down and plays with my clit, and it's too much. I sink my teeth into his shoulder, biting the flesh until the skin breaks. I rip my mouth away when my orgasm tears away at my consciousness, and my vision blackens.

"Rohan!" I call out to him with every spasm of my walls gripping his cock.

SKIRT

"I'm going to come," he warns, kissing me as he plants himself as far as he can go with every spasm of his orgasm. He's warm inside me, filling me to the rim. Skirt brings his mouth to mine, kissing me gently while we both try to catch our breaths.

I don't think I'll ever fully breathe the same way again, not with how consuming Skirt is in every way, shape, and form. He suffocates me, yet at the same time, he brings me back to life.

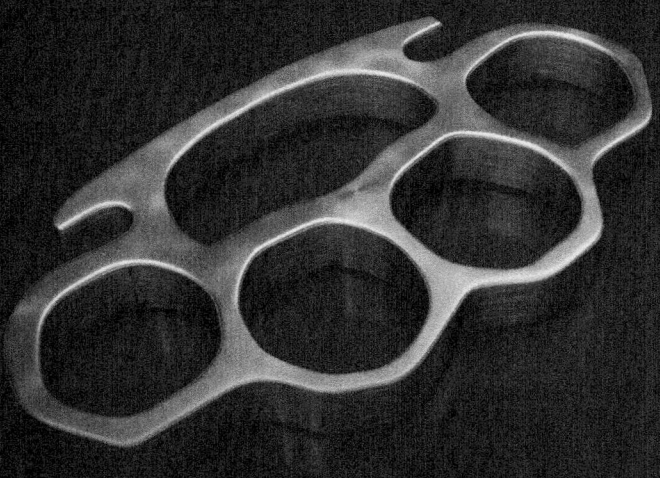

CHAPTER TWELVE

Skirl

I'M ON FUCKING CLOUD NINE.

No, cloud one-hundred. Is that possible? No wonder blokes feel so much better after getting laid. I don't think I'll ever be able to go a day without being inside Dawn. No fucking way. I can't even remember how many times we fucked last night. I was raw, and she was sore, but not even that stopped us.

We can't get enough of each other.

Only one thing can bring me down today.

I'm giving Reaper the cut I made from the fight. He isn't going to be happy with me, but I'm willing to take the punishment because I have a lead on Cohen since Badge can't seem to find one.

My phone buzzes in my hand, and I look down to see it's a text from Maximo.

Be here at seven tonight. Sharp.

Fuck.

I stare at the duffle bag in my hand, the one stuffed to the brim with cash, and I debate if I want to give it to him now.

"I know what you're up to," Tongue chuckles darkly in a creepy corner.

Always in a damn corner.

"I don't know what yer talking about."

"I followed you last night. Didn't like the vibes you were giving off. I don't like a liar." Tongue steps forward from the shadow, and the blade he has in his hand shines. "Saw you fight."

"Tongue, what yer talking about. Ye have no idea what's going on."

"I suggest you inform me," Tongue sneers.

It's never good to be on Tongue's bad side. The man is insane on a good day, on a bad? He is beyond reasoning with, beyond trying to convince. He only has one intent, and that's to cut and kill.

I'm about to open my mouth to answer him, but Reaper's announcement silences me. "Church! Now!" he roars as loud as he can and slams the church door shut.

Oh, shit. He's furious.

Something bad happened.

"Saved by the bell," Tongue growls, sliding the tip of his blade down my arm. It's a slight touch, not usually enough to cut the skin, but since Tongue keeps his knives sharp, my skin parts on the surface and a trickle of blood flows out. "You better hope I don't find out you've turned your back on the club, because if you have, I'm going to rip that Scottish tongue out of your mouth." He slams his shoulder against me which causes his knife to dig deeper into my skin.

Tongue finally pulls the blade away and wipes it on his jeans before stuffing it in his sheath. Fuck, the man scares the hell out of me. I rip my sleeve off my shirt and tie it around my arm to stop the bleeding. Tongue is always going the extra mile before he learns the truth. I should be glad the only thing he did was cut my arm.

I'm glad he didn't just reach in and cut my tongue out.

All the men march into church and the cut-sluts are left alone in the main room. I wipe my forehead on my good sleeve and step inside, and the world stops moving for a minute when I see Maximo standing next to Reaper.

Fuck. If Reaper finds out I'm fighting for Maximo before I tell him, the punishment will be severe for being dishonest.

I lean against the wall and set the bag down next to me. Reaper is waiting for the rest of the men to enter before he begins. When the door closes, he smashes the gavel on the table, and everyone quiets down.

My stomach is in knots. I can't believe Maximo is here. This cannot be good for me.

Reaper pinches his eyes closed and rubs them. He seems older lately. He has silver hair around his temples and crow's feet next to his eyes. This isn't an easy job, and it has taken its toll. Being part of an MC means giving up your life of peace in exchange for turmoil, and I think our peace at the club is over. It has to be if Maximo is here.

"Everyone, this is Maximo. New owner of Circus, Circus. Head of the Moretti Mafia."

"No shit. He's Moretti's family?" Tool asks, flipping his screwdriver between his fingers.

Maximo gives a slight bow. "I am his brother. I hate to see my brother in the state he is in. All I can hope is that he pulls through."

"How do we know you aren't full of shit?" Tongue drags each word out then stabs the table. "Moretti has been in that bed for a while now, and you're just now coming around? Sounds like a bunch of bullshit."

"There were many things I had to take care of before I came to Vegas. Remember, my family is from Italy. That's where I was before all this happened. I had to put someone else in charge there before coming here."

"Maximo has been repaying the money back we invested in Moretti's casino before it blew up." Reaper's eyes land on me, and I can't tell if he knows or not that I'm fighting behind his back. "He has news," Reaper blows out a breath and starts to pace. "You tell them, Maximo, before my anger gets the best of me."

"Of course," Maximo says and sprawls his hands out on the table. He always dresses in black, making his demonic features even darker. "We have a problem in our city. I've had my men keep a close ear to the ground. I know you don't, partake in many illegal activities as I do and I respect that, so when I hear something disturbing, I know I can come to you. My men have told me there are two new MCs. They aren't in Vegas, but they are on the outskirts of the city. Regardless, it isn't good for an MC to encroach on another's territory, especially without making themselves known."

Reaper grunts, and the rest of the guys bang their fists on the table.

"Your President has informed me that you are looking for a man, a fighter, who might have kidnapped a child? I've heard they have been seen with one of the MCs."

"Ye've seen Aidan? Where? Tell us. I'll go get him now."

Maximo's eyes search for me and when they find me,

they soften around the edges. "I do not know. I'm sorry. I've informed Reaper of my fighting ring, and that it is probably his best bet to find Cohen there, along with the other MCs. All are welcome as long as they bring cash."

"That's where you come in, Skirt." Reaper stops pacing and runs his hands through his hair, then twists his neck left and right, cracking the bone. "You're going to fight for Maximo. You're going to fight every damn fight until Cohen catches wind of it."

"Oh, I think he already has. He has taken down one Blackwood brother; I'm sure he would love to take down the other," Maximo adds, and my brothers growl from the threat against me.

"There's something else," Reaper says and rubs his hand over his scruff. "NOLA chapter called—"

"God, can't they leave us alone?" Tool gripes.

"Shut up, Tool. I'm not in the mood for your bullshit," Reaper cuts him off with an evil eye.

"Yes, Prez," Tool relents.

"NOLA called me and told me they have had a large number of kids disappearing. There are new flyers of missing children appearing every day."

"Fuck." Bullseye laces his fingers behind his head and leans back in the chair until he's staring at the ceiling.

"They think whatever is happening, NOLA might be the hotspot, the epicenter of it all."

"Ye mean, Aidan can already be there, and we would have no idea. And that's if Aidan is there. The tunnels for human trafficking go on all over the world. Fuck!" I kick an empty chair and feel completely helpless. I'm invested in this. If we get him back, he's my kid too since I'm with his ma. I want him back. I already feel connected to Aidan in a way I can't explain, and I want to say it's because I'm falling hard for his ma.

"Get it together, Skirt." Reaper points the gavel at me, and his tone of voice has my back slamming against the wall. "You're our chance at getting Cohen. I need you at your best. You need to fight."

"Aye, Prez. I'll do whatever it takes." Obviously. I've fought for my dead brother, for his revenge, but what's more important than fighting for the living? A kid needs me. I'll be killing two birds with one stone.

Fight to avenge my brother.

Fight to bring Aidan home before it's too late.

"We might have to go to NOLA. Everyone be ready. It will be a moment's notice if we find out we're going. I don't want to hear any complaints." Reaper cuts his eyes to Tool, and the screwdriver-wielding man stares at the table, ashamed. Tool has some apprehensions with the NOLA chapter, all because Seer freaked him out with his 'sight' ability.

I'm a skeptic, but it's near hard to deny since Seer helped with Juliette's situation.

"I'm obviously at your disposal. My brother wanted to be allies with you, and I want to extend that opportunity. You need anything, you let me know, and I will get it for you." Maximo checks his watch and then his phone. "I need to leave, gentlemen. Reaper, I will see you tonight."

"Sure thing. Thanks again," Reaper holds out his hand, and Maximo doesn't hesitate to shake it. Maximo might be a shady guy, but I can't say he isn't honest. So far, he has been nothing but genuine. People can't be that nice. He has to have another angle in all this.

"Any information I come across, I'll let you know." Maximo leaves, and his goons push off the wall to follow him.

Everyone lets out a breath when they hear the front door slam.

"That man freaks me out."

"I know that's right, brother." Poodle holds up his fist, and Slingshot taps his knuckles.

"Anything else that needs to be addressed now?" Reaper asks, eyeing every brother around the table.

"I'll keep an eye out at Kings' Club. If anything seems off, I'll be sure to let you know," Tool says. Kings' Club has been very profitable for the MC. It's where most of our legal profits come from; that and the garage, which Braveheart has taken over since Tool now spends most of his time at the club.

"Good, man. Okay, dismissed." Reaper hits the gavel on the table, and my brothers file out. "Skirt, I want to talk to you for a second."

Fuck.

"Good luck." Tongue gives me a smug, crooked tilt of his lips as he shuts the door behind him. Crazy bastard. I swear, he wishes pain on everyone around him.

Reaper and I stare at one another. It's quiet. My heart races and makes blood rush in my ears. My cheeks heat. He fucking knows, and he's waiting for me to say it. I swallow my fear and pick up the duffle bag, tossing it on the wooden table that has the Ruthless Kings logo in the middle of it. Reaper cocks a brow at me and laces his fingers in front of his face, creating a steeple with his index fingers as he presses them against his nose.

"That supposed to mean something to me?" he asks.

"Aye."

"Open it."

I walk around the table and lean over, gripping the zipper between my fingers and pull it down. Stacks of money are piled high. There has to be close to eighty-thousand there. "I fought for Maximo last night."

Reaper gives me a quick, sparing look before he pulls a pack of cigarettes from his cut pocket. He places a smoke between his mouth and lights it, as always. He's smoking more and more these days. It's only a matter of time before Sarah finds out. He leans back in the chair, throws his boots on the table, and blows out the smoke through his nostrils.

I rub my hand over my face. This is torture. "I'll accept any punishment for not telling ye and going behind yer back." I yank off my shirt and kneel, preparing for his blade to slice through my skin.

His boots pound on the floor and the chair rolls back as he stands. The smell of smoke comes closer, and his hand takes hold of my ear and yanks. "Get the hell up and put your shirt on. I know you fought last night. Who do you think called Maximo and told him?"

I grab my shirt and yank it over my head. "What do ye mean? How?"

"Maximo and I are in on the fighting ring together. I miss getting my hands dirty. We both want the same thing—money—but we want the fights to be fair, nothing fishy. When he said he needed a fighter, I offered you, and I knew you'd take it. You're just like Tongue needing to cut and Poodle needing to kill; you have to fight, and I knew you wouldn't turn Maximo down. When I found out about Cohen, I knew fighting would be a way to draw him in. You're his damn bait."

"Ye used me?"

"Yep. Don't you feel dirty?"

"Little bit." I scratch my head, confused.

"Get over it. We would have problems if you didn't end up telling me, but I knew you would. You don't let pride get in your way."

"Have you considered that I could lose a fight?"

Reaper bores his eyes into mine, and he snags me by the cut. "No, and you better not lose because that's the only way you're going to get in that cage with Cohen. Regardless of the piece of shit human being he is, he's one of the best fighters in the world. We need that kid back. I don't fucking like it when people hurt kids, and I have a feeling your lady wants her son back and you want your lady happy. Am I right?"

I tilt my chin down, submitting to the Prez.

Losing is not an option.

"Good. Now, go update Dawn. I'm sure she's going to want to know there's a little more hope now."

"Hope? About child sex trafficking? That will destroy her."

"So will knowing the truth too late. Tell her now, let her wrap her head around it. The sooner she knows, the better." Reaper puts his cigarette out on the table and takes out four stacks of cash. "The rest is yours."

He pats me on the back as he leaves, and I'm left staring at money and too much information swirling in my head. The weight of this entire situation is on my shoulders, and the only way to get rid of it is to win.

I'm not like my brother. I'm a good fighter, but I'm not great. "Conor, if ye can hear me right now, I really need ye help. I can't do it alone. Dawn needs me, Aidan needs me, the club is depending on me. Send down some of that fighting ability that ye took with ye to the grave." The black bag of cash taunts me, and the first thing I think of is buying a new bike for myself

138

since my other one is in the junkyard behind Kings' garage. It can only be used for parts now.

Conor is silent, which I figured would be the case, but one can only hope that spirits and shit are real. I snatch the bag off the table and stomp my way toward the door. When I open it, Tongue is there, arms bracketing the way out.

"Tongue, I'm not in the mood."

"I'm never in the mood. Some of the club is going with you tonight. I'm your bodyguard."

A bodyguard? At a fucking fight?

If I'm lucky, I'll be the one stopping Tongue before he kills someone. Great, now on top of everything, I have to fucking babysit.

I'm only one man. There's only so much I can do.

CHAPTER THIRTEEN

Dawn

"I'M GOING TO THIS FIGHT," I YELL AT SKIRT WHEN HE DARES to tell me I have to sit here on my ass, staring at the fucking wall, waiting for him and half the club to come back.

"Ye can't. I won't be able to focus on the fight if I'm worried about ye. Please, just listen to me."

"Aidan could be there."

"He won't be there!" Skirt shouts back at me, and I flinch. I know he won't hit me, but I can't stop the impulse. "Lips…" He pulls my head toward him by gripping the side of my jaw, his thumb laying on my bottom lip. "I won't ever hit ye. I don't mean to scare ye, but what if Cohen is there and he takes ye from me? I only just found ye, Dawn. I can't focus on finding ye and Aidan. Please."

I tangle myself in his embrace. I want to cry. "Skirt, I need to go. I'll stay near Tongue or someone equivalent to him. I need to. Don't take this from me. Please," I beg.

"No," he says.

I wrench away from his grasp and shove him. "I'm going to find a way there. Whether you like it or not."

"If ye go, I swear, Dawn, I'll—"

"You'll what?" I hiss, pushing his chest again. "I'm going!" I scream until my voice breaks, and his chest rises and falls in heavy beats.

He grabs the shoulders of my shirt and picks me up, tossing me on the couch. "Ye aren't going! That's fucking final." He rips my shirt off and bites my nipple so hard tears spring to my eyes.

I cry out, frustrated, angry, and turned on.

"Tell me ye won't go."

"No," I say defiantly.

"Yer a fucking headache, ye know that."

"I guess you haven't met yourself because you're a bigger pain in my ass than that damn cactus in yours!" I shout. "I'm going, and there is nothing you can do about it."

"Maybe this will shut you up then." He flips up his kilt and pushes my head down toward his cock, but I push him away. He thinks I'm playing our game. Push and pull, shove and slap, but this is a hard limit for me. I don't suck cock like this, not when Skirt is mad. I can't do it.

"Get off me!" I roll away from him, and he stares at me with regretful eyes.

"Shite, I'm sorry, Dawn." He reaches for me, and I scurry away from him, tears rolling down my eyes. I can only see Cohen. Cohen forcing me to suck his cock. Cohen fucking my face. Cohen not caring that he's hurting me by shoving his cock so far down my throat I can't breathe.

Before a fight and after a fight. My mouth was his.

"Christ, please don't be scared of me. I'm sorry. I thought… I thought we were playing. I'm so fucking sorry." He falls to his knees on the ground and inches his way toward me. "I didn't know."

A sob catches my throat, but all I can do is nod.

"I'm going to kill him," Skirt says, pulling me to his chest.

"He made me—" I hiccup at the thought. "He'd leave me—" But it's useless. I can't get the words out. All I can feel is the humiliation, the pain of being used.

"I'll never do it again," Skirt swears, pulling me onto his lap as I cry.

I feel so stupid. Why would Skirt want to be with someone like me? A woman who can't even manage to suck her man's cock? Am I going to freak out every time he tries? I hate Cohen for ruining me.

"Ye can go, but I swear, you have to stick with the brothers, okay?" He tilts my chin up to look at him, and his face is blurry through my watery eyes. His finger brushes over the yellow bruises that are quickly healing. "I can't stand the thought of anything bad happening to ye."

"Nothing will as long as I'm with you and your brothers."

A knock at the door interrupts us, and it's Tongue, the creepy guy who always has the knife. His hair hangs in his face, and his stares at us on the floor. "We need to go." He turns on his boot that jingles as he walks away, and Skirt exhales, placing his forehead on my shoulder.

Why can't everything be normal? Why can't we stay here on the floor, happy in each other's arms? Why does the world have to be so cruel?

"Come on, Lips. We need to get going. If I'm late, I forfeit, and I can't lose." Skirt stands, and I expect him to place me on my feet, but he continues to hold me. "I like ye here. I think I'll hold ye till we get to the cage."

I lean my head against his chest, relieved that Skirt is the type of man to accept things as they are. He didn't push me when I backed away from him, unable to give him head, unlike the cut-sluts. A sliver of fear makes its way into my bones, and something makes me wonder if being unable to suck him will be a problem. I know it was for Cohen. Anytime I denied him, he made me push my ass up and my head down, and when he was done, he'd fuck my face anyway.

I clutch Skirt's cut, as he calls it, and hold onto him as if he's the only thing keeping me fixated on this earth. Gravity is giving way from under me, and Skirt is holding me tight, making sure I don't float away. His strength, power, and tenderness is compelling, enthralling, and addicting. A woman could get used to being with a man so viral, so electrically charged.

It would be all too easy to give up everything for Skirt. He's my anti-gravity, the space where there is no force, no strain, no weaknesses, just a safe place to be, to soar and be free.

I suck in a breath and close my eyes as Skirt carries me to the truck. Everyone uses it when they need it and since Skirt doesn't have a helmet for me yet, we'll be riding in it tonight. When I hear the doors open, Skirt somehow finds a way to keep a tight hold on me while he sits in the back seat.

The leather is hot, and the cab of the truck is stuffy which makes it hard to breathe. Fluttering my eyes open, Tongue is in the driver's seat and Knives is in the passenger seat, pretending to throw his ninja star through the windshield. A roar of bikes sound behind us, and I don't need to look back to see them following. They're coming to support their brother.

I flinch when I think of seeing Skirt hit and plummeted with fists, and I hold onto him tighter.

Without saying a word, he tightens his arms around me in a hug, and we drive down the road. I'm tracing the patch on Skirt's cut, outlining his name with my finger. His lips find my forehead, and I close my eyes, relishing in a touch so soft, simple, and tender.

He's an enigma, leather and brass on the outside, warm and gentle on the inside. I get to experience all of it.

All too soon we stop, and Skirt unwraps his arms around me, leaving me cold and with worry.

"Ah, so glad all of you arrived."

It's a voice I don't recognize. I meet the man's curious gaze as he stares at me, and he holds out his hand. I go to shake his, and he tilts my hand over and brings my knuckles to his lips. "Why, who is this beauty? She is magnificent. I am Maximo, beautiful. Who are you?"

"She's mine," Skirt steps in front of Maximo, blocking the Italian's hungry eyes.

"Oh, she is Dawson?" The edge of excitement is hard to miss as his voice raises. He looks around Skirt's shoulder. "You are famous, beautiful. I have longed to meet the woman who has a man bleeding his knuckles for. And you are worth it, aren't you?"

I jerk my hand away and lay it in the middle of Skirt's back, rubbing my hand over the buttery leather of his vest. The bottomless orbs of the skull embroidered in the back of his cut stare at me, reminding me of the deep void leveled in my chest.

SKIRT

"She's worth it all. I'll fight, Maximo, but she's mine. My property. My woman. Ye fuck with her, ye fuck with me, and I will kill ye. Do I make myself clear?"

Hearing Skirt's claim has a rush of lust replacing every blood cell in my veins, and the only liquid my heart is pumping is desire. I've never had a man claim me so openly before. Skirt's body shakes with waves of rage. His fists clench, and I can tell he's seconds away from punching Maximo in the face. I rub his back in soothing circles, hoping my touch relaxes him, and his shoulders sag from my attempt.

It's working.

"I see. I am sorry to step on any boundaries. She is yours. I understand. You're a lucky man, and that Cohen is a fucking fool. I hope he comes tonight."

"I don't," Skirt admits and holds out his hand to help me out of the truck. "I don't want Dawn anywhere near that fucking arsehole."

I keep my lips shut and walk hand in hand with Skirt toward the hotel/casino. It looks nice, in repairs with its new hedges along the front entrance and automatic swiveling door as people enter and exit. I clutch onto Skirt's arm as we slither through the maze of people gambling and laughing. The song of slot machines ring, and someone screams with joy as they win the jackpot.

Maybe when life calms down, I'll be able to gamble and enjoy a night out like this.

"After you," Maximo holds out his arm and winks his chocolate eye at me.

I flush, and Skirt sneers at Maximo and tugs me close to his chest, pulling me against the front of his body as we find ourselves on the elevator. Maximo hides his mischievous smirk

145

under a broad palm and swipes a card to the basement after all the MC brothers climb on the elevator.

"I hope this elevator holds the weight of all of you. You aren't exactly small," Maximo teases. A blinking red light catches my attention under the B button. Red is never a good color. It says, 'danger' and 'beware.' The elevator slides down, dinging until it passes the B level, then it comes to a sudden stop, the white light on the button turning red to signal our arrival to Hell.

I assume that's what this place is.

Once the silver doors slide open, I know I'm right. Red seems to be the theme for the night. A light hangs above the cage, burning bright red, the color of hot flames and blood. As we walk down the aisle, the ground itself is dirt and the crowd is shaking the fence blocking them off from us, screaming and shouting, roaring for the fight to start.

The fence reminds me of lace, a barely secure barrier made to block the true object of obsession, and to tease the mind to want more.

Skirt shrugs off his cut and slips off his shirt, and hands them to me. I clutch them to my chest, inhaling his scent of sweat and leather. I've never been allowed so close to the cage before. I always had to wait in Cohen's private room, watching the fight on the TV. When he was done, that was when I would get undressed and get into position.

The Ruthless Kings circle the cage, looking into the bleachers for Cohen O'Roarke. My skin doesn't tingle. The hair on the back of my neck doesn't stand up. Nothing inside me is screaming that Cohen is here.

I'm equally relieved and devastated because it means another night without Aidan.

SKIRT

"It will be okay. Skirt is a good fighter. Sometimes a bit slow, but no one can be perfect." Tongue sucks his teeth by running his red appendage over them and then pulls out his knife to start flossing them.

I shiver from disgust. How much blood is on that blade that he's putting into his mouth?

Skirt reaches into his pockets and pulls out a pair of brass knuckles and slides them on his fingers. He grips my chin, and the brass is cold as it presses against my skin. It's odd. In a few minutes he will be bashing his fists against someone, but as the weapons lay against my flesh, I know he'll never use his weapons to harm me.

"Give me a good luck kiss, Lips." His other hand tangles in my hair, and his breath ghosts over my lips, tingling my flesh and tightening my nipples. This isn't the time or place.

"Anything you want." I smash my mouth against his, and the crowd roars and the impulse to give them a show has me jumping onto Skirt and wrapping my legs around his waist.

A menacing rumble vibrates the back of his throat, and I can feel it sink into my chest, even over the crowd's ruckus. "I think ye are an exhibitionist. Ye want to fuck in front of someone, Lips?" He brings his lips to my ear and moans. "Maybe later we can listen to one of the guys fuck again. Do ye want that?"

I nod, completely breathless and slump against the fighting cage. The thought of listening to others have sex relaxes me.

What the hell has gotten into me?

"Good, now I have something to look forward to." He lays one last kiss on my lips, then my nose, and climbs up the cage, which has to be eight-feet tall, and then descends down the other side.

The crowd stomps their feet, and the dirt on the ground begins the bounce from the bass.

"I could slice everyone's throat in here." Tongue scans the area, his eyes hungrily eating up every face in the crowd. "Every single one. I bet they would deserve it being in a place like this."

"Does that mean we deserve it?" I ask him, and his murderous, cold eyes lock onto mine. His long black hair reminds me of a curtain of evil when only half of his face shows.

"We all deserve it."

A beefy arm wraps around me, and I turn my head to the left and see Bullseye, and my face turns a pink. I wonder if he knows we listened to him fuck Candy the other day. "Don't mind Tongue. He's all fucked up in the head." Bullseye tightens his arm protectively around me then nods toward Skirt.

Poodle, Skirt's best friend, I think, watches me too.

Everyone is watching me. It's unsettling. I throw on Skirt's cut, needing to feel secure, and bring the leather to my nose and inhale.

The elevator opens again, and the man who runs down the aisle is three-times the size of Skirt.

"Oh, that's a big motherfucker," Bullseye says, which doesn't make me feel better.

The man scales the cage in half the time and jumps into the ring, landing on two feet and tree trunks for legs. Skirt doesn't look nervous, but one hit from this giant could kill Skirt. The man has scars all over his back, lashes, maybe from a whip, and he as a scar running from the side of his mouth to his eye.

Maximo stands to the side with a microphone in hand. "Everyone welcome, Rohan the Red and Joker," he announces, and the crowd goes wild.

"Well, that makes sense."

I hold Bullseye's hand and hold my breath. Tongue takes a step forward and cocks his head. "Well, hell. I'm the one who put that scar there ten years ago. I'll be damned, the fucker lived. Cut him with this blade too." Tongue rips the knife from the sheath strapped to his chest and points it at the giant, taunting him.

"Stop it! If you get him angry, it's only worse for Skirt!" I hit the hand that holds the knife, and it falls to the ground.

"Good," Tongue sneers, his lifeless eyes darting between mine. "Skirt thrives off danger. Don't ever fuck with me and my blade again."

I'm scared, terrified actually, but I throw my shoulders back. "Don't fuck with Skirt again and maybe I won't."

"May the blood be in your favor, gentleman," Maximo sings and lets go of the dangling microphone.

The giant is holding something that looks like a bat with small metal spikes circling the body. I hold my stomach, squeezing the skin violently until it hurts when I realize there are no rules here. One swing of that bat and Skirt is a dead man.

"This just got interesting." Maximo stands beside me, and Bullseye's fingers tighten on my shoulder a bit harder to protect me. "I believe in Rohan. This giant is dumb."

The giant swings the bat, and Skirt ducks, barely missing the sharp metal teeth protruding from the bat.

I hold my breath and wait for the longest night of my life to come to an end.

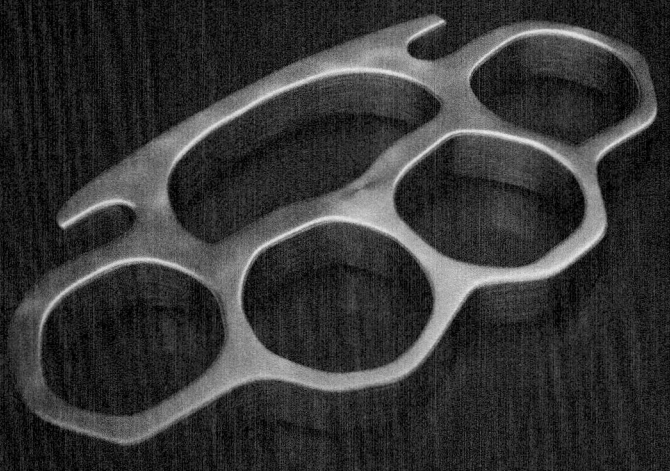

CHAPTER FOURTEEN

Skirl

WHAT BIG BLOKES DON'T REALIZE ABOUT BIG WEAPONS IS the amount of time it takes to use it, gives me enough time to react. I duck and slam my fist against his side, right where his kidney is. The brass knuckles do their job, and the giant doubles over and drops his meat grinder of a bat. I send an uppercut to his face, knocking him out in less than a minute.

He falls in slow motion as I dance on my toes and his teeth snap together as he hits the ground, and the cage floor shakes. I guess it's true what they say. The bigger they are, the harder they fall.

There are no breaks in this cage. Just as soon as they drag the big bloke away, another one climbs in, and this one has a sword. What is it with big weapons? Don't they know that's how they lose about a second or two in time, giving me the opportunity I need?

I'm swearing as I dance around the sharp blade, and I glance over at Tongue to see him staring through the fence in awe, watching the silver blade slice through the air. Then my eyes land on Dawn. Her eyes are wide, and she's holding Bullseye's hand, clenching it every time I dive and dodge.

It's a distraction.

She's a distraction.

And it costs me.

The blade slices through the skin on my back when I don't dodge in time. I bite down the pain, but the burning is unimaginable. The trickle of blood pools down my back, and Dawn's cries are loud, nearly piercing over the roar of the crowd.

"Now I'm mad." I flex my shoulder, welcoming the burn, and act quick on my feet, letting the dust from the ground make its way into my lungs as I inhale, reminding me of when me and my brother would fight as kids outside in the field.

I slide to my leg and trip the bastard, step on his wrist with my boot until an orchestra of snaps play up his arm, and he releases the sword. I bring my fist up and slam it against his cheek over and over again until I see bone through the split flesh.

"Fuck ye and ye damn sword. Even I know not to carry mine to a fight." I gather a wad of spit and spew it on his chest.

Maximo gives me two thumbs up, and Reaper stands there with a smoke in his mouth, staring at me with concern.

Not pride.

Not joy.

And I get pissed off because he set all this up. If he's worried about me taking it too far, he's probably right. I spread my arms out and toss my head back, releasing a feral roar that builds up in my throat.

I want more.

I want Cohen.

I feel it. The electricity burning through my body, blazing, blistering under my skin to let the animal out, to kill, to feast, and to bury. I need it. I'm almost hard from the madness taking hold of my brain. The line isn't blurred. It's gone.

Another victim enters the ring, a man with a hatchet.

He has no idea what he's entered and who he's facing.

I'm in bloodlust. He doesn't understand the visceral need in my veins to break every bone in his body with my fists. The man throws the hatchet over his head, and I dodge left, staring at him in disbelief that he just willingly lost his weapon.

I pick it up and flip it in the air, like one does with a baseball bat. "Ye need to learn how to throw an axe before ye threaten a man with it." I've tossed a thousand axes and can do it with one hand. Without warning, without batting a damn eyelash, I toss it through the air so fast that when it lands between his eyes, the sick thud quiets the crowd as the man falls to his knees.

I squat and tilt my head, his eyes wide as he stares at me, realizing that the last few seconds of his life is upon him. A small trail of blood escapes his wound, dribbling down his nose, lips, then falls free from his chin. Poor bastard. I don't even know his name.

And I don't even care.

"Maybe ye'll practice in heaven, boyo. Ah, ye probably going to hell." I stand, towering over the man's weak attempt to speak. He can't with an axe in his head. I wrap my hand around the handle, placing my boot against his shoulder, and kick him free.

I toss the hatchet aside and watch the life leave his eyes and the blood pool around his head.

They take his body next.

And I'm only left hungrier.

You can't tempt a man who longs for blood and not expect him to become addicted to it once he has it.

I search the crowd for Cohen, but every face I see blurs to one. I shouldn't have to prove myself. I'm Conor's brother, for fuck's sake. That should be enough for him to come out of his fucking shadow and fight me like a man.

"That's enough for the night," Reaper says on the other side of the cage.

I stomp toward him and grip the fence, curling my fingers through the metal until the brass knuckles clink against the cage. "I say when it's enough. Bring on the next one!" I roar, and the crowd goes nuts. Maximo claps his hands together and licks his lips. He can taste the money he's making.

"Get the fuck out of there," Reaper commands.

"I'm the god in this cage; not ye, Prez," I dare say, but I can't stop myself. I'm too fucking high on endorphins to care.

I pace the cage like a wild animal, snarling and watching the elevator open for my next opponent. Reaper talks to Maximo, and I'm not sure what is being said, but Maximo hurries over to the microphone and grabs it from the air.

"The night is over. Leave at once. No questions." Maximo's statement has the crowd dispersing quickly, like sheep listening to their handler.

All too soon the crowd is gone, and the buzzing in my mind gets louder. I'm surrounded by my brothers, and Dawn stares at me with absolute terror in her big green eyes that make my knees weak. I shake my head to clear the haze, the need to keep fighting, but as Reaper climbs the fence, takes a knife from Tongue, and jumps down in front of me, what I've done hits me like a ton of bricks.

"You want to fight, Skirt? Fight me," Reaper says, circling me like a shark. He digs the knife into the cut on my back, and a shout of pain rips from my lips. "I said fight me!" He shoves. "You want to prove you're a god? Fight your President."

"I'm sorry, Reaper. I don't know what got into me. I wasn't thinking clearly."

Heat radiates off him, his anger, and he whispers so only I can hear, "You do not disrespect me like that. Do I make myself clear?"

"Aye," I say, knowing what's coming.

No matter what state of mind I'm in, I will never fight Reaper. He's the one man I will not go up against because I know he'll kill me.

"We have company," Maximo says as a few men crawl in under the large garage door.

"Table this shit for later. I'm nowhere near done with you." Reaper slashes the blade across my back, and my knees give out. That knife hurts more than the damn sword that etched my skin earlier.

The men are in leather cuts too. They aren't armed, but that doesn't mean anything. The guy up front has a patch on his cut that says VP, so Tool pushes off the side and charges at the stranger to take him out, screwdriver in hand.

"Stand down," Reaper orders, and Tool doesn't take another step.

"We aren't here for trouble. We heard about the fight and

knew this would be one of the ways we could meet you all. Word around town is you've been looking for someone. I have information."

"Introduce yourself," Reaper says, his voice echoing off the underground cage.

"I'm Whistler, VP of Demons Fury. We just moved in on the outskirts of town near the dam."

It isn't our territory, so they have every right to claim it. Still, I can see how much Reaper doesn't like another MC encroaching like this.

"We want to be allies. My President isn't trying to make enemies."

"Then, where is he?" Tool spits, flicking his screwdriver over his knuckles.

"Home, with his ol' lady. She's on her death bed, and he ain't ever going to leave her side."

"Sorry to hear that." Reaper climbs up the fence and jumps down to stand in front of the strange biker.

I level the cage, ignoring the stinging pain in my back that is close to my spine and sail through the air, landing on two feet.

Barely.

"This is One, my Sargent at Arms." Whistler points to the man to his left.

"One?" Reaper and I say together. What the fuck kind of road name is that?

"Yeah, he only ever needs one bullet," Whistler explains.

"This is Skirt," Reaper points to me with Tongue's knife. "That's Tool, the one with the screwdriver. And that's enough pleasantries. What do you want?"

"You're looking for a kid, right? And that Cohen guy? He came to us for help, but we denied him."

"You saw him? You saw my son? And you did nothing?" Dawn screams from behind me and when I look back, she rips out of Bullseye's hold and marches up to us with a look of hatred in her eyes, swirling like emeralds on fire. She doesn't hold back. She swings and punches Whistler in the face. "You fucking bastard!" She lifts her fist again, and Reaper catches it mid-air.

Reaper doesn't say a word. He doesn't have to. He's fucking furious. At me. At her. And when he cuts his eyes to me, I know what he wants to say.

I need to get a better hold on my ol' lady if I know what's good for her.

"Emotions are running high, fellas. I apologize. This is the mother of the kid you saw, and the man who has him is on our shit list."

"That's what we heard from Maximo," Whistler says.

Reaper lifts a brow at Maximo. "Someone has loose lips. I don't like that," Prez sneers.

"I have a job. I'm on the strip in Vegas. I need to know who is worthy around me and who isn't. They are. I told you about them earlier." Maximo rolls his eyes, annoyed from Prez's outburst.

"We want to help with this. We are new to the area, and we don't want to start on a bad foot. We didn't realize who the guy was at the time, or we would have stopped him. We think he went to the other MC when he ran out of options. The Hellhounds MC. They're no good. They have their hands in some fucked-up shit."

"What kind of shit?" Reaper asks, losing his patience.

Whistler wipes his lip with his tongue and grins. "Your ol' lady packs a punch. You taught her well."

"She taught herself," I say with pride. I like that my woman knows how to protect herself.

Whistler ignores my comment and stares Reaper straight on. "The kind of shit where they are putting pretty price tags on things that shouldn't have price tags."

"I'm going to be sick," Dawn gags and runs to the side of the cage, retching her guts up.

"You help us get this kid back, you'll forever have allies with Ruthless and all its chapters."

Whistler's brows shoot up so far, I thought they were about to leave his forehead. "Fuck yeah, Prez." He holds out his hand and Reaper grips it, hard. Reaper pulls the man forward until he's staring him down. Whistler isn't a short man at all, Reaper is just that fucking big, and being at the end of that stare, I fucking hate it. Whistler probably wants to piss his boots.

I don't blame him.

"Let me get one thing straight to you, Demons Fury. If you are fucking with me, if you are lying to me, if you are thinking about double crossing me, I will rip your fucking hearts out and then shove them down your throat, and then I'll have my craziest fucking member cut all your tongues out. Do not fucking ruin this, or I will bring so much death to you, so much pain, not even the fury you demons possess can save you. Do I make myself clear?"

"Crystal," Whistler says, a slight shake in his voice.

"Good. I want a meeting with your Prez. He comes to me. There is no negotiation on that."

"He won't come until she passes."

Reaper nods and lets go of Whistler's hand and turns toward the Ruthless Kings. "Let's roll." Reaper turns around and then stabs the knife in the wood of the cage floor. Tongue runs to the knife's side and yanks it out, kisses it, then sheaths it again.

"That's the guy who cuts tongues," I say. One's eyes go wide when Tongue slides his thumb along his neck, smiling at the promise of spilling the Demons Fury blood.

"Look at us, making new friends." Maximo claps his hands together and slaps me on the back. I hiss, almost punching him in the face with my knuckles, but I catch myself in time. "I need everyone to get the fuck out, okay?" He smiles, and the twists and turns of his attitude give me whiplash.

"Hope yer smart and really consider siding with us. Ye have no idea how fucked up we are." I head toward Dawn just as she wipes her mouth. She's in damn tears again over the idea that her son might already be sold.

I lay my arm around her shoulder and guide her toward the exit. Once we're alone, she stops in front of me. "You killed a man tonight," she says with a wobbly lip.

"Aye."

"You liked it."

"Aye." No need to lie about it.

"You're a killer."

"Aye."

"Stop fucking agreeing with me!" she screams.

"Aye," I say again, but she pushes against my chest until my back is against the wall of the casino. The rough stucco digs into the open wound of my back.

I've put a few things together when it comes to Dawn, my sweet lips. When she's emotional, she needs an outlet. It's like me with fighting.

"Stop it! Stop. You killed a man. You liked it. You wanted more! Do you want to do that to me? Do you want to hurt me?"

"No, Lips. I never want to hurt ye."

"Seeing you fight like that did," she says. "Seeing you become that man…" She trails off and stares at the ground, crossing her arms over her chest. "Skirt was gone."

"Aye."

She rears back and slaps me across the face. It's the first time all night I've been hit by someone else's hand, and since it's hers, my cock rolls beneath my kilt and comes to life. "Stop agreeing with me."

"Do it again," I say.

She backhands me next until my cheek is on fire. I should not be turned on right now, neither should she, but she and I both are running high on emotion, and this is how we take it out.

On each other.

"Again."

"No."

I flip us around until it's her back digging into the rough concrete. I push her shorts to the side and slide my fingers through her wet cunt. "I said *again*."

"I said no! I won't hit you again."

"Yer defiant…" I shudder, loving how much she fights me.

"I can't get the thought of you killing that man out of my head."

I shove my hand over her mouth, lift my kilt up, and plunge my cock into her heat. "Get used to it, Lips. I'd kill again for ye." I thrust in and out, rocking furiously. I can't believe we're fucking right now, but adrenaline is high, and it needs an escape. "And *again*." I take all my anger and frustrations of the night out on her, plundering her deep, wet crevice. "And *again*." My back burns, stings, and I can feel fresh beads of blood swelling up and flowing down my back.

Dawn screams into my palm and her inner walls massage me, forcing cum from my sack. It's the quickest, dirtiest fuck I can imagine us doing. I spill my seed inside her and smash my mouth against hers, spearing my tongue between her lips. She sucks my red muscle, and my eyes roll back, and another wave of cum leaves me as her cunt strangles me from her orgasm.

"We're fucked up," she whispers against my mouth as the humid air swirls.

"Aye, but we can be fucked up together."

Dawn knows what I need without me saying it, and the same goes for her. We are fucked up. I don't know another couple that loves to rough house like we do. I like the slapping she gives me when she wants my cock and doesn't just come out and say it. It's a soft punishment that I've longed for. It isn't often I get hit, and I need to feel it, fucking *need*. It's an aphrodisiac.

"Hey! Tuck your cock in. You can fuck pussy when we get back. We aren't waiting around for you forever!" Poodle yells down the alley, and his voice reminds me that the Prez is waiting, and I'm getting lower on his list by making him stand around.

I slip out of her heat and push her panties and shorts back in place.

Here I am, knowing I'm about to get carved more than a piece of wood, and all I can think about is how my cum is pooling in her underwear and slicking up her folds for me to use later.

Yeah, I'm fucked.

CHAPTER FIFTEEN

Dawn

WAYLON JENNINGS BLARES FROM THE JUKEBOX IN THE MAIN room. Everyone is going on with their lives, drinking and having a good time, but I know what's really going on. The music is turned up, people are drinking, but in the next room, Skirt is getting a heart carved in his chest.

"Tool has one," a beautiful brunette woman sits next to me, green eyes like mine, but a tad lighter. She has two dogs next to her, Yeti and Tyrant if I remember correctly. Yeti is the reason why Poodle's dog, Lady, got pregnant and had puppies. Skirt bought one, but he hasn't had time to care for it yet, but maybe I can for him. With all the shit going on, he'll never have time for a dog.

"One what?" I take a swig of beer.

"A heart on his chest. Tool got it for disobeying Reaper about staying away from me."

My eyes linger on her curvy frame. She's wearing a leather cut too, and as she bends down to pet the dogs, I see "Property of Tool" on the back. I want one of those. Unless Skirt doesn't really view me as his ol' lady. "They have their own laws around here. It's just how it is. It might not seem like a big deal, but not listening to Reaper is one of the biggest crimes a brother can commit."

"You act like Reaper is God." I tilt the beer to my lips and take a few greedy swallows. My eyes land on Jasmine, who's giving me the evil-eye along with Candy, the slut I throat punched. I'll happily do it again if they don't get their damn eyes off me.

"Here, he is, and you'll be smart not to question that," Juliette advises, and another woman sits to my left. Sarah, if I remember right.

"She's right. Reaper can be brutal, but he has to be for the club to take him seriously," the blonde says, and then catches thing one and thing two looking at us. "What the hell is their problem?"

"Me. Jasmine is mad that I fuck Skirt, and Candy is mad that I throat punched her when she tried to attack me because I said the guys had no standards." I shrug, guzzling the rest of my drink until I'm fresh out. How long does it take to carve a damn heart?

Juliette and Sarah howl with laughter, slapping their knees as if it's the funniest thing they've ever heard. Sarah's cheeks are red, and Juliette snorts since she can't control her breathing.

"That's great. I love it. I like you." Sarah wiggles a finger at me, and Yeti jumps up and licks it.

Jasmine struts over to me, swaying her hips in her red mini

skirt and cheap pink lipstick. She's only wearing a black leather bra, and her belly button is pierced. Candy is next to her as back up, and her tits are so big, she can't even cross her arms over her chest. Her lips are just as fake as her blonde hair, along with her lashes. Is anything real on her?

"How can I help you skanks?" I ask as nicely as I can. I'm not really in the mood. I've had a hell of a night. I'm somewhat closer to getting my kid, saw Skirt kill a man, fucked next to a dumpster because apparently I have no class where I drop my panties for Skirt, and now he's getting his chest scarred for life because of me.

I mean, if you think about it, all of this is because of me. If I'd never showed up, if he'd never found me on the road, none of this would be happening to them.

"We have been here a lot longer than you," Jasmine slurs, her fruity drink splashing over the rim of the plastic cup as she teeters on her heels that are three inches too high. "We deserve them. Not you."

"Well, none of them picked you, did they?" Juliette spouts, flicking her thick brown hair over her shoulder.

"They fucked us." Candy has a satisfied grin on her lips as if that is supposed to make me jealous.

I laugh because I know my man hasn't fucked any one of them. Only me. Only ever. I'm not about to tell them that, but I know the truth. "You think that makes you special? Sweetie, you were another pair of legs to help get on with the day, but you don't have their hearts. You will always be a cut-slut. Now, why don't you go spread them for a brother who isn't taken?"

"Fucking bitch." Jasmine tosses her drink on me, right in my fucking face. All I taste is vodka and punch, staining the white shirt Sarah let me borrow.

Candy takes a step back, the first time in her life that she's probably ever been smart, as I stand. I don't know why I can defend myself here and I couldn't with Cohen; maybe it's because of Aidan. I had to take the abuse so my son never got it, but Cohen isn't here, and Aidan is missing, and the only thing keeping me somewhat levelheaded is Skirt.

And I'm not about to let these women ruin that for me.

The song on the jukebox is turned down, but lightly plays in the background. Conversation comes to a halt as everyone stares at us.

Without thinking, I snag her by the extensions in her hair and push her to the ground, then drag her to the front door. I'm so sick of people thinking they can walk all over me. I'm done with that. It's time to show people who's boss, who's in control, and it's not some whore who had Skirt's cock in her mouth for less than a minute.

When we get outside into the cold night, my breath can be seen, and the bonfire that Braveheart, Tank, and Doc are sitting around is warm and inviting. When Doc sees what's happening, he stands on his feet from the stump on the ground.

I slam Jasmine's head against the porch, and she whines, "You bitch!"

"Yeah, you've been saying that a lot lately." I kick her down the steps, and she cries when she hits the ground. I mean, ugly sobs as she tries to get to her feet. I hurry to her side and push her, and if Doc wasn't in the way, Jasmine would have been set on fire. "Let me get something straight to you—Skirt is mine. You might have had a taste of him for a moment, but I get it for a lifetime. I fuck him. You don't. You don't like it? Leave. I have other things to worry about than a selfish whore who thinks she has any say over the men here because she waves her ass in the air for an easy ride. Leave me alone, and I promise I won't take Skirt's brass knuckles and fucking beat you with them. Are we clear?"

"Yes." She stares at the ground, not even able to look me in the eyes.

"You owe Sarah an apology for ruining her shirt. Reaper will deal with you later for it, I assume. Isn't Sarah the one thing you aren't supposed to fuck with? Her or her belongings?" Her eyes widen, and her face turns ashen; even with the glow of the fire, she's terrified. Why can't Reaper carve a heart in her chest? Why the hell does the MC have sluts hanging around all the time? It isn't like they can't go to Vegas and get a piece of ass whenever they want.

Having women here is a constant reminder for us ol' ladies, like a slap in the face.

I stomp my way up the steps and slam the door behind me, take a deep breath, and make my way toward the bar. Tongue is behind it, and whatever beef we have is gone when he opens up another beer and sets it in front of me; the cool fizz of the cap coming off is like music to my ears.

"You're a bad bitch," he says, clinking his drink with mine. "I've never seen an ol' lady take out the trash before."

"Well, you know what they say, if the garbage is full..." I trail off, not wanting to sound like a complete idiot.

"You can then use the bag as target practice."

I give Tongue an incredulous look of how he put our expressions together. If the garbage is full, you take out the trash, but Tongue doesn't think like other people.

"I suppose so," I say.

"Is she running?" He lays his elbows on the bar and leans across it. "It's been a long time since I've had a moving target."

I spew my beer out of my mouth, and it soaks Tongue. His hair is dripping with it, and his skin is wet. His eyes remain open, and he licks the beer from his lips. "I see what all the fuss is about you."

Before I can ask what he means, the door to Church finally opens. Reaper storms out, and Sarah runs to follow him to his office. Reaper banned me from entering the room when we got back tonight, and it took all I had in me to obey him.

I've been obeying a man for more than the best part of my life, and I'm tired of it, but for Skirt, I have to think about my actions because whatever I do, he can get punished for it. Tool comes out next and heads toward Juliette. Skirt staggers to the doorway, sweat beading along his freckled forehead, and he closes his eyes a second, composing himself. I run to him, my feet pounding along the floor in tune with the drums banging in the song. I stop before I bulldoze him and stifle a sob when I pull his cut away to see the angry, seared heart on his chest.

Jesus.

Reaper is an animal.

"Oh my God, Skirt."

"I'm okay. I deserved it."

A door across the clubhouse slams, and Skirt sighs, knowing it's Reaper still ticked off.

"You don't deserve this. You were only doing what he wanted."

"Until I didn't listen," he finishes, then snatches the beer from my hand and drinks it down in three swallows. "I'm lucky I didn't get more than this. What I said could have been taken as a challenge." Skirt gives me a quick peck, and I can smell the beer on his tongue. "I don't want to talk about it anymore, okay? I just want to move on with the night."

"Don't you need to get bandaged? I can get Doc."

"No, it's fine. The wound itself is cauterized. It looks worse than it is, promise."

Somehow, I don't believe that for one goddamn minute.

Skirt's face is pale, he has dark circles under his eyes, and he seems like he's about to fall over. "Do you want another drink, or do you want to go to bed?"

"I need a drink," he says. "It's been a hell of a day." The front door opens, and Jasmine walks in with tears on her face, mascara lines down her cheeks, and all I want to do is throw the bitch in the fire again. Skirt looks toward the door, and his red eyebrows pinch so close together it looks like a unibrow. "What the hell?" He glances down at my shirt, then back at Jasmine, and having his attention on her instead of me, makes me want to slap him.

And I would if he didn't have a gaping wound on his chest.

"You have two seconds to get your eyes off that whore and back on me." I slide onto the barstool, and Tongue places two beers in front of us. I've never been happier for a day to almost be over. I've been dealt my fair share of abuse, but the way they do it here makes me wonder if I'm cut out for this life. Do I want to be around more men who think they can control me?

My question is answered when Skirt pulls the stool I'm sitting on closer to him, dragging it along the floor until I'm right in front of his face. "I'm betting you have something to do with Jasmine walking in here with her tail tucked between her legs," he says, impressed and if I'm not mistaken, turned on.

"Oh, you should have seen it, Skirt." Tongue doesn't bat an eyelash at the nasty, burnt skin on Skirt's chest. It's not hard to miss. Reaper had to have gone in with a hot blade. "Jasmine and Candy mouthed off. Jasmine tossed her drink in Dawn's face."

Skirt's eyes grow wide, and then he laughs; even if it is laced with pain and exhaustion. "No shit, seriously?"

"She dragged Jasmine out by her hair. I don't know what happened after that, but Dawn is a female version of you, always ready for a fight."

Which is funny, because I never fought a day in my life until I was free of Cohen. I try to convince myself that the fight I dealt with before is different now. I had to sacrifice myself for the sake of my son. I'd do it again too.

"Sounds like my woman," Skirt says. "It's fucking hot too."

"You're seriously horny?"

Skirt, through his pale skin, blushes from my surprise. "Aye, ye have that effect on me, but I am tired. Ye think we can go to bed?"

I'm confused. I lean in and whisper, "Which one? Your cabin or back there where Bullseye is."

"Ye killing me, Lips. The cabin. As much as I want ye again tonight, I'm sore all over. I need to go to bed."

It's my turn to blush. I can't believe I fucked a man next to a dumpster.

"What are ye thinking about?"

"Yeah, what are you thinking about?" Tongue repeats Skirt's question and sets his chin in his palm.

"Nothing," I say too quickly and hop off the barstool. "Come on; let's go." I help Skirt up and snag my drink. He tosses an arm around my neck, and we hobble to the back door, not saying goodnight to anyone.

What the fuck has been good about it?

A whole lot of nothing. Just pain. Torment. A tornado in the midst of a hurricane, that's what tonight was.

"I'm fucking hurting, Dawn."

"I know, baby," I say, taking more of his weight with every step because he's getting weaker.

"I had to make face for a bit, to show the club that I'm not a pussy."

"After everything you did tonight, you felt like you had to have a drink at the bar?"

"It's different when the punishment comes from Reaper."

"I guess." I still don't understand the dynamic of the club. Reaper holds all the power. He makes the decision on what's right and wrong. How can he be judge and executioner? I'm sure I'll learn more as time passes, but right now, if I'm being honest, that little issue with authoritative men is still affecting me.

The cold desert air hits us in the face when we make our way out the door. It feels good since I'm sweating, carrying this heavy man across the way, even if it's just a few feet. I open the door to the cabin, and he groans from the relief of being home.

We don't say anything as I strip him of his dirty clothes. I bite back tears when I see the cuts on his back, the angry red skin welting from being parted by a sharp object. I need to be strong. He needs me to be. Once he's naked, I help him to the shower, turn on the hot water, get undressed, and hold him under the stream of water.

"Even through the noise, through the pain, when I look for solace, I look for ye, and everything is right in my world." The whisper of his words is drowned out by the water, but I heard him.

I always hear him.

We hold each other, limbs wrapped around each other, water slicking us, and his lips prying mine open until all I drink down is him. He pulls away when a rip of pain tears through him, and I shake the lust out of my head.

"Come on; I'll bathe you."

"No, I can bathe myself."

"Don't make me slap you. You're in pain. Let me take care of you."

"Can't believe ye'd slap a man when he's down."

"I only slap one man when he's down, baby." I playfully smack his round, firm ass, and he chuckles, letting me bathe him with his pine-scented soap.

"Don't make promises ye can't keep, Lips. I'll spank ye ass if ye don't."

The man is insatiable, even when he's all carved up like a broken heart.

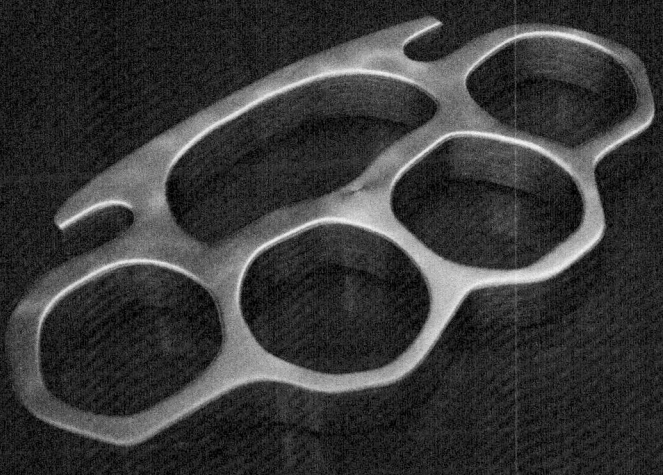

CHAPTER SIXTEEN

Skirt

SOFT KISSES MAP AROUND THE HEART REAPER CARVED IN MY chest yesterday, waking me from my deep sleep. I'm drowsy, sore, and fucking hurting everywhere. I wouldn't mind a bottle of that rum Pirate always has in his hand right about now. Poor bastard. Reaper sent him to a rehab center to get help.

I'm afraid my friend will die there. Pirate isn't the kind of man someone locks away. He'll get out and drink himself to death, or he will kill himself in isolation. I'm not too sure which one is better.

A tongue swirls around my nipple, yanking me from my thoughts as teeth bite down on the pink, sensitive bead. "Fuck," I hiss and arch my back, loving the feel of unexpected nipple play. I glance down and see Dawn's strawberry blonde hair running down my chest like a silk sheet. Her lashes flick up at me, and those green eyes take me to another world as she abuses my nips, something no woman has ever done before.

Her hand dips below the sheet and bypasses the long, tender cock, then she presses her index finger below my sack, rubbing it back and forth along the sensitive spot. "Oh, shite," I curse, my body shaking from the over stimulation. I knew I was sensitive, but I didn't know how sensitive until this moment.

"I bet you could come like this," Dawn purrs, still lapping at my nipples like a thirsty kitten.

"I bet I could too," I say, not having any fucking doubt that if she keeps stroking me like she is, I'll bust. "Ye drive me mad, woman." The sheets are hot as my body heats, and a sheen of sweat breaks over my skin. She's consuming me with a desire that's only found on a nuclear level.

"You better stop, or I'm going to come," I warn her. Now that she has me all riled up, I want to fuck that sweet pink cunt until the sun fucking sets and rises again.

"I want you to come."

With a snarl, I wrap my arms around her and flip her over, throwing the sheet over her body. I drive into her in one solid stroke. "I want to come too, but I'm going to come inside ye where I belong." I ignore the pain in my chest and the cuts on my back as I pull out, only to thrust inside her again. I never thought pussy could feel so good, not ever fucking before. I didn't know what I was missing.

Now that I have it?

I don't think I can live without her warmth and slick gripping my shaft. And it can't be any woman, just this one; just

Dawn. The more I think about how much I need her in ways she can never fully understand, I slow my movements as my heart expands and warms in my chest.

Hell.

I've fucking fallen in love with her.

What do I do with that?

I slide my arms under her back and tighten the front of her body to mine, then lay my lips over hers, massaging a slow kiss from her. My hand buries in the back of her hair, cupping her skull to keep her close to me while her channel grips me to keep my cock in when I pull out.

Unwrapping my arms from her back, I sit up which breaks the kiss. I stare down at the beauty writhing beneath me. Her lips are swollen, wet, and red from our kiss, and her eyes are closed as she soaks up how we are making each other feel.

"Skirt..." My name leaves her parted lips in a blissful sigh.

I want to always hear my name coming from her mouth like that.

I pause when she opens her eyes, and they shine as she stares at me. I stop moving, keeping my cock buried, and push her hair out of her face. "Did I hurt ye? Are ye okay?" I wipe the tear gathering in the corner of her eye, and I think back to the last few minutes and try to determine what I did to cause her pain.

"No," she says with a tiny shake of her head. Her palm lands over the open wound on my chest. "I've never felt so close with someone. I've never had someone give me what I need in so many ways."

I press my forehead against hers and nod, speechless, because I know exactly what she means. She gets me. Dawn wraps her legs around my waist and urges me to turn over onto my back. I do as she wants, keeping myself lodged in her still. I grip her hips, digging my fingers into the flesh until I feel bone.

No wonder men love it when women are on top. The fucking view is priceless. "Don't move, Lips. Don't fucking move." I'm two seconds away from coming seeing her propped up on me, big tits free and bouncing, nipples hard, and her trimmed blonde bush between her legs rubs against mine.

She fucking moves. A sly and knowing stretch of her wicked lips, and I'm done for. I thrust my hips to bury my cum as deep as I can, groaning like a man who has never had a woman on top of him before.

I haven't.

The familiar feeling of my cheeks blazing burns my face, but I'm not going to let my inexperience ruin this. She swings her leg to get off me, but I hold her to me and rock her hips back. "I'm not ready to see you climb off me yet." I push and pull her waist, grinding her against me fast and relentless. Her tits bounce, and I reach my right hand up to tug and pinch that sweet rosy red bud.

"Yes!" She tosses her head back and her long hair tickles my thighs. "More. Faster, Skirt. Faster."

I do as she says, rocking her harder, quicker, causing my arms to burn and my chest to ache. The wound splits open, I can feel the healed skin pulling apart as her nails rake down my pecs. It fucking hurts, but it isn't enough to deter me from making her come. Her creamy flesh hypnotizes my eyes as I devour her.

She's flawless, fragile porcelain trusting my hands not to break her, but she's broken me.

"Rohan!" Her hips stutter, and her finger digs into my stomach as she tightens around me, pulling my seed against her womb with every electrical wave spasming her muscles. She moans and sways, her body drifting and floating in the post orgasmic space. I rub my hands over her body, unable to decide where to touch, so I touch her everywhere.

I sit up, thrusting into her again, sliding through the wet collective of us. Her hands hold onto my shoulders as I take her for another ride. I spin her on my cock until her back is against my front, and the globes of her arse are plump and begging for my palms. I bring both of my hands down, watching the pale flesh turn a bright shade of pink. The flesh jiggles, and my mouth waters to see her cheeks clap again.

Letting go of the apple bottom, my hands soar through the air and spank her as she rides me reverse cowgirl. Her pink star flutters when I part her cheeks and right below it is where she's taking my cock. My shaft shines, fucking glitters like a diamond from her cream and mine. Her hands land on my thighs, her nails biting the skin as she bounces on me, using me like a fuck toy.

I need to invest in some toys. I'd love nothing more than to shove a plug up her arse while fucking her. The thought has me sliding my finger over my cock, soaking it with our slick, and I bring my digit back, circling her star before pressing to the knuckle.

"Fuck, Skirt!" she hisses, but she doesn't stop fucking me. If anything, she fucks me harder, with more wild ferociousness.

She's octane, and I'm going to make her explode.

"Greedy fucking girl, using my cock and my finger plugged in her arse. Yer dirty, but I should know that since you love hearing people fuck, don't ye? Do ye wish we were doing that right now? Hearing Bullseye fuck that slut? Or maybe ye want someone to watch us? Ye want that? They can sit in the corner and jack their cocks to ye fucking me, Lips."

Liquid flows out of her cunt from my words, dripping down my balls, and I debate if I want to pull out and make her clean me up. I decide against it when she lays her sweaty back against my front, panting for breath, and wraps one arm around my neck. I slide my finger out of her forbidden hole and I lean us back until I'm laying flat against the bed, my other arm is wrapped around her middle, and I'm thrusting into her hard and fast from the bottom. My lips are right at her ear and I growl, something deep and dangerous coming alive in the back of my throat.

I want to fucking rip her cunt apart and put it back together. I want to destroy her so she can't even think about being with another man. I'm the only one. I need to know her fantasies so I can make them all come true. "Tell me, Lips. Tell me what ye want, but know this, ain't no other man touching ye. Only I touch ye. Ye mine, only mine." I bite down on her earlobe, and a moan erupts from her throat, sexual sounds pouring out her. Damn that's what she is, once she explodes, she leaks lava; instead of burning me, it slicks her up for my cock.

My hand dives between her legs and finds her hungry, swollen clit, slippery from her cum. I pinch the erect pearl, wishing I could see it and kiss it, but once I roll the bundle between my fingertips and tug, she's crying out, gyrating her hips and pussy undulating around me.

"I'm not ever going to stop fucking ye until ye tell me," I repeat, then flip us over so she's on her back.

"I want to listen," she says between swallows, trying to catch her breath. "I wouldn't mind someone watching. I don't know. I need to trust them. You won't share me, right? I don't like that."

The heat, the passion, the yearning, the desire to stamp my claim on her in this moment, vanishes because the red hot lividity takes over me. I grip her chin and make her look at me. "Did he do that to ye? Share ye with other men?"

She glances away, and her silence speaks loud enough.

I let go with a growl, a primal animalistic howl gnawing at my throat as I grab her hips, lift them in the air, and pound into her like a man possessed. I am. There's no doubt about it. She's mine. No man will ever touch her. No man will ever use her like that again. Only me. Mine.

"Yours," she replies.

I must have said that out loud. I don't care. She needs to know I won't let anything happen to her. I fucking love her.

She's coming again, and this time I fall over the edge with her. I bring my lips down on hers. Her pussy weeps for me as she orgasms, soaking me with her nectar of tears.

I collapse to my side and wince when the wounds on my back hit the sheets. Fucking hell, all the aches and pain are hitting me now that the endorphins are crashing.

"Oh my God." She giggles and throws her arm over her eyes. "Never in my life. That was so good." The sweet sound of her drunk laughter makes me smile.

Hell, it makes me puff out my chest with the pride of a peacock. I've made her delirious. If that isn't good sex, I don't know what the hell constitutes the definition of good.

"I'm lucky to have you." She snuggles up next to me, and I wrap my arm around her shoulder. My thumb lazily strokes her inner bicep. She's soft, silky, heated velvet that I find comfort in. "I bet if Aidan met you, he'd love you. It's impossible not to."

Is that her telling me she loves me?

"We're going to bring him home to us. I'll die trying, Dawn. Yer my family which means he is my family."

She sniffles and shakes her head. "I can't talk about him right now. I feel too helpless. Tell me about you. Tell me about your family."

I stare up at the ceiling, watching the blades of the fan turn in a circle. I haven't talked about my past in a long time, and I'm not too sure if I want to start now. She's given herself over to me, and it's only fair that I do the same. She's trusting me to keep her safe, to protect her, to bring her son home; the least I can do is tell her about me.

She presses a kiss on the side of my stomach that fixates to the depths of me, settling in my ruthless bones. A life-long, ever-present, deep-rooted emotion replaces everything I thought I wanted, with everything I need.

Love.

Bikers like me, men like me, we aren't supposed to love. Our hearts are too wicked, too dark, too far gone for anyone to take a chance on us. No one ever really took a chance on me before, so Dawn jumping in with both feet excites me and terrifies me.

"I wasn't always in an MC," I start by saying, wondering where I should begin my story, and I might as well tell it from when everything changed.

"When did you come here? Why did you join Ruthless?"

I let out a sad breath, one that is full of good and bad memories. "I used to live in Scotland. When I was younger, my parents moved to the United States. We lived in Georgia or something. I fucking hated it, especially since my brother decided to stay in Scotland. He was a fighter, the greatest in the country, so he stayed behind, and I visited him in summers and any school breaks I had. My parents were afraid I'd become just like him, and that's why they moved me clear across the world." I clear my throat and hold Dawn a bit tighter. "He died fighting Cohen. Cohen never fights fair, and right after the ref blew the whistle to stop fighting, Cohen cold-cocked him, in the temple." I lay my finger against her head to show her where. "Killed him on the spot."

"I'm so sorry, Skirt."

"His funeral was the hardest. It rained that day, heavy fucking sheets of it, and it was cold. The weather matched the mood. I was so mad at him for dying, mad that I lost time with him because my parents dragged me everywhere with them. I should have had more of a backbone and stood up to them, but I was gentle, a bit softer than my brother."

She props herself up on her elbows and holds her head in her hand. "You? Soft?"

"I know, but that day changed me. The weather sunk into me I guess ... I don't know. My insides felt like they were raining, if that makes sense; just so much pain, and the thundering of it never stopped."

"I understand."

I know she does, especially with Aidan missing, but at least I have the comfort of my brother dying; she has no idea if Aidan is alive or not. That's worse.

"Anyway, I sat on his grave for a bit, and Ma came and told me it was time to go. Told her I didn't want to, and she snapped. She hit me across the face. My ma had never hit me a day in her life. She said she wished it was me in the grave, that I was dead instead of Conor. She said she never wanted to see me again, so she hasn't. The night of his funeral, I climbed into Conor's bedroom window, packed up a few things, including all of his damn kilts, and found a letter addressed to me. He told me to come to Vegas, something we were supposed to do together. So I came here and met Poodle; he told me about this club he was a part of, and I figured, why not? I don't have anything else, might as well. He became my sponsor, and I haven't looked back. This is my home now."

"Don't you ever want to go back home? Don't you ever wonder how your parents are doing?"

"Aye, I do, but I'm not welcome there." I want to change the subject. I don't want to talk about this anymore. I feel more open than the heart Reaper engraved on me. "I didn't always like kilts, ye know. I always used to wear pants, but my brother always fought in them, so I gave it whirl, and I never looked back."

"You look good in jeans. I love seeing the material hug your ass. Makes me want to bite it." Dawn play bites the air and lets out an adorable little growl that makes me laugh.

"Are ye a chihuahua? One of them ankle biters?"

"I'll bite you, alright. You better watch yourself."

I pause. I let her think I'm done talking to her, and then I attack my fingers on her sides, tickling her until she's screaming and crying with giggles. She's kicking me, trying to get away, and I'm grinning so hard my damn cheeks hurt. I stop the maddening wiggle fingers against her sides and slid up her body. Both of us are huffing from fighting one another.

"I think I love ye, Dawn. You've become an escape I never knew I needed."

She reaches down and grabs my cock in hand; it's hard and leaking since she was fighting me a second ago, and I guide it to her still drenched hole. "I think I love you too, Rohan."

I'm a lucky man to earn that. I have everything I'll ever need.

Almost.

I have the gal. I have her love.

Now, I'm even more determined to get Aidan back. When I do, I'll make sure nothing ever hurts him again—hurts *them* again.

They are mine.

My family.

CHAPTER SEVENTEEN

Dawn

I WRAP A FUZZY MAROON BLANKET AROUND ME AND TAKE A PEEK over my shoulder to see Skirt asleep. He's so big and takes up all the space in the king-size bed that my only option is to cuddle him. I don't mind. Being close to him is not a hardship; it's a gift.

But I can't sleep because he keeps kicking the blanket off because he's sweating. I get cold, and I don't want to cuddle against his wet skin. His hand scratches his stomach, and he flips over to snuggle me, but he grabs my pillow instead.

The man is a marshmallow; I don't care what anyone says. I caress the top of his head, and he nestles his cheek against me—the pillow—and I stifle a laugh.

I don't *think* I love him. I know I do. It's more love than I've ever felt for a man and a man who's good for me? It's like I keep hitting the jackpot over and over again until I'm the richest woman alive.

I stand and look out the window to see a clear, starry night, and decide a nice walk and fresh air will do me some good. I drop the blanket and throw on a pair of panties and one of Skirt's shirts that says Ruthless Kings. It falls to my knees, but I don't care. I like that his shirts are big on me. It reminds me of how much larger he is than I am. All muscle, red hair, and tattoos.

I need to get out of here before I jump him again. The man, for never having sex, is a fucking god at doing it, and I'm addicted. I pick up the blanket and tuck it around me like a toga, then give Skirt a kiss on the cheek.

"Dawn," he mumbles on a sleepy smile and whimsical sigh. "Love you."

"I love you," I tell him, watching him fall back to sleep with that silly little grin on his face. I bet no one would have thought the big bad biker would talk in his sleep. It suits him. I hurry out the bedroom door and tiptoe through the living room, easing the lock as I turn it and slip outside.

I'm restless, but I don't know why. I want nothing more than to sleep. Tomorrow, Skirt fights again, and I don't know if I have it in me to watch him turn into that man. I hate to see him lose himself like that. He wouldn't be that man if it weren't for me. I swear, some days I think he is better off without me.

A burst of laughter comes from the front of the clubhouse, and a faint glow appears from a fire. A few of the guys are rough housing at three in the morning. With a faint smile, I turn in the other direction, away from the noise of the club brothers. I need time to myself. My feet are bare.

Damn. I forgot shoes.

It's fine. It's only desert out here anyway. My feet sink into the red clay and since the moon is full and glowing it's light down on me, I'm able to see where I'm going. I bypass a few cactuses and giggle when I remember that less than two weeks ago, Skirt had needles plucked from his butt because of me.

Jeez, has it really only been two weeks? So much has changed, so much pain, newfound love, and yet I feel like I'm at a standstill, watching the world pass me by since I don't have my son.

"Please, send him back to me," I whisper to the sky, to anyone listening, God, the devil, the stars, fucking aliens for all I care. Just someone hear me.

Please.

I take a seat in the middle of the field and look around. Crickets chirp and something buzzes in the distance. A faint howl of a coyote ripples through the air and makes the hair on my arms stand up. Glancing around, nothing seems out of place. The breeze sweeps through, kicking up a tumbleweed, and the roll of twigs stops at my feet.

Aidan is going to love it here. All this space to roam and run. He'll be the only small kid here and that worries me, but I know in time more kids will come, especially with how Reaper and Sarah trying so hard.

I stare up at the sky, trying to find the Big Dipper when a pair of hands slide down my shoulders. I bite my lip, excited that he found me. "I'm glad you're joining me. I was wondering when you were going to notice I was gone."

The hands move around my neck and squeeze. "I fucking noticed, bitch. Because of you I have nearly every MC and every mafia soldier looking for me, wanting to bring Reaper, whoever the fuck that is, my head." He spins me around and every ounce of courage, strength, and fear drains out of me into the ground. I can't remember how to fight. My body is frozen as Cohen's blue eyes stare at me.

"Cohen, please—" He smacks me across the face, and I tumble to the ground, my hand falling on a small cactus. My cheek aches, and I try to crawl away from him, but his foot lands in the middle of my stomach. My knees and hands give out from under me, and I lay face-down in the dirt, Cohen straddling my back and gripping me by my hair.

He jerks my neck back, and all I see is the side of his face and the twinkling stars above. Even in the midst of violence, constellations still shine, and the light inside me slowly dissipates. "Go ahead, bitch. Beg. You know I love it when you do." He licks my cheek and inhales the scent in my hair. "I should kill you, drain your blood right here and now." He dips his tongue into my ear, and I whimper. The noise sets him off, and he stabs the blade into my left hand. As I open my mouth to scream, he covers it with his own, forcing his tongue into my mouth. He tastes like eggs and smoke, which makes me gag as I cry out because the knife is pinning my hand to the ground.

His dominant hand, the one that always leaves the final blow on his opponent, is still around my neck, squeezing me, while his other hand fondles my breast.

"I've missed this body, bitch. I've fucking missed it so much. Can't wait to get you back in bed where you belong, ass up and pussy open for me."

I rear back and my head connects with his nose which makes him fall off me. "I'm not going anywhere with you." I try to get my hand free, but even as I pull on the handle, I can't get the blade out of the ground. I wiggle and panic, watching as he starts to come around. He shakes his head and blood drips down his lip. I open my mouth to call out, but he tackles me to the ground and yanks the knife from my hand, laying the bloody steel against my throat.

"Make another fucking sound. I dare you. You're tempting me." He clicks his tongue. "You're tempting me to kill you. I don't like your disobedience, Dawson. Have you learned anything?"

"Fuck. You," I spit in his face as I struggle to breathe.

"Oh, you will. Maybe right here, right now." His hand lowers down my belly and lifts up Skirt's shirt and cups my pussy through my panties. "Maybe I'll slice your goddamn throat and while you bleed buckets, I'll fuck you, using your blood as lube. Do you want that?" he sneers and then spits in my face, right on my lip.

I don't say a word. I'm too scared to move. If I push him far enough, he'll do whatever he wants to me. I want to open my mouth to scream, but I'm afraid he'll kill me and then I won't see Aidan or Skirt again.

"Be a good little bitch, and I'll take you to your son."

"You have him? Where is he, you sorry son-of-a-bitch." I struggle against him, my left hand throbbing from the cut. I try to unwrap his hand from my throat, but he exhales, completely annoyed by me. His left fist flies through the air, smashing against my other cheek.

He stands and picks me up by my throat as he pushes me toward the back of the property. "Don't fucking talk. Don't fucking ask questions. Do what I say, okay?"

I struggle to look over my shoulder, but I get a glimpse of the small cabin Skirt built for himself. If there is any chance for me to come back to him, I have to obey. I miss him already. Will I see him again? Were the two weeks here the best and worst of my life? Best because I fell in love, the worst because Cohen has my son.

Or will I die never knowing what a future will be like with them?

My feet trample through the dead brush, the dry twigs, and sharp pins stick me. I'm whimpering with pain, tears pouring down my face, and the further we get away from the clubhouse, the chance of survival decreases.

When we get to the iron fence around the edge of the property, I see there's a section that is broken, but it's welded in such a way where it opens like a door. He pushes against it and throws me through. To my left is a small tent where he has been staying, covered in leaves and twigs. It blends right in.

"Aidan?" I hurry to my knees and desperately crawl over to the tent. I don't care about the burning in my hand, the blood I'm leaving as a trail, and how badly my feet hurt. I want my son. I spread the lapels of the tarp and see a sleeping bag, water bottles, and a lamp. I rustle through the sleeping bag, knowing Aidan isn't here, but wishing like hell he was. "Where is my son?" my voice rasps.

"Safe for now," he says, grabbing me by my hair. "Get moving."

I trample my way through the woods, snapping the twigs under each step and shivering from the cold. The blanket fell back at the compound. I hope someone notices it. The further we get away, the less likely it will be for Skirt to find me.

When we break through the trees, there's a van at the edge of the road, a complete rust bucket that looks like it has seen better days. "Are you going to take me to my son? Please, I'll do whatever you want, just take me to him. Where did you keep him? Why did you do this?"

"Because of your disobedience!" he roars, pinning me against the truck. He lifts my injured hand and licks the blood and dirt that is caked around the cut. "You need to fucking listen to me. Why do you think I dumped you in the desert? For you to spread your legs like a whore for some biker scum? No. You were supposed to come back to me, on your knees, ready to take my cock down your throat with how sorry you were for disrespecting me in front of a fellow fighter. And you didn't come back to me. Do you not care for your son at all? Are you so selfish to just fuck your way through life and forget all about the poor little baby who seizes and needs you?" He pouts his lip. "Taking care of that damn burden is annoying. I didn't want to be stuck with him. He's broken. He's disgusting. I wish he was never born; that's what I get for fucking you bare, right?" Cohen gets himself worked up and runs his hands down body, cupping my breasts and rocking his erection against my stomach. "I'll continue to fuck you like that too, all raw, until there is no doubt you're pregnant again. Maybe you'll learn your place, bitch. At home. No back talk. Raise my kids, fuck me, feed me, and repeat. Am I clear?"

I sneer, hating him more every second that he spews his venom. He puts the knife between my legs and the tip of the blade cuts through the cotton and sharp edge presses against my clit.

He is crazy. Crazier than normal. Keeping me alive is important to him, but why?

"Come on, baby. Don't you remember how good it was between us? It was hot. Sexy. Don't you miss it?" He opens the passenger side door and pushes me in, keeping the knife trained on me.

"I never miss anything about you." The words are dead as I speak.

"I'll be glad to remind you later." He hops into the driver's seat and cranks the engine. A belt screeches and causes my ears to ring as he pulls away, keeping his hand on my thigh and knife pointed to the space between my legs.

I lean my head against the window and have a small pity-party. Why is this happening to me? I don't understand. How did I get mixed up in Cohen? How can I escape him? My fight is leaving me. Cohen's cruelty outweighs me. He isn't the kind of person to share strength with; he's the kind of person to soak it up until there's nothing left.

He seeks to destroy.

Skirt brings out the best in me. The strength, bravery, the will to fight for myself, and Cohen, he steals it. He doesn't want a woman who is as strong as him, so his goal is to always put her down.

A tear rolls down my cheek as we drive off into the night, away from the place I've called home for two weeks, away from the man who taught me more about love in two weeks than I knew in my entire life, and I hope this time, love is strong enough to lead him to me.

If not, I'll die. As long as Cohen has his way, he will be the one to murder me. I can't allow that to happen. I need to fight for my son. I can't give up now. I'm tired, so tired, so fucking bone exhausted that it causes me pain, but I have to push through it. I have to dig deeper for the will to live.

I clutch my hand to my chest and shut my eyes when we hit a pothole and the jostle causes the knife wound to throb.

"Sorry about stabbing you, bitch."

I hate that he calls me bitch. He always has, as if it's a pet name or something.

"You were really pissing me off."

I keep my lips sealed, not wanting to entertain his sick mind. We drive twenty minutes in the opposite direction of Vegas. The city lights flicker in the distance and turn into a faint glow the further we get. When we come to an abandoned warehouse on the left and motorcycles parked all around, I swallow.

Death lives here.

And I'm about to knock on its door.

The building is old, the half the roof is sagging, and it looks like it's about to collapse any second. A bunch of bikers are outside, smoking, and by the smell of it, it isn't cigarettes. The Ruthless Kings don't smoke pot; they drink, a lot, but I've never seen drugs. Now I see the stark differences between what a 'good' MC is compared to a bad one.

"Get out." Cohen pushed my left shoulder, and I hit the passenger side window with the other half of my body.

"I'm going," I say weakly, and step out of the van in nothing but a t-shirt and torn panties. I've experienced pain. I've known fear. I've lived and breathed it every day of my life. I've been through abuse, tears, and broken bones, but staring at the men in front of me, I truly believe everything I've ever gone through won't be as bad as what I'm about to experience here.

One man is older, burly, and as he walks toward me, I notice his hairy shoulders and thick mustache. He sucks on a roach, the ember lighting up in a faint orange hue before blowing out the murky cloud in his mouth.

"Told you I'd deliver. Isn't she fucking hot?" Cohen says, throwing an arm around my shoulder and grabbing my ass. "I've been in this cunt, Prez. There ain't nothing like it."

"You've done good, Conrad."

"It's Cohen."

"What the fuck ever," the Prez says, inhaling his weed

again as he circles me like a shark. Hands roam down my back, and he hums in appreciation. "Damn, boy. You really out done yourself. She's a fine piece of ass. Bitch will do well here."

"We have a new toy, Prez?" another man asks from the dilapidated porch, leaning against the rail. He has long legs encased in blue denim jeans, and he isn't wearing a shirt; just his cut. He hops down from the porch to get a closer look, and a different man turns around and walks inside. That's when I see the logo on the back.

It's a growling two-headed dog, and in red words above it says, "Hellhounds MC."

"Looks like it," the Prez finally answers his brother when he's done inspecting me. "I can't wait to get in here. All the other bitches inside are going to be so fucking pissed."

"Whores," Cohen says as if it's an excuse, and all the men roar in laughter.

"What do you say, bitch? How about you go inside and get comfortable with your new surroundings, and I'll be down in a few to welcome you home." The Prez rubs his cock against me, and instinct takes over, like the idiot I am.

I kick his shin and rip out of Cohen's arms and run. The hounds howl to the moon and give chase. I don't get very far either. Someone wraps their arms around me and bites my earlobe, dragging me back to the hounds to feast.

"Better calm down, bitch, or I'll have them fuck all your holes right here and now," the Prez growls into my ear. I kick and scream, doing my best to get out of his arms, but all he does is laugh. "Looks like we got a fighter, boys!" The Prez whispers, "I love breaking the fighters."

I'll make sure I die before he even gets the chance.

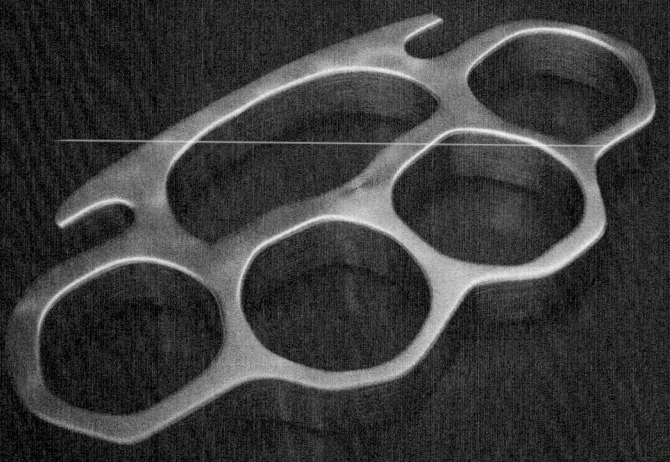

CHAPTER EIGHTEEN

Skirt

I ROLL OVER AND MY ARM HITS NOTHING BUT AN EMPTY SIDE OF THE bed where Dawn is supposed to be. I flop to my back and yawn, while my arm searches the spot for any heat. It's cold. I rub my left eye, then stretch, and every bone in my damn body cracks into place. I groan in relief then twist my neck like I always do. "Lips!" I call out to her and scratch around the skin that's burnt. It's itchy. While my chest is sore and my back aches, it's nowhere near as bad as it was yesterday. "Dawn? Where are you?" I yell for her again, but all that answers is the sound of my own voice.

She must be over at the clubhouse with the other ol' ladies. They love to get together in the morning over gossip and giggle and shit. It tickles me that Dawn fits in so well with them. I love it. It's important our women get along when we can't.

Like Poodle and me.

Even though it's more on me than him now. Life's too short to be petty like this. I'm going to talk to him this morning, right after I talk to Bullseye and find my Lips. I need a good morning kiss.

Rolling out of bed, my cock is hard, aching for Dawn. Beads of pre-cum dribble out of the tunnel, and I fist every inch, stroking my morning wood until it starts to soften. I don't know what it is about the mornings, half the time I'm hard and not even wanting to fuck. The moment I give it a good squeeze, it deflates, which makes the rest of the morning go by a lot easier as I get dressed and am not thinking about sex.

Okay, I'm kind of thinking about sex now that I've been having it all the time, but it isn't giving me a painful erection 24/7.

I go to the bathroom, piss, wash my hands, and brush my teeth. When I look in the mirror, I turn my body around to get a good look at my back. "Fuck me," I whisper in awe. It looks like I've been to war and back. I have the slashes on my skin, but the red lines jettisoning down my back and chest from Dawn's talons look more painful than the actual injuries I have. "Shite, Lips. You tore me up." Seeing her mark on me, I'm getting hard now. I want to fuck her against the nearest surface while she tries to get away from me.

Fucking love it when she does that.

I comb my fingers through my beard and leave my hair the mess it is. I don't give a fuck. I slip on a kilt and shirt, then head to the front door.

It's open.

A slither of something I can't quite put my finger on

alerts me. I study the room, trying to see if anything is out of place. The door is open because she went to the clubhouse.

"Idiot," I chastise myself as I make my way outside. I inhale, and my mood is fucking glorious. I prance down the steps with a happy little trot and open the side door that leads to Reaper's office, and if I follow the hall to the kitchen, I'll find some pie.

It's been too long since I've had pie.

"Morning, Badge," I wave at the man sitting at the computer desk, staring at five screens, typing furiously, then zooming in on different monitors.

"Morning," he grunts, not wanting to be bothered.

I wonder if he's had any luck on finding the kid. Ambling down the hall, I enter the kitchen and go straight for the fridge. With a smile on my face, I take a look inside and then in the next instance, I'm frowning. "There's no pie." I don't think I've ever been so devastated. "There's always pie. How is there no pie?" The fridge is empty besides a few bottles of beer and a mountain dew. There's a tub of butter, but I don't feel like eating that again.

Damn dares. That butter fucked up my stomach for weeks.

"What are you bellowing about?" Bullseye lumbers in the kitchen and heads straight to the pot of coffee.

Ah, just the person I need to see. "There's no pie."

He nods while sipping his coffee enthusiastically, a strangled moan leaving his throat as he drinks. "I swear, coffee is better than sex in the mornings."

"Yer fucking the wrong women if ye think that, Bullseye."

"Well, all of us aren't lucky enough to find an ol' lady. My day will come. Until then, coffee in the morning and whores at night. That's all I'll ever need."

"Spoken like a true romantic in search for his everlasting love," I tease, shutting the fridge door with a bit more gusto than I planned.

"Fuck off." Bullseye flips me off and pulls out a chair to the dining room table, taking a seat. This is my chance. I grab a mug from the cabinet and pour my coffee, then sit in front of him, sipping and staring, then I tap my fingers along the ceramic. I don't know how to have this conversation with him. He lurks over the coffee cup, his tired eyes narrowing in irritation. "What the hell are you looking at, Skirt? Out with it. I don't have all fucking day. I have to go meet Maximo in about an hour."

"For what?"

"Don't know. I'll find out when I get there. Spill." He sighs and rubs his temples. "I swear if this is going to be about eating the last piece of pie—"

I slam my mug down and stab a finger in his direction. "Ye! How... The audacity!" I place my hand to my chest, hurt from his betrayal. "I thought we were friends."

"Skirt, you know we are."

"Ye a backstabbing little dart, ain't ye?" I pick up my coffee mug again and take my time drinking it. I cross my ankle over my knee and get my thoughts together. I'm a jumbled-up mess now. I can't remember what I wanted to talk about.

"There was nothing left in the fridge—"

"Blasphemy. Traitor. You ... you broke the most sacred—no—you know what?" I pinch the bridge of my nose and inhale a calming breath of air. "Forget it. It isn't important. I need to talk to ye about ... uh ... things." I clear my throat, cough, and take a scalding gulp of coffee.

Bullseye crosses his arms and chuckles, leaning back on

two legs of the chair. "Oh, you're blushing. This is going to be good."

Damn it! I hate my pale skin. Gives away all my emotions.

My stomach clenches, but then I think of how turned on she gets listening to other people. I lean forward and crook my index finger for him to meet me half-way.

The chair falls forward, and the wooden legs hit the ground with a loud thud. "I'm not kissing you, Skirt." Bullseye scoots the chair forward, and I deadpan him an incredulous glare.

"What? You're being weird. I'm not going to kiss ye. Ye not my type."

"I'm everyone's fucking type," he boasts about himself.

"Will ye listen? I'm nervous as fuck asking ye about this, but I trust ye. I can't ask anyone with an ol' lady. I have to ask someone who is single."

He lifts a brow at me, and his curiosity only makes me more nervous.

I spin the mug in my hand, the ivory scratching against the table. "Dawn likes to hear people fuck."

Bullseye spits his coffee out mid-sip, and it lands all over my face.

I should have planned better. Mid-sip is never a good idea to take someone by surprise.

"No shit? Kinky. You lucky bastard." He slaps my shoulder. "So what does this have to do with me?"

"Well, I was hoping ye'd kind of be the guy we listen to? In the next room."

"Not going to lie, knowing she wants to listen to me is giving me a hard-on. Fuck yeah, I'd be honored to be her honorary audible fuck." He wiggles his brows and leans in further. "Can we go do that now? I'll grab Candy—"

"Can't be Candy." I know how much Dawn hates her.

"Eh, I wanted to switch it up anyway. Candy is getting clingy. Clingy Candy." He slaps the table when an idea strikes him, and I jump. "That's her new name."

"There's more."

"More?" he says, the whites of his eyes wide on display.

"So, she wants to know if she likes someone watching us. Ye can't touch her because I'll kill ye, like fucking murder ye with yer own darts. If ye sat in a dark corner, touched yerself, whatever; she just wants to know if she likes it." Why is this so hard to talk about?

Bullseye's mouth is open, and I reach up, lifting his chin so he doesn't catch any flies.

"You're serious?" he asks, staring at me skeptically. He runs a hand over his lips, exhales, then locks eyes with me again. "You realize any single guy here would want to get in on this right?"

"I don't want all the guys, Bullseye. I need someone I trust. She's my ol' lady. My fucking one, okay? Just watching. I want to make her happy even if I'm not 100% comfortable with it. Maybe I'll like it."

"So I'm like, your booty call, kind of, right?"

I groan and thud my head against the table. "Kind of?"

"Fuck, yes! I'm in. I'm so fucking in. Can we go do it now? Shit, this is going to be so hot. I need another coffee."

"No touching her, Bullseye. I mean it. You can watch, get close, but ye can't touch her."

"Deal. No problem. I don't mind being someone's fantasy test drive. Zoom zoom, bitches. I'm coming to rev some engines." He laughs and holds out a hand for me to high-five.

Christ.

I slowly lift my hand, and he smacks it with vigor. "That a boy! You just made my fucking day." He claps his hands and rubs them together evilly. "So, let's go wake up your girl and get this show on the road."

"Wake her up? She isn't in bed. She's here."

Bullseye's fun facade is gone, and the Sargent at Arms mask is in place. "Skirt, she isn't here. Not even the whores are here right now. Sarah is awake with Ellie, and they're playing with the puppies. Skirt, she has to be in the cabin."

My cup trembles in my hand and the coffee splashes over the rim, burning my skin, but I don't fucking care.

"There has to be a reason. Don't panic yet."

Too late.

I drop the cup, and it fractures on the floor into tiny pieces. I push away from the table and run through the club-house. "Dawn! Dawn! Lips?" I shout her name with hysteria. "Dawn?" I bellow. My legs are shaking, my heart is thumping, and my mind is drawing fucking blanks. I'm spinning in circles.

"Dawn!" I scream for her again.

"What the fuck are you yelling for?" Poodle scratches his head, his hair a poufy mess. Melissa puts her arms around his waist.

I run my hands through my hair and then haul arse out the door. "Dawn!" I shout at the top of my lungs, letting my voice carry over the flat desert. "Dawn, love! Lips!" My voice breaks from how loud I'm crying out for her.

"Skirt." Poodle runs down the steps after me, but I'm searching the property for any sign of her.

"Dawn! Dawn, baby? You okay? I'm here. Where are you?" It's been five years since I've cried.

Today, the streak has ended. My eyes turn to those fucking lagoons, and I let the tears fall. I don't give a fuck that the guys see me losing it. They don't get it. They don't understand how she anchors me.

I'm no longer a wayward soul, not with her directing me to the safest place I can be—her soul.

She's my fucking home.

"Skirt, I need you to talk to me. What's going on?"

"Dawn!" I ignore him, even when he stands in front of me and grips my shoulders, shaking me in hopes it brings me back to reality. "Dawn!" I taste the blood in my throat from straining my vocal chords.

Poodle slaps me across the face, and the burn is exactly what I need to stop panicking. "Stop. Fucking focus. What is going on?"

"I can't find Dawn. She isn't in the cabin. I thought she was in the clubhouse while I was fucking chatting it up with Bullseye, but she isn't even here! She isn't fucking here!" I pound my chest while staring at my best friend. "She isn't here," I say softer, broken. "Poodle, I need her. Christ, I fucking need her."

Poodle nods. "I know. I know you do. We will find her. She has to be here somewhere. There's an explanation. Okay?"

Yeah, there's one that's going to make me sick to my stomach. This piece of land is huge; what if she's dead? What if she's laying there in a ditch, and she cried out for me, but I was fucking sleeping, hugging her pillow like a damn fool? I wasn't there for her when she needed me.

Why can't I ever be there for the people I love?

Poodle slaps me again. "Don't. Don't blame yourself." All the MC brothers run out of the house, and Reaper buttons his pants as he jogs over to us. "Lady!" Poodle calls for his prissy dog and places two fingers in his mouth, letting out a ear-ringing whistle.

Right. She's trained in search and rescue, which isn't expected since she prances and her fluffy white hair bounces with the bows she always has in her hair. I watch toward the front of the clubhouse, and Lady runs at the speed of light to get to her owner. She has pink bows in her hair today. At least she will look good doing it.

"Skirt, do you have anything of Dawn's?"

"What? Yeah, yes! I'll be back. Lady, I'll be back," I say to the elegant dog. She sits at Poodle's feet and cocks her head at me. I run toward the cabin and kick open my door, breaking the hinges off from the force. I trip, right myself, and hurry to the bedroom to pick up the shirt she wore yesterday. I bring it to my nose and inhale her scent, wild like a fucking rainstorm in fall.

Hurrying outside, I jump off the porch and toss the shirt at Poodle. He catches it mid-air by and then lowers it for Lady to sniff. She buries he black nose in the material, inhaling Dawn's scent. Lady is my only damn hope. Thank God Poodle has her.

Nothing else matters. The problems, whatever happened between us, I just need Dawn back. I'm happy Poodle isn't the kind of guy to keep Lady locked away when she's the only chance I have at finding her.

"Search, Lady," Poodle gives Lady a command and her head is down, nose to the ground as she sniffs. Poodle claps a hand on my back. "We'll find her."

Lady barks about twenty yards away, and a stampede of bikers run to where she sits.

I bend down and pick up the blanket that Dawn has claimed for herself. "There's blood. Fucking goddamn it, Poodle.

There's blood." I pinch my eyes shut and try to rub the burn away. I have to keep it together.

Lady barks near the fence and I take off, Poodle and Reaper right behind me. There's more blood. It's dotted along the sand and a few small bushes, then there's blood along the iron rods of the gate.

Please, don't let it be her blood, but I know better.

It's hers, or Lady wouldn't be telling us to search here.

"Look at that," Reaper says with unhinged anger as he pushes the fence, and a makeshift door swings open.

I crawl through the gate and see a rundown tent and supplies, covered with leaves and shit. "What the fuck is this?" I shout. "Reaper? What the fuck is this? Who's doing perimeter sweeps? Who missed this?" I throw myself on the tent and tear it down, kicking the tarp and bottles of water until I'm breathless.

Lady barks from the road, and I know one thing—there's no way to track a scent if the person being searched for is in a car.

It's a dead-end, and I don't care if I have to fight every man in the city. I'll get Dawn back. I'll feel those lips again, and whoever stands in my way, I'll kill them with my bare hands.

I'll paint the city red with blood for her.

CHAPTER NINETEEN

Dawn

THERE'S A LEAK COMING FROM THE ROOF THAT IS DRIVING ME crazy.

      Drip.

Drip.

Drip.

Since my hands are tied behind my back, I can't scoot the rag over, probably a cum rag, to stop the water from splashing onto the concrete floor. I bang my head against the wall and look around the room. This place is a shithole. The men are disgusting, and the women... the poor women.

Don't get me wrong, I hate the club whores at Ruthless. I hate seeing Jasmine's face every day knowing her lips touched Skirt's cock, but the guys treat their sluts so much better than the men here. Half of the women are on cots, half-naked, dried cum on their thighs, and a needle in their arm. In the furthest corner, there's a girl with blue lips.

I think she's dead. She has to be dead.

She's naked, and her body is pale without any signs of the slight pink color the skin has with blood actively pumping through it.

What the fuck has Cohen gotten me into?

The door opens, and two bikers stare at me, running their beady eyes up and down my body before going to the girl in the corner and checking her pulse.

"Damn, another stiff. Let's dump her," the guy smoking a cigar tells the other younger biker who has a prospect patch. I've seen those patches. They aren't full blown members yet. He looks like he isn't made for this rough life. He's my chance at getting out of here.

"Is she dead?" I ask, wondering if that's what 'stiff' means.

"Shut up, bitch. None of your fucking business," the man mumbles around the end of the cigar, blowing smoke from the corner of his mouth as they carry the dead woman. She was someone's daughter, sister maybe, a mother? Who knows, but she's gone, and the family is better off not knowing what happened to their child. They would be horrified to find out she was probably drugged and repeatedly raped before dying.

Oblivion can be a bittersweet little bitch.

I try to slip my hands free of the zip-tie, but when I get nowhere. I want to hit myself, if I could, for not watching that damn YouTube video on 'how to get free of zip-ties.' Like anyone, I was thinking, 'I'll never find myself in that situation.'

Yet, here I am.

Zip-tied, surrounded by half-dead, drugged-out women, my future if I can't get out of here. A club whore walks through the door with one of the members, and for a moment I'm confused. Why do they need this room full of unwilling women when they have club whores?

Because they like unwilling women.

"Hey, new bitch!"

My eyes fall onto the road name on his cut, but I can't make it out; he's too far away.

"Come on, Chrissy. Show the new bitch what's in store for her here." The man pushes the woman toward me, and she falls to her knees, and he unzips his pants to free his cock. I look away, not wanting to watch this, even if the woman wants it. It leaves a bad taste in my mouth.

"You're going to fucking watch." A cock of the gun has me turning my head, and I shiver when I stare down the barrel. "Because I want you to take note of how I like it." He aims at the woman on the floor and pushes the gun into her head to urge her on. "Suck it, bitch." The woman giggles and pulls out the man's dick. It's tiny, but she stares at it as if it's the biggest damn thing in the world.

I close my eyes and a gunshot rings out. I scream as the hot barrel lands on my foot, and I cry out from the singed heat.

"I said watch, you stupid bitch. Can you not listen?"

My eyes flutter open just as the club slut takes the small cock into her mouth, sucking it with more enthusiasm than the guy deserves. I wish she'd bite down, but she won't because she's probably just trying to live another day. Her red lipstick smears and the mascara under her eyes smudges as she gags, which is not possible since his cock is so little.

"Yeah, just like that. You takin' note, new bitch? I'm going to have those hot lips around my cock in no time."

"Believe me, you don't want to come near me with that thing," I sneer, half-daring him to try so he can see what will happen.

His eyes are glassy, and he has track marks on his arms from needles. He fucks the girl's face, and in less than a minute he's groaning, coming down her throat. I gag when I see a dribble slip from her mouth, but she hums, licking her lips as if he's the best dish she has ever savored.

"Damn, Chrissy. You're my favorite. Love that dirty mouth."

"What the fuck do you think you're doing?" the Prez's voice has fear slithering around the biker. The woman gets to her feet, and he tucks his cock in his pants, leaving the button unclasped.

"I'm just showing the new bitch how things will be around here. I didn't touch her, Prez. I swear."

"You better not have; she's mine."

"I swear, Prez. I was enjoying Chrissy and giving our new guest a show; that's it. Ain't that right, bitch?" the guy asks me.

I should lie. What happened? I hate him and what they do here.

"He's lying," I say, my voice trembling with fear. My eyes water, and I enhance my fear by a hundred. "He touched me, burnt me with his gun."

"You stupid whore!" the biker yells and lunges for me.

Another gunshot rips through the air, screams echo, and blood splatters all over me. On instinct I close my eyes. When I open them, the biker who just had his last orgasm is on his knees, bullet-hole right between the eyes. The woman who sucked him off screams at the top of her lungs when the dead man falls over.

"Shut up. You're fucking annoying." The Prez cocks his gun again and fires, ripping a hole in her chest.

More blood sprays over me, coating me in red. I'm shaking. Instead of being curious, I'm fucking terrified. A tear slips down my cheek, and my body quakes from the shock.

Prez squats in front of me and twists the end of his mustache with his finger, curling it up as he ponders his thoughts. "I never liked him anyway. And Chrissy wasn't all that great at sucking dick." His eyes fall to my mouth. "I bet those lips are made for sucking cock, aren't they?"

"They sure are," Cohen says from behind the Prez, who just took out his own brother. Cohen is wearing a leather cut that says prospect on it. "Believe me when I say firsthand, you're going to get a lot of pleasure out of her."

"Where is Aidan?" Nothing else matters. I just need to know where my son is.

"Aidan is long gone, Dawn. Sold him. Made a pretty penny. Cut a deal with the Hellhounds here, and now we have a pretty good business going."

"You sold him? Where? You asshole! Where is my son! I'm going to kill you! I'm going to fucking kill you if you don't take me to him," I sob, spitting out the rotten blood that landed on my lips.

"You're never going to see him again. Maybe now you'll learn not to be disrespectful toward me. Don't worry, if you're good, I'll give you another one." Cohen rolls his eyes, speaking as if Aidan is easily replaced.

"I don't want another one. I want Aidan! I don't want anything else. Just take me to him, please. I'll do anything," I beg. "Sell me to the person you sold him to. Please, I just want to see him. Is he okay?"

"No more questions." Prez stands and lights another joint. "Gather a few men and have them take out the trash." He kicks the dead biker's foot, then grabs me by the arm and forces me to stand. My feet slip on a puddle of blood and I lose my footing, but Prez doesn't seem to care; he drags me from the room, leaving behind the women and two dead bodies. "Don't bother me. This room is off-limits!" Prez's patch says Mercy.

Mercy.

What fucking mercy?

He slams the door, locks it, and I run to the other side of the room, shivering so much my teeth are clinking together.

"You don't need to be afraid of me," he says, turning to me with a different look in his eyes.

"I am. You need to stay away from me. You have no idea who is looking for me! You've really stepped in the shit, buddy!" I mouth off and then pinch my lips shut to stop myself from digging my own grave.

"No, you don't need to be afraid." His voice is even different, lighter, smoother, not so deep and threatening. "I'm not Mercy or the Prez," he whispers.

"You just shot two people!" I scream, and he holds out his hands, gesturing them down, which tells me to lower my voice.

"They were dead anyway. Sometimes this job has consequences, and sometimes innocent lives are sacrificed, but I don't think that guy was too innocent, do you?"

"Who are you?" The man takes off the cut and throws it on the bed, then reaches into his back pocket to pull out a wallet. My back stays against the wall, wishing like hell the damn thing would give and take me away to another planet.

He unfolds his wallet to show a badge. "I'm FBI. I've been undercover for a very long time. The Bureau has been building a case against the Hounds for years. There are so many activities they have their hands in."

"There are women here. Someone died. How could you... You're just as bad as they are!" I spout.

"The girl that's dead isn't dead. She's an agent too. This is real shit. It took me years to build up trust with this group. Years. If you're going to ruin that for me, I'll shoot you. I won't have my case compromised. When Cohen came to us, he had already used one of the members to ship your kid off, or I would have found a way to put him in protective custody. He's gone. I can find him, but in order to do that, you have to let me trade you to the seller."

"You're a good guy?"

He rubs his graying mustache, his bulging bicep flexing against his shirt. "I'm better than most, but I wouldn't say I'm good. I do what I have to for my position to look real, to be real, and for the most part it is. I do things that you won't like. I have to. I'm close. I need to bust this child ring they're running, and then I can take these bastards down once and for all. You need to cooperate, okay?"

This horrible man is claiming he's an FBI agent. I find it hard to believe, but whatever fucking universe I have crossed into is most definitely real. I mean, who the hell shoots two people to keep up appearance?

My eyes well with tears, fucking lagoons as Skirt calls it, and I let out a sad laugh that turns into gut-wrenching sobs. I want to go home. I want my son. I want Skirt. Why has my life been so damn difficult and uphill.

"I know, I know. It's an emotional time. I get that. I need you to get your shit together, okay? I can't have you losing it on me in front of twenty bikers who will tear me to shreds."

"I want my son," I tell him. "Promise me you will find my son, and I'll do whatever you want me to."

His hands land on my shoulder, and he stares into my eyes, the sinister side of him gone. "I promise to do everything in my power to bring your son home to you."

He doesn't say he'll find Aidan or bring him back, but his promise to try is better than nothing. "What are the chances of getting him back? How many kids have you saved?"

"Do you want me to lie?"

"Yes."

"All of them," he says as he takes a knife from his pocket and cuts the zip-ties from around my wrists.

I rub my wrists to ease the ache. "Don't lie to me," I say instead.

He clenches his jaw and tucks the knife back in his pocket. "Bathroom is that way. Get cleaned up. Stay in this room. Borrow one of my shirts. I need to go set up the exchange for you. Once you leave my hands, I can't promise protection, Dawn. Where you're going, you're going to have to hope I get there with my team in time."

"How. Many. Kids." I don't give a damn about me. "No more lies."

"None. Every trail goes cold because the ring moves around so much."

It's a punch in the gut that has me doubling over. The pain is unbearable. The thought of my little boy lost in this world forever is too much to bear. "Thank you," I force out, even if it comes out more as a whisper, a sound being carried in the wind.

"Don't thank me. Not yet. I'm sorry for grabbing you when you got here. I fucking hate doing that. I hate being this man," he says. "I can't wait till this job is done."

"Your road name makes sense now." I point to his cut lay-ing on the bed. "I was wondering why you were called Mercy."

"In the club? It's because I don't show any."

"Outside of the club, you do."

"This conversation never happened, Dawn. Please, don't make me kill you."

"If my son isn't found, you might as well," I say, numb to the core as I make my way to the restroom. His arm blocks the doorway, and when I look up at him, his mustache twitches.

He runs his hands through his graying hair and leans down. "Don't ever give up on him. He'll always be out there. I won't. It's my job. I care. I will search until it kills me, Dawn. I will do this job, be in this club, until they lead me to whoever they are working for, trading people, human fucking beings, drugs, and weapons. You can't let this break you because the obsession of not knowing what happened to your son will eat you alive."

He walks over to the plastic bin he uses as a dresser and pulls out a shirt and a pair of boxier briefs. "I know it isn't much, but it's better than what you're wearing. While you're here, you're mine, so you'll listen to me. Got it?" He holds out the clothing and then sees how much blood I have on my hands and folds them neatly on the bathroom counter.

"Got it," I say, impressed with how clean the bathroom is. The warehouse is a piece of crap, but his area is clean. The sink is plain, the tile is a bit rotted, and he has a rug covering most it, but the edges are peeling and black, giving away the mold growing in here.

"You have to listen to me or this won't work."

"I'm an ol' lady. I know how it works." I step inside the bathroom, and he enters with me, slamming the door behind him and locking us inside.

I step back and crane my neck to look at him. He's intimidating to say the least. Over six-four, wide, built like a Mack truck, and now that he's in this small space with me, door locked, I wonder if he's going back on his word.

His wingspan is bigger than the width of the bathroom as he presses his palms on either side of the wall. "You're an ol' lady? To who? Where? Tell me everything."

"You don't know? Cohen didn't tell you where he got me? How can you be an FBI agent and not know of the chapters around you?"

"Because I don't look at shit like that. My plate is full. We were just supposed to be passing through, but a few brothers liked it here. It lead me to Cohen, and Cohen got me a new lead, even though it meant it was your son, and now you're here. What chapter are you affiliated with?"

I still don't trust him. "I'm not telling you anything, Mercy." The last thing I want to do is be loose lipped to a guy who claims to be an agent. Even if he does have a badge, I've learned lying comes easy to a lot of people.

"Smart girl. You're learning." He leans in again. "But if you tell me, I can let them know where you are. I'm sure your guy is going out of his mind with worry."

I want to tell him. I'm torn. What if Mercy ambushes Ruthless? "If you really want to know, you'll figure it out for yourself. I'm not giving you any ammunition."

"You might survive this, Dawn," he says, impressed.

I hold my head up high and turn on the shower. "You might too."

"I need to go out there."

"No." I wrap my hands around his wrist and stop him from walking out that door. "Please, don't leave me alone showering with men like Cohen waiting to get me. I'm 'yours,' remember? Can't you stay?"

His eyes soften around the edges, and he flops the toilet seat down and sits, the hard plastic groaning from his massive weight. "Yeah, I can do that."

I step in the shower and close the curtain, thankful that the material is black and not clear. I toss the shirt over the rail and it lands with a sick, wet plop on the ground. The water flows dark pink as the blood is washed from my skin. I bite back more tears as my eyes tingle with the emotion I've been holding back.

I'm about to break—no, shatter.

And Skirt isn't here to pick up the pieces.

"Thank you," I say to Mercy, and he gives me a grunt in response. Any man outside this room would get in the shower and force me to their will. Mercy doesn't do that. He sits there, waiting patiently, and gives me the peace of mind I need by protecting me.

He shows more mercy than he thinks he does, and I'll be forever grateful to him being a light in a really dark, twisted, fucked up, haunted tunnel.

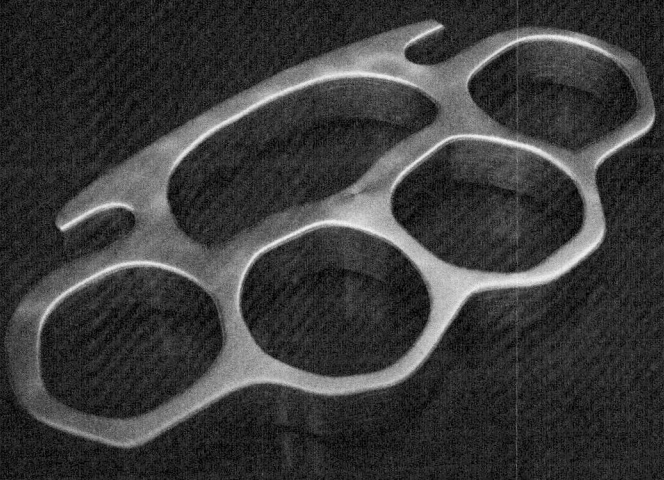

CHAPTER TWENTY

Skirt

CHURCH IS HEAVY.

I'm sitting at the table, mourning, my head bowed and my hands clenched tight into a ball. This cannot be my reality. Last night I had her in my arms. She was right there. I felt her. She was safe. I remember her warm skin pressed against mine, the sound of the words of love falling off her lips; all of that was real.

The guys have never seen me like this. My eyes are red-rimmed, and I know bikers aren't supposed to cry. We aren't allowed to be soft. There isn't room for emotion when it comes to big decisions concerning life and death.

I'm loving Dawn in ways I never thought I'd be able to do. If I lost her, the absence of love would be too much to bear.

Bikers can fucking cry too.

We aren't heartless. Those bastards are the ones who feel the most. The tough exterior doesn't mean shit when the interior is in strife. Havoc might swirl in our lives, but we like the calm after the storm just like everyone else.

"Skirt," Reaper breaks the silence by saying my name.

I don't lift my head.

Poodle is next to me, and he squeezes my shoulder, trying to make me feel better.

"Do you think Cohen did this?"

"Without a doubt," I say in an instant and press the heel of my hands against my eyes. "It has to be him."

1,440 minutes.

86,400 seconds.

That's how many minutes and seconds are in a day, and Dawn has been missing every hour of it. With every tick of the hand on the clock, my mind has been on her. Her absence is eviscerating.

"Maybe that other MC has something to do with it," Tool says. "Maybe we need to reach out to those Demon Furry's."

"Fury. Demons Fury," Reaper corrects him, and a few guys chuckle, but there isn't any humor in it. It's automatic because Tool is trying to lighten the mood.

"I'm just saying, maybe they know something."

"It's not a bad idea. Tongue, ride out to the dam. Take Knives with you. Get a location on the Hounds. Bullseye? Any update on Maximo? I find it odd that he's been quiet through all this."

"When I met with him, he said he's keeping his ear out. He says the Hellhounds are bad news, but that's all he knows. He hasn't heard anything about Dawn."

"Keep an eye on him, Bullseye, and take Tank with you."

"Prez—"

"If you want to prove yourself fucking worthy, Tank, you're going to go. How long do you want to be a prospect? Go with Bullseye, and I swear, I don't want to hear from either of you until you have something useful. Either information or a dead fucking body."

"Yes, Prez," Bullseye says, stands, and picks up Tank's huge ass by his prospect cut and drags him out the door.

Braveheart, Reaper, Poodle, Slingshot, Doc, and Badge are the only ones at the table. "We always find our women," Reaper states, trying to make me feel better.

"Aye, I know."

A soft knock taps against the door. None of the guys knock that way. The door creaks open and Ellie, Poodle's daughter, peeks her head in the crack.

"Ellie, what did I tell you about coming in here? Prez, I'm sorry."

"It's okay. Everything okay, Ellie?"

She blushes and steps in, holding Chaos in her arms. "I know Skirt is sad. I wanted to bring him his puppy in hopes it will make him feel better."

Reaper's eyes soften as does every other guy in the room, especially Braveheart.

"I'd really like that, Ellie. Thank ye." I stand and squeeze behind the chairs to get to her. She places Chaos in my hands, and the bush on top of his head has gotten bigger, but his body hasn't. Chaos whines and licks my nose, and I hold him close, feeling his little heart racing against my shoulder. His nose is cold and whoever said dogs were therapy deserves a damn reward because I feel lighter.

Dawn would love this pup. "Hey, Chaos."

He whimpers, sensing my sadness.

"Thank ye, Ellie."

"Anytime, Skirt. Sorry, President Reaper. It won't happen again."

A few of the guys snicker from hearing her say "President Reaper." It's cute and naïve. We never want her to change.

"Good job, baby. I'll be out soon, okay?" Poodle kisses his daughter's forehead, and it spreads another ache in my chest.

Aidan is still gone. I'm such a goddamn failure.

Chaos growls and sinks his sharp puppy teeth in my neck.

"Ye little shite!" I press my hand against the spot where he bit me and see if he drew blood. I bop his nose, a light love tap, and slightly scold him. "I'll let that go cause ye cute. No biting."

He latches onto my finger and growls, those damn teeth as sharp as Tongue's blade. "Damn it! Ye menace." A small smile breaks my face, the first one I've had since Dawn went missing. Chaos removes his bear trap of a mouth from my finger and licks it, sensing my mood shift. "Yer alright, Chaos. Ye alright." I tuck him to my chest and take a seat.

"That dog is damn ugly," Badge says. "Pidoodles were not, and still are not, a good idea."

"Don't talk about Lady like that," Poodle and I say at the same time.

"Okay, alright. I'm glad to see everyone's mood has shifted, but I know the heaviness is still felt. Skirt. I know the pain won't go away until she's home. We will find Dawn and her kid. No one fucks with women and children. No one." Reaper punches the table with his fist and the guys that are left in the room cheer and holler.

Badge's phone blares, the sound of an alarm before a tornado, and in a hurry he pulls his cell from his inner cut pocket and taps the screen. His lips press into a firm, pissed-off line. "That was Braveheart. We have a visitor, Prez. He's alone."

"Who is it?" Reaper asks, reaching into his gun holster to pull out a .44 Magnum pistol. The damn barrel seems to be a mile long, and the gun itself looks heavy. He definitely upgraded from his last gun.

Badge's eyes cloud with rage, and his mouth tenses before he speaks. "Seems to be the Prez of the Hounds. He's alone."

I stand and thrust my dog out to Badge. "Hold my fucking Pidoodle." Badge grabs onto the pup, and I run through the house, slipping my brass knuckles in place as I go. I'm going to kill this sorry excuse of a man. I'm not going to stop until his skull is in pieces and scattered amongst the desert.

"Skirt! Stop. We need to know what he has to say," Reaper calls the order out from behind me, his tone full of warning, but all it does is push me to keep going. If it means I earn an arrow through the heart on my chest, so fucking be it.

The air is fucking dry and hot as I sprint out the door, choking me with the mugginess. I jump down the eight steps and land on both feet, a cloud of dirt engulfing me. The biker rides down the long dirt path toward us, and I run to him, head on, like knights about to joust. I dodge left to miss the tire and fling out my arm at the last possible second. His neck slams against my forearm and the man flies off the back of his bike. His Harley swerves right and crashes to the ground, his mirror snapping off.

I press my boot against his neck and bend down. "I hear that's seven years bad luck." I punch him across the face, brass knuckles making contact with his skin, and the feral fighter within spurs me on to keep going until he's nothing but hamburger meat.

"Enough!" Reaper places the .44 against the back of my head. I know he won't shoot me, but the slightest possibility that he might has me lifting my hands. "I said to stop."

"This fucker—"

"We don't know shit yet. For all you know, he's innocent."

"Something tells me he ain't." I lift my boot to crush his throat, and Reaper cocks his gun. If that bullet leaves that gun, it won't leave a hole in my head; it will blow my damn head right off my neck. I take a step away and kick the ground. "Fuck!" I scream.

Reaper turns the gun off me and aims to the Hound. "You better get to talking before I let him loose."

The man nods and groans, pressing his hand against the wound on the side of his cheek. "You have a hell of a hook, man." He struggles to get to his feet and shakes his head, probably trying to get the bells to stop ringing in his head. They won't for a while.

"Shut up and talk before I lose my patience and shoot you dead."

The guy presses his forehead against the barrel, daring Reaper to pull the trigger. "Do it. Have fun with the feds on your ass." The guy tosses his wallet to me and I open it to see an FBI badge staring back at me.

"Shit, Reaper. He's FBI."

Reaper's sardonic smile plays on his lips, reminding me of a sinner about to dance on a few graves. "I don't give a fuck if you're a fed. Nothing a few buzzards can't help me fix. Explain why an FBI agent is a Prez of an MC."

"I'm undercover. Been undercover for a while so I can find this child sex-trafficking ring these fuckers sell kids to. It hasn't been an easy few years. I've had to do things I never want to do again, killed a lot of innocent people, and the only fucking trail I have right now is Aidan."

"How the fuck do ye know about Aidan!" I roar and slam my body against him, taking him to the ground.

"You must be Skirt," the agent says, bleeding from his cheek.

I grab his cut and bring him so close to my face, he has no choice but to smell the fury on my breath. "How do ye know me?"

"Cohen brought us Dawn. I came here to tell you of the plan we have, okay?"

"Ye have Dawn? Where is she? I want her back! Tell me, or I swear to fucking God I'll kill you and not give a damn what the consequences are."

"Dawn and I made a deal. She was sold to the same people who have Aidan. It's the first time I've had contact with them. Usually it's one of the other members handling this shit."

The breath leaves my lungs, and I fall onto my arse. "She isn't here? She's gone? Ye sold her? Ye son of a bitch! I'm going to fucking kill ye!" I wrap my hands around his throat and squeeze.

"I have the location of where they are! I have it! I'm getting a team together. She will be okay."

"Where are they?" Spittle flies from my mouth and lands on his face.

"New Orleans," he chokes through my hold. He rolls to his hands and knees, gasping for air. "You know, I had to look for you guys on my own to prove my intentions to Dawn. She didn't tell me shit about your club. She was afraid I was lying."

Good girl. God, when I get her back, I'm going to kiss

the fuck out of her and make love to her until she can't take anymore.

"Call Pocus, Skirt. Looks like we're going on a road trip to NOLA. I'll call Tongue to see if the Demons Fury want to join us. I have a feeling it's going to be a shit show."

"The feds will be there," Agent Fake President says. "You all will get arrested if you go."

"Well, that's why you're going to tell us when they're getting there so we beat them to it. This is a fucking club matter. One of our own. That's the law, Mercy," Reaper reads the nametag on his cut. "Either get used to it, or go back to your federal building."

Basically, nut up or bitch out.

"I can buy you the time you need," Mercy says.

Reaper tucks his gun in his holster and pulls out his phone. "Tool is going to be excited to see his friends down in NOLA." He walks far enough away that I can't hear what he's saying, but by the aggravated expression, he's pissed at Tool.

"She's okay?" I ask Mercy.

"For now. Cohen is with her for the trip. He has my order not to touch her."

I punch the ground until the dry clay cracks and creates a web of fractures. That fucker always gets away. Not anymore. When we get to NOLA, he's mine. I'm going to enjoy ripping him from limb to limb and throwing his body parts in the Mississippi.

Actually, not the Mississippi.

I'll feed him to the gators.

Alive.

CHAPTER TWENTY-ONE

Dawn

I'M NOT SURE HOW LONG WE'VE BEEN DRIVING, BUT THE VAN IS starting to smell like body odor, and I really need to pee. They have refused to stop to use the restroom. One girl pissed herself, and they threw her out of the back of the van in the middle of the night. I hope she survived, but I doubt it. Being thrown from a moving vehicle at seventy-miles-per-hour doesn't leave much hope.

"We're here," the driver says, the brakes squeaking as we come to a stop.

Cohen slides the door open, and I look away from the sudden burst of light; the sun has my eyes wincing and watering. I've been in the dark for too long.

"Come on, bitch." Cohen grabs my arm and yanks me out the door. I don't have my footing yet, so I fall to the ground, banging my head against the sweltering pavement. Warm liquid drips from my forehead, and blood blinds my left eye. I can't wipe it away either because those damn zip-ties are back.

Cohen picks me up, bruising my arm with his fingers as they dig into my flesh so forcibly. "Get the fuck up. Come on. I have a big pay day waiting for me." His hands run down my back and palm each cheek, then he brings his lips to my ear, rotten breath permeating the air I need. "Maybe I can get one last feel of you, huh? Would you like that?"

"I'd rather die than feel you again," I sneer, which earns me a backhand across the face. He hit me so hard, I worry my neck might break.

"Don't worry. A few days in here, you might." He shoves me forward, walking me to a rundown house next to a swamp.

I look out into the dark, murky waters. Algae floats along the top, making certain sections appear green. Dragonflies flutter their wings around the trees growing in the water, scaling the air. Gauzes of moss hang from the branches, broken and tattered, skimming the surface of the swamp. A few heads bop out of the water, and black, beady eyes are staring at me.

Alligators.

How many women and children are thrown in the water for food? Oh my god, what if Aidan isn't alive? What if he's in a belly of the swamp? No, I've come this far. Mercy says Aidan is alive, and I'm going to believe him. I'm close. I have to have faith. I can't give up now.

My feet crunch along the long grass, squishing against the soft ground. The driver, another Hound, leads us to the door of the haunted house.

It looks like it would be. The wood is rotten, a few boards are missing, and the windows are broken and shattered. Tarps hang on the inside to cover the deceit on the other side. The steps groan and bend under my weight as we climb up the steps. The driver knocks, and Cohen keeps a firm hold on my arm.

"Password?" a voice says from the other side of the door.

"Peaches and cream," the driver replies, and the door opens on a painful moan, echoing all the fears this place has undoubtedly holds.

Cohen pushes me forward, and I'll have nightmares for the rest of my life after what I see. Along both sides of the room are small dog cages, the kind someone puts in their backyard to keep their pet in. Locked inside are children.

While dirty, as I walk by each cage, they seem healthy. They have an abundance of food and water. Some are crying, others are sleeping, but they don't seem to have been abused. They are fully dressed and staring at me with curiosity.

Hope is a foolish thing to have right now, but I feel it when I see that the children are safe and without bruises. Maybe the monsters aren't as monstrous as I imagined. Still, these men are what nightmares are made of.

Another thing I notice, there are no adults.

"I have someone interested in a mother child duo, so this works. I never do this, but the payout is worth it," the man leading us to the back informs the driver and Cohen. "Luckily the little brat is still here. No one seems to want a child who is broken."

Aidan.

Oh God. I bet he's had so many seizures.

The water beneath us splashes against the wood, and that's when it hits me that we're on a houseboat. The breaks between the floorboards show the rippling of the swamp beneath us, and I know there are gators under there just waiting to take a bite.

We stop at a cage to the left, and in the back is a small figure curled up in a ball on a bed of blankets. Just like a dog, but it's my son.

"Aidan! Aidan, baby! I'm here. Mommy is here," I cry when I see his small body curled up on the floor.

"God, shut up!" Cohen tightens his grip, and I do as he says, but the overwhelming joy is impossible not to feel. It's been too long without Aidan.

The man opens the cage, and Cohen cuts the zip-ties from my wrists and tosses the plastic inside. The greasy old man shuts the gate, and his pointy chin reminds me of a witch, but the scabs on his face tell me he's a drug addict. The man locks the cage in place, and his eyes never leave me. "You're goin' to make me good money," he says.

I crawl over to Aidan. He's still sleeping. I shake him awake, but he doesn't move. I snap my head in the direction of the men who think they have the power of God. "What's wrong with him? Why won't he wake up?"

"He kept cryin' and seizin', so I got some medicine from a doc and knocked him out."

I'm not sure if I'm thankful or terrified that the man drugged my kid. "How can you care about their health when you treat them like this?"

"I don't touch 'em. Don't believe in that sort of thing. I have a business to run. I got bills to pay. They are fed, taken care of, so why you bitchin'?"

"Because the people you sell them to probably do."

"Ain't my problem, lady." The chain hanging from his hips jingles as he walks away. Cohen squats and tilts his head, eying me from head to toe.

I hope I never see him again after this.

"I'm going to miss you. I know you find it hard to believe, but I hate breaking new bitches. You can't be trusted anymore. So this is the consequence. At least Mercy was kind enough to reunite you with your son. Honestly, I wouldn't have cared so much."

I cradle Aidan's limp body to my chest and kiss his forehead. He's burning up, and I can't tell if he has a fever or if it's this Louisiana weather. I'm so glad to have him in my arms again. "What will you do now?" I ask.

"Well, we have to stay around here for a few days, wait for the rest of the club to come down. I think the Hellhounds might make New Orleans their new home. Lots of business here. The Mississippi is a great way to transport the goods we need."

Goods.

That's what he's calling human beings, these poor children. The families that will never see them again… It's devastating to even fathom. "I hope you burn in hell," I say to him, hoping that hell does exist because men like him don't deserve to live.

Cohen's acerbic grin has my skin pebbling in the broiling heat of New Orleans. "Bitch, I was born and raised in hell. Who the fuck do you think is in charge? It sure as shit ain't Satan. And you better hope I don't buy you two from under that old man's feet. Can you imagine?" He stands from his hunched over position and chortles malevolently as he strides down the aisle.

Cold fright numbs my core. Dread is now a forcefield surrounding my soul that guards any positive emotion out of my psyche, trapping the bad ones in.

"Aidan, baby? Aidan," I whisper, grab his face, and shake him. "Hey, angel. Come on, wake up. It's me; Mommy is here. Come on, baby, open your beautiful blues. Let me see them.

Come on, wake up, Aidan!" I beg with tears in my eyes, but his beautiful face is still as he sleeps. "Okay, baby. Okay, you rest." I rub my hand through his hair and hold him tighter. "I missed you so much. I love you. I love you so much. I won't let anything happen to you again. I swear." I rock us back and forth hope by some miracle Skirt finds us.

The little girl next to us grabs on to the metal, her small chubby fingers curl, and she stares at me with large brown eyes and thick lashes. She's beautiful. "Are you a mommy?" The little girl looks around, making sure she's speaking low enough that no one can hear.

I give her a watery smile and nod. "I sure am. I'm his mommy. This is Aidan. I'm Dawn, sweetheart. What's your name?" I ask her.

She turns around and grabs her blankets, then pushes them over to the side of the cage closest to me, and she sits down. "I'm Maizey." Her chocolate-colored hair almost matches the tone of her skin. She's older than Aidan by a few years, maybe six or seven since she's missing a front tooth.

"Maizey? Wow, that's such a pretty name. I like that." Talking to her helps me keep calm, and Maizey seems to want to talk to an adult who doesn't scare her. The bang of a cage opening and closing has Maizey turning around, but I reach out and hold her hand, stopping her from looking at the child being carried out and will probably never be seen again. "Hey, sweetie. Tell me your favorite story. Who is your favorite princess?"

"I love Princess Elsa. I want to be just like her when I'm all growed up." She pops the P at the end, then laces our fingers together. "Can you be my mommy too? I don't have one anymore." The statement comes out of nowhere and breaks another chunk of emotional control off me.

"Of course, I will be. Do you want a bedtime story? How about you rest, along with Aidan. I'll wake you up if anything changes." I lift my eyes above her shoulder to see the child going out the back door, hand in hand with the old greasy man I met previously. The best thing for these kids to do is sleep.

"Okay! I haven't had a bedtime story in so long. Can it be a happily ever after?"

I squeeze her hand and stare into her doe-like eyes and grin. "Of course. What other kind of ending is there?"

"A bad one. I'm tired of bad ones," she mumbles through a yawn and lays down, keeping a tight hold on my hand.

I lean my head against the cage separating us, keeping Aidan tucked against my chest. I try to think of something happy this little girl's imagination can get lost in while she sleeps. "Once upon a time, on the tallest cliff near the sea, with the cloud-high trees soaring in the sky, was a pink castle."

"Pink!" she gasps, blinking up at me in shock.

"Pink," I say. "It's the Princess' favorite color. Since she lives all alone, it's the only thing left that keeps her truly happy."

"She's alone? That's so sad."

I look around to see a few other children at the front of their cages, watching me, listening, needing to hear something magical and happy. I'm their source, and I can't disappoint them.

"It is sad, but things for the Princess are about to change." I try to think of anything, something children will find even the least bit interesting. "She's sitting near the window, and the ocean's breeze caresses her face when she sees something in the distance. The Princess is brushing her long, purple hair—"

"Purple! Cool. I want purple hair!" Maizey says.

"While she's brushing her hair, she stares at the dot in the sky that's coming closer and closer. The Princess gasps when she sees…" I look around to see the kids have wide eyes as big as the moon staring at me. "A dragon!"

"Wow," Maizey blinks at me in awe.

"And on the dragon is a man, but not just any man—a knight! He has a sword in his hand, ready to fight whoever to free her from the tower. No man has ever been able to get inside the castle because there is a spell that doesn't allow anyone inside. Only love stronger than the spell can break it, freeing the Princess once and for all."

Maizey's eyes droop shut as she listens to the made-up fairy tale.

"But the knight on the dragon isn't any knight; he's her knight. He jumps off his dragon and lays his hand on the door like so many others before him, hoping on all hope that he'll free his true love. With a twist of the knob the spell breaks, unlocking the castle. He runs inside to save the Princess. They share their first kiss, and true love wins once and for all. The knight helps her onto the dragon, and they fly into the sunset, living happily ever after together, with no more chains, no more spells, and no more evil."

If only real life was as good as a fairy tale.

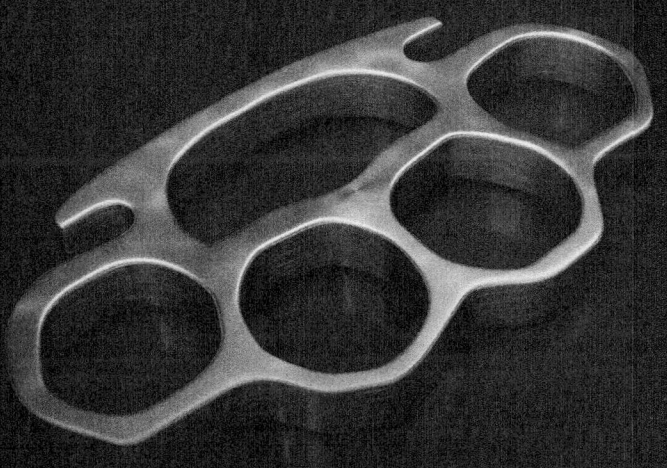

CHAPTER TWENTY-TWO

Skirt

"**W**ELL, IT'S GOOD TO SEE YOU AGAIN, REAPER. HATE the circumstance," Pocus greets us, clasping Reaper's hand in a friendly shake.

"Maybe when all this is said and done, you guys can show us how NOLA really is, Pocus."

"Don't think you city boys can keep up, Reaper."

Pocus and Reaper share a few laughs, and I try not to get annoyed by sharing pleasantries. Dawn is out there. We only have about five hours before the feds roll in, and we need to get going. The sooner this is over with, the better. For everyone's safety.

"Long time no see, Tool. Well, I guess I can't really say that. I saw ya'll were comin' round yesterday," Seer taps his temple, and Tool gives the guy a wide berth, not greeting him.

I stand outside as the rest of the guys walk into the old plantation house. I never thought a badass group of bikers would own something like this for a compound, but whatever works, I guess. The lot is big too, filled with trees, and the swamp is a few miles back. The clubhouse seems to be on its last leg, needing some big repairs.

Seer stands out there with me and leans against the towering column that holds up the second floor. "I'm sorry I couldn't warn ya ahead of time." His Cajun accent thick and hardly understandable.

"I know that's not how yer... gift works," I say, sitting on the broken porch step. "I know you would have called if you saw something."

"I have to say, when it comes to ya situation, I haven't seen anything, Skirt. The future is undecided still."

"The fuck ye mean undecided? We're here. We're about to leave to go get her! There's nothing undecided about that. I'm going to get her back."

"My gift isn't set in stone. The future changes. Nothing is certain, okay? Everyone tinks dat is how it works, and it ain't, mon amie. Being the only man here with the power of sight, it ain't easy. Everyone expects it to work every second of every day. Some are skeptical. Some live and breathe for it, waitin' to see if I know what the winnin' lottery numbers are. It's annoyin.' I cannot see when there are selfish motives."

I can't imagine feeling like an outcast like that. I thought him and his MC brothers shared similarities, but if it's just him, then that must be lonely.

Seer slaps a hand on my shoulder and inhales a gust of sharp air. I stand as fast as I can and see a distant expression on his face, his eyes are vacant, and a gust of wind blows as thunderclouds fill the air.

Seer lets go of my shoulder with a huge gasp and doubles over, holding his stomach, gagging.

"Pocus!" I yell for the Prez of the NOLA chapter and kneel on the ground to see if Seer is okay.

His dreads hang in his face, and his mixed skin tone seems paler than usual.

"Are ye okay, Seer?"

"We need to go," Seer pants, reaching out for the column to brace himself. "We need to go now."

Pocus runs out the front door with a few other guys behind him. Seer is the VP, and the big guy named Bones must be the Sargent at Arms. Makes sense since he's the biggest motherfucker I've ever seen.

"What is it, Seer? What did ya see?" I reach out to stabilize Seer when Pocus slaps my hands away. "Whatever happened has to do with ya. Don't go touchin' him. We don't know all he can handle."

"The girl. Dawn?"

"Ye saw her?" My stomach drops when sweat drips off him like a leaky faucet.

He nods, and Bones hands Seer a bottle of water. Seer pours it all over his face, cooling himself off. "She's safe. She's in a cage with a boy, but not for much longer. They already took one kid. They are getting a boat ready. We only have an hour."

Reaper storms out the door and mounts his bike, my brothers following suit. I run down the steps and jump on my own hog, not wanting to wait any longer. "You coming or am I leaving your ass here, Pocus?"

"We have ya back. Hex, Shadow, drive the truck since we don't know how many survivors there will be. Sage, Hemlock, ya in the water. Take the boat. Everyone else, we ride in front of Ruthless. Seer, ya take the lead."

"I know where we need to go."

"No, ya don't. They changed location. If it weren't for me, ya'd be fucked." Seer hops on his deep purple custom bike and cranks it.

Reaper curls his top lip in, but stays silent, which isn't like him. Once he starts his engine, the rest of us do the same, and dozens of growls rumble through the air. We sound like a feral pack of wolves circling the last prey on earth.

NOLA's clubhouse isn't guarded like ours. The driveway is worn grass and dirt, wide from all the bikes coming and going. We speed down the backroads of New Orleans, following Seer as we make our way deeper into swamplands.

The further we ride into the darkness and evil the swamp holds, the tighter I clutch the handlebars. The trees even have a gloomier appearance. There are weeping willows, the long branches piercing the flesh of the water like a knife to skin. A murder of crows fly above us, hundreds of them, and Seers swerves off the road when he sees them.

I'm not really a superstitious kind of guy, but that shit is questionable. I know Seer is analyzing what it means and believes that a group of crows are called murder for a reason.

About twenty minutes later, Seer pulls off into the woods. There isn't a road or a path, and as we turn in, the bikes get scratched, branches slap me in the face, and my suspension isn't really helping with the shaking and bouncing.

One by one, the motorcycles turn off, and there's a moment of quiet eerie, and the hair stands on the back of my neck. Shit is creepy. We park our bikes and hop off. Everyone's boots snap against the twigs on the leaf-covered ground.

Everything is covered in mud, and the mosquitoes are a real fucking bitch.

I slap my hand against my neck and pull my palm away to see a giant dead insect twitching, then wipe it on my jeans. Fucking hate humid weather like this.

"She's about a mile away. I didn't wanna get too close 'cause the bikes are so loud," Seer says.

"Lead the way," Reaper says, holding his gun in the air. "Weapons out. Be ready. I have a feeling this is going to be a shit show."

As a large group, we stay in the shadows of the trees so we aren't seen.

Is there ever a normal person anywhere in an MC? I'm starting to highly doubt it.

I'm not sure how long we walk. It feels like an eternity. My arse is sweating, my eyes sting from the salt, and the swap smells like dead bodies.

Seer stops and signals us to stay down, then points up ahead. There's a houseboat floating on the water, old and ready to sink to the bottom of the swamp. There are a few men pacing on the porch, wearing Hounds' cuts. I'm going to kill every single one of these arseholes.

Then I see him.

Cohen.

He's leaning against a beat-up Toyota truck, as if he's on top of the world as he fans money in his face.

Money because he brought Dawn here.

"Don't." Reaper's palm splays against my chest, stopping me from launching through the bushes to kill the man. "We have the upper hand. They have no idea we are here. You do that, we might be fucked."

My eyes never leave Cohen. I watch as he pushes off the old tire and makes his way back onto the houseboat.

"We can take out the first two," Seer says, and Pocus nods in agreement.

Right as the words leave Seer's mouth, a low, silent hum rips through the air, and the men pacing on the porch collapse.

Dead.

"Well, damn," Reaper says.

Tongue is with the Demons Fury. The man who calls himself One throws the rifle over his shoulder and comes out of the woods on the other side.

We step out from the tree line, and Tongue hurries to the porch. He tilts the dead men's heads back, reaches into their mouths, and cuts their tongues free. "Finally," he moans, his cock hard and visible through his jeans.

The man is nuts.

He lays down on the porch and holds the tongue in the air, calling for the gators like they are kittens.

"You called. We came," Whistler says. "And that guy is fucking nuts."

"Pretty gator." Tongue pets the top of the gator's head.

"Yeah, we keep him around because of that. Thanks for coming, Whistler."

"Anytime, but we still have work to do." We stare at the houseboat, and it bounces along the small waves of water.

I can't wait any longer. I climb up the steps and knock on the door.

"Password?" the sicko asks.

"Let me the fuck in," I growl. My brass knuckle-covered fist punches through the flimsy wood and hits the man in the face.

"What the fuck?" He stumbles back and touches his broken

nose to see that it's bleeding. I kick the door open. Fuck order, fuck listening—I'm done.

Dawn is here.

Aidan is here.

My family needs me.

I don't answer the guy. I crush with a quick jab to the throat. He can't breathe. There's no going back as I watch the life slip out of his eyes, the black pupils dilating to onyx drops.

"Holy fucking shit," Whistler whistles behind me as he peers around the room, seeing cage after cage of children locked inside.

A gunshot reverberates the air and slams against Whistler's shoulder. He tumbles back and hits a cage and the kid screams, fat tears rolling down her face like a hurricane slinging rain. The back of the houseboat fills with Hounds, a row of black and ugly fuckers who have no right to call themselves bikers.

Reaper and One lift their weapons and fire, careful to make sure they don't hit a kid. Bullet shells falling onto the floor is the only sound in the houseboat. Tongue runs through the crowd, somehow not getting shot, and plunges his knife into someone's head. He then slices the throat, digs his hand inside the man's neck, and yanks his tongue out.

It's fucking sick.

Blood is everywhere, dripping through the cracks of the wood, and the snapping of gators can be heard below. They smell food. We will give it to them too.

While my club brothers fight the Hounds, I search the cages for Dawn. I try to open the gate to each cage, but they are locked. I need a key. "Hey, I'm going to get ye out of here, okay? Sit tight. Yer going to be fine," I say to a little boy who can't be more than five-years-old.

"Are you the knight?" a girl asks, gigantic brown eyes and hair of the color of garnet.

"What? No, little lassie. I'm here for someone I love, though. Have ye seen her? Her and a wee boy?"

She nods, then points to the back doors where a few Hounds are fighting with Demons and Ruthless Kings.

"She told me a story. About a princess being saved by a knight. Are you the knight?" She stares at me like I'm some savior, some Prince Charming in a fairy tale. "They were right next to me, but the mean man, the bad guy, he come and tooked them away." Her eyes well and her bottom lips puckers out.

Those damn lagoons get me every time.

"I'm going to get ye out of there, okay? I am. I need to know where Dawn is. I need to save her like the knight in the story saved the princess, okay? I'll be back for ye."

"You swear?" she asks.

"On me life, little lassie." I grip the fence one last time, making myself turn away from the terrified girl, and get ready for the fight I've been waiting for far too long. I give my knuckles a good crack and swing my arm through the air, knocking the guy out in one swift hit, then I take his head and smash it against the other one, leaving them unconscious.

I kick open the door and see Cohen getting on a small jon boat. I see Dawn's strawberry blonde hair and two little boys next to her. I don't know who is who, but it doesn't matter. Those kids, that woman, they are my responsibility.

"Don't even think about getting on that boat, O'Roarke. Yer time is up."

He pauses as he unhooks the rope from the dock, then stands straight. "Damn, if it ain't the second Blackwood brother. You want to die too, right?"

"I'm not the one dying today."

The door kicks open, and Tongue throws a body on the dock, a Hound. Reaper comes through next and drags two out, then Whistler, even with a gunshot wound, drags a body out. Every member, Ruthless and Demon alike, throws bodies on the ground.

The only one left is Cohen.

And he is mine.

Tongue lifts his knife, but I grab onto the blade before he can throw it, letting the edge cut into my palm. "He's mine, Tongue."

"Ya need to hurry; Feds will be here in thirty," Seer says, tossing one of the dead Hounds in the water. A gator's jaws wrap around the head and death rolls to make sure his food is dead before taking it to the bottom of the swap.

I want to finish this how it started—fighting.

"No guns, no weapons." I take off my brass knuckles and pop my finger. "Just ye and me."

"I'm a better fighter than you," he taunts. "I'm a champion."

Cohen isn't wrong. I know he's the better fighter, but where he has training, I have skill and natural ability. We circle each other while the guys throw the bodies in the water to get rid of evidence. I'm never the one to make the first move. I like to see what my opponent is going to do and read his body language.

He dips left and swings his right fist, a hard jab, which if it hit me, would have taken me down, but I'm quick. I duck and hook my left fist and punch his stomach, then lift my knee right between his legs. He groans, but he doesn't let the pain of getting kneed in the balls stop him. He tackles me to the ground, my head hitting with an unforgivable thud.

I'm on my back.

It's never good to be on my back. It gives my opponent an advantage. I can't afford Cohen to have the advantage; too much is at stake. I manage to push my knee between us and roll us. Grabbing his head, I slam it against the dock. I reach for my brass knuckles, slip them on, and wail him in the face.

"You said no weapons!"

"And ye killed my brother after the round ended. I'm fighting too fair with ye." I punch him again, splintering his front tooth. "I'm fighting to kill ye." The sound of his skull crunching under my fists is liberating. I don't stop. I can't stop.

Left. Right. Left. Right. My arms burn. My knuckles sting. I hate him so much.

"Skirt!" Reaper grabs my hand before I can punch the man under me again. Cohen's face is nothing but blood and broken skin. He coughs, and a fountain of blood leaves his mouth. "Let the gators take care of it. You have someone who needs you."

My brows pinch for a second. I forgot where I was for a minute. I turn to look over my shoulder, and Tool is helping Dawn and the two kids off the boat.

"Dawn," her name rushes out of me as I stand.

"You came for me," she sobs, taking a small step forward, like she's unsure if I want her or not.

"Lips, I'll always come for ye, till my dying breath." I gather her and the boys in my arms and give them a tight hug. I'm not sure which kid is hers, but it doesn't matter. The children are safe.

Dawn is in my arms.

We won.

"Told you we always get them back," Reaper reminds me.

Sirens sound in the distance as Tongue throws the last body in the swamp for gator meat.

"Damn, can we do that again?" Tongue asks, then rinses his knife off in the swamp. "Good swamp kitty." He pats the gator's head; it seems to enjoy Tongue's touch.

This fucking day needs to end if Tongue is now a gator whisperer.

"This is Aidan. Aidan, this is Rohan; people call him Skirt."

I glance down at the little boy who is holding on to his mom's leg, hiding behind it. He has chestnut brown hair and bright baby blue eyes. "Nice to meet ye, Aidan. I've heard a lot about ye."

Aidan's hold on his mom loosens as he takes a step near me, but then his eyes roll back, his legs give out and I catch him just in time before his body seizes.

The battle might be won, but the war is not over.

CHAPTER TWENTY-THREE

Dawn

I NEVER THOUGHT HOME WOULD FEEL SO GOOD. WHEN I THINK about it, I've never had a home before. Not like this one here with Skirt. Nothing can ever compare to being here. Especially now that I have Aidan back, everything feels complete.

My soul is saved by a ruthless biker, who at times, can be anything but ruthless.

"How are you feeling, baby?" I pet Aidan's hair as he lays in the bed in Doc's treatment room. Doc has him on medication, and luckily, there has been no brain damage from how many seizures he's had the last few weeks.

"Better." His small voice mumbles. "Tired."

"We are going to take care of that," Doc says with a kind grin. "This stuff? It will help you sleep, okay?"

Aidan looks to me for reassurance, and I bring his hand

up and kiss it. "It's okay. Doc is a good guy." Aidan hasn't been sleeping since we got back four days ago, and Doc is worried it will make his seizures worse, so he is going to give Aidan a strong dose of sleep medicine. He might be out until tomorrow morning.

Aidan's eyes start to close, and he struggles to keep them open because he's scared. Finally, his eyes shut, and the steady rise and fall of his chest brings me comfort. I let out a heavy breath. "Thank you, Doc," I say as he moves to the next child.

Badge ran all the kids through missing person reports. More than half the kids got to go home, but five of them had no one. Reaper has no idea what to do, but for now, the kids are staying here and are getting medical care.

Sarah has practically lived in the basement, reading kids bedtime stories. She met Maizey and immediately felt a strong connection to the little girl. Reaper has voiced more than once not to get too close to the kids, but Sarah has clung onto Maizey.

He's worried Maizey's parents will come out of nowhere and take her home, leaving Sarah devastated and more depressed than she was before.

"It's not a problem. I live for this. I'm thankful none of them have been abused. It's rare for their situation. All of them are well nourished, a bit dehydrated and bone fucking tired—I mean, really tired." Doc coughs to cover his slip up. "They are lucky. This never happens. They will have mental trauma, but damn it, it could have been so much worse. So much worse," he repeats, laying his stethoscope over a little boy's heart.

It's the child that I thought I would never see again when I was telling Maizey that fairy tale. When Cohen found out the Ruthless Kings were there, he dragged me and Aidan out of the cage and onto the boat where the scared little boy was.

"I can't believe how healthy they sound. It's a fucking … it's a miracle."

I giggle from another curse he tries to hide.

"This is going to take some getting used to," he says. "Why don't you go get some rest? He isn't going to wake up anytime soon. Go eat, shower, relax. He's safe here. Reaper is having a new electrical gate installed so what happened doesn't happen again. Security is tighter. Breathe easier. I'll be down here with them."

"Me too!" Juliette says in the blue scrubs she insists on wearing. "I passed my test! I'm officially an RN!"

"Thank fu—thank fudge, I mean. I need all the help I can get."

"You have a bad habit to break, Doc."

"I know, I know. And I'm not even the worst one. Everyone is going to have to learn how to bite their tongues around these little ones." Doc moves to the next child and checks their heart rate, listening closely for any inconsistencies.

"Yeah, but something tells me they won't mind. They might be big, bad bikers, but they are softies at heart," Juliette states, tucking a blanket under another kid.

"Don't let them hear you say that," Doc chides. "It will be a pissing match."

We all share a laugh because we know it's true, and then we quiet down when the sounds bounce off the walls. I lower my voice to a whisper, "Are you sure it's okay to leave? Maybe he will need me. I'm nervous to leave him alone."

Doc stands in front of me, and his broad chest takes up my view. I tilt my head back to be able to look at him, and his massive paw of a hand takes mine. "I promise. I have him. I'm not going to let anything happen to these kids. They are probably the safest they've ever been."

I know he's right, but that doesn't mean I'm not scared; not after everything that's happened. "Okay, but call me if anything happens. If he wakes up, screams, cries—"

"Go. It's fine."

"Doctor's orders. Get on out, missy." Juliette pushes me toward the staircase.

"Fine. I'm going. I'm going." I amble up the stairs, as slow as possible. I look back at Aidan, sleeping soundly, then I continue into the kitchen. A few guys are sitting around the table, tired from the trip to NOLA. Tongue is even falling asleep while sharpening his knife.

Tool slaps the back of Tongue's head and he startles awake, pressing the blade against Tool's crotch.

Tool stands on his tiptoes and backs away. "Woah, hey now. No need to go crazy. You were falling asleep while making your blade nice and deadly. I was just trying to help."

"I'm going to hit the hay," Tongue snaps, sheathing his blade as if it's a sword. "Don't fuck with a man holding a knife, Tool. "

"Don't fuck with a man holding a knife, Tool," Tool acts childish, mocking Tongue like a little boy in a high-pitched tone.

"I'm too tired to even deal with you." Tongue stomps off down the hall and opens the door where Sarah used to sleep, slamming it shut.

"Was it something I said?" Tool questions.

"No," Poodle says in a way that is condescending toward Tool.

I grin at their antics and make my way to Skirt's cabin. It's a simple chalet style log cabin. Three bedrooms, two baths, and what's even better is that he built it himself. Skirt is a man of many talents.

I open the door, and there are a few things missing, like the couch. The hardwood floors have been replaced with foam material that look like puzzle pieces. What the hell? As I make my way toward the master suite, I see a tool box sitting near the door along with a tool belt.

There's childproof locks on everything. He might have gone a little overboard. There's even foam covering the vent. It warms my heart that he cares so much, but Aidan knows not to go near the vents. I unlatch the foam from the puzzle piece and carry it with me to the bedroom.

Skirt is sitting on the bed, rummaging through an old, tattered cardboard box. On the side it says, 'Conor.'

His brother.

I drop the red foam piece on the ground and crawl on the bed, then wrap my arms around Skirt. "You okay?"

"Today's his birthday. I miss him," Skirt breaks my heart with how soporific he sounds.

"I'm sorry. Is all of this stuff his? Do you have a picture? Why haven't I seen him yet?"

"It's been too painful to have his photos up without getting revenge. I guess, I can hang them on the walls instead of being shoved in a corner." He buries his hand in the box and pulls an old picture frame out. The glass is cracked, but that's alright; it can be replaced. "Here he is. He was older than me by ten years."

With a gentle touch, I take the picture frame out of his hands and hold it as if it's the most precious thing in the world. Simple black wood holds the picture in place and while I look through the glass, I see a pair of eyes that I see every day.

"Oh my God." I rub my thumb through the dust on the glass to show Conor's face more.

"What? What's wrong? Did the glass get ye?" Skirt goes to take the picture out of my hand to check me for cuts, but I hold onto the frame tighter.

"This is Conor? This is your brother?" I ask.

"Aye, it is?"

My voice softens when I ask, "He's dead," emotion clogging my throat.

"Aye, why?"

"That's ... that's Aidan's father." A tear drips down my cheek and off my jaw, cleaning a spot on the glass. "One night. That's all it was. Saw him at a bar in Scotland before I made my way to Ireland. We got drunk, and I woke up the next day and slid out of his bed because I didn't want it to be awkward."

"Aidan is my nephew? Are ye kidding me?" Skirt jumps off the bed and cheers. "Holy shite. I'm a bloody uncle. I'm an Uncle! My brother has a kid." The laughter stops a moment later when he falls to his knees. "My brother has a kid, and he will never know. You're sure? You are positive that he is Conor's child?"

"I'm positive. His eyes are the one thing I will never be able to forget. A frozen blue, like if the Caribbean Sea was ice. He was beautiful."

"He told me about you. I remember now. The girl from the bar. He had a picture of you two on his phone, but it was a bit blurry."

"The whiskey," Skirt and I say at the same time.

"I can't believe it." Skirt's hands lay on my neck and he presses his forehead against mine, his tears falling onto the glass too. "I was meant to find ye, Dawn. Ye were meant to be mine.

I have no doubt now that my brother sent ye to me. I have no fucking doubt because I don't think I would have found ye or Aidan without him."

"It doesn't bother you? That Aidan is your brother's?"

"Are ye kidding? Ye just made me the happiest man in the entire world. Aidan is my flesh, my blood, my brother's son." Skirt places his fist over his heart. "It's a damn miracle."

"I never thought I'd see him again. I had … I had no idea of his name or anything. I didn't know he had died." Emotions stuff my throat when I see Aidan's father staring back at me. "I tried looking for him, but—"

"He was the best fighter in Scotland, how did you not know?"

"I didn't know anything about that life then. I didn't meet Cohen until after."

"I've had five years to absorb his death; are ye okay?"

"Yeah, I'm fine. It's just really sad that I didn't get to know him more and that Aidan will never know his true father."

"I'll make sure he does," Skirt promises, placing his hand on top of the picture. "I'll make sure Aidan knows everything there is to know about Conor Blackwood."

It's hard to believe everything happens for a reason, especially when everything seems so bad, but then I have this moment with Skirt, learn about the father of my child, and have the comfort of having my son safe.

That is the reason.

And everything bad that's happened, led me right where I belong.

Property of Skirt.

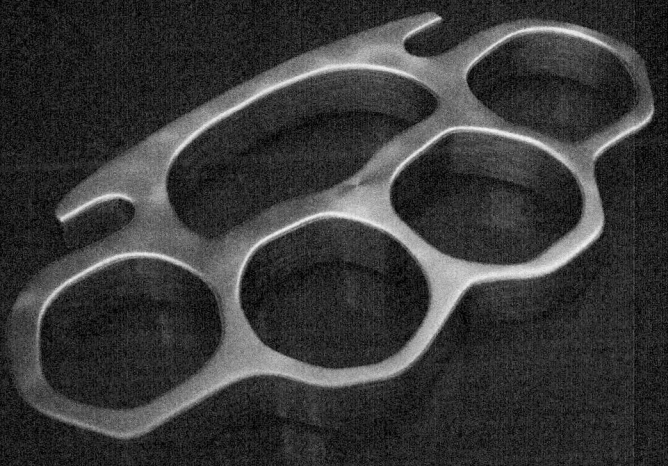

CHAPTER TWENTY-FOUR

Skirl

TODAY IS THE DAY.

Holy shite today is the day. I want to puke.

I have everything all set up. It's perfect. Nothing can go wrong. "Okay, are ye ready?" I hold my hand over Dawn's eyes as I guide her through the house.

I pass Knives who is at the kitchen table, taking a bandage off his arm that shows new ink, something he has never gotten before. I want to ask about it, but I have something much more important to do.

"What's going on?" Dawn asks, taking apprehensive steps since she can't see.

"Trust me." I nip her ear.

Opening the door to the fuck rooms has never been so thrilling for me. The hallway is dark, a low glowing yellow light to set the mood to fuck instead of a bright fluorescent one. The smell of cheap booze and cigarettes permeates the air, which is not romantic at all, but this isn't about romance.

It's about making fantasies come true.

Steering her through the doorway, I kick it shut and lay her on the bed, which has clean sheets on it. I'm not fucking my woman on a cum-stained bed without a barrier.

"Skirt?"

I tug my shirt off and wrap it around her head to blindfold her so she can't see a thing.

"What's going on?" she asks again.

"Ye'll see if ye hush that sexy mouth, Lips." I unbutton her pants and throw them over my shoulder, growling when her soft, silky legs come to view. I roam my hands down her legs and hook my fingers over her panties then tug them down her thighs.

A wet spot forms in the middle of her crotch, soaking the material. With a hungry rumble in my belly, I bring the damp material to my nose and inhale. "Ye smell so fucking sweet, Lips. I can't wait to taste this cunt."

She moans and buries her hands in my hair, arching her back as I run my tongue up her inner thigh. I bypass her juicy sheath and grab the hem of her shirt with my mouth, pulling it up to expose her slender ribcage. I pepper kisses along her belly, and my hands dive under her shirt, gripping her big tits. I moan when her nipples harden under my touch. Straddling her, I rip the shirt off her head, then unhook her bra from the back with a quick snap.

She's naked. Her creamy flesh is elegant and too pretty for the likes of this room, but what happens in this room isn't going to be pretty. It's going to be carnal.

The door opens again, and Bullseye slides inside. His eyes land on Dawn, and he adjusts his cock under his pants. I don't have the urge to claw his eyes out because I know I can trust him. He knows the rules, and Dawn is beautiful to look at. She has an hourglass shape with her round tits and thick thighs.

It's almost selfish of me not to share her, but I want to be selfish. Bullseye can watch, and that is all he'll ever be able to do.

Bullseye settles in the corner, strips off his shirt and pants, and his cock is already hard. He sits on the loveseat and slowly jerks himself. He looks at home. Maybe he has done this before?

I take off my kilt and toss it on the ground, then straddle her belly, my cock slapping against it. Pre-cum dribbles from the tunnel, pooling a small drop on her stomach. I tug the makeshift blindfold free, and her lusty eyes set on mine.

My hand drops between her legs, and I rub my fingers through her sweet petals, causing her to moan. "Tell me if ye don't want this, and we will stop," I inform her and with my free hand, I turn her head in the direction Bullseye is sitting, lazily touching himself to the sight of her.

She gasps, but not in horror; her eyes lock on Bullseye's, her sweet pussy drips onto my hand, and her clit becomes erect between her folds, needing an orgasm.

"There are rules, Lips. Do ye want to hear them?" I tell her, bending down and plucking a sweet nipple into my mouth.

"Please," she whimpers, rocking against my hand for friction.

"He can't touch ye; ye can't touch him. He will not ever fuck ye. This cunt is mine and only mine, but I know ye like hearing people fuck and like the idea of someone watching, so I want to see if ye want to entertain that thought. If not, I'll kick Bullseye out right now."

"He can't touch me?" she asks with relief.

"No, love. Just me. Only my touch." I slip two fingers inside her, and Dawn shatters under me, her orgasm pulling my fingers deeper.

"Oh, I think ye like being watched. Ye my dirty fucking woman, aren't ye?"

"Yes," she hisses, turning her head to look at Bullseye again.

The sound of skin slapping tells me he's fucking his fist in earnest now, and her walls flutter around my fingers.

"Skirt, please," she begs, clawing my back. Dawn reaches for my hips, but I pull away, wanting to tease her a bit more. "Skirt! Please, I need you inside me. Fuck me."

"Yeah, Skirt. Fuck her. Make her scream," Bullseye pipes in.

I slide my fingers free and stuff them into her mouth. "Taste yerself." I choke her with my fingers, fucking her mouth as I shove my cock to the hilt in one hard thrust.

She keens, the hum of her voice vibrating through my fingertips.

"Lap yerself up. That's it," I urge her as her tongue rolls around my fingers.

I flip her onto her stomach and squeeze her fat arse with my palms and fuck her long and hard. The bed slams against the wall, and the light hanging from the ceiling sways from side to side. She grips onto the edge of the bed and screams at the top of her lungs while I rail her tight channel. My cock is dripping with her slick, her walls still spasming from her last orgasm, and it won't be long before she's going over the edge again.

Bullseye stands and walks closer, then sits on the floor, still a safe distance away. Dawn lifts her head from the bed, and I grip her hair to yank her back so she can get a good look at what she does to him. "Look what ye do to him, Lips. Look how hard he is watching ye."

"You're gorgeous, Dawn. I love seeing your tits sway and ass jiggle as he fucks you. I can't believe you're letting me watch. It's a fucking treasure. You like what he's doing to you, Dawn? You like how Skirt fucks you real hard? What else do you want?"

She doesn't answer, and I tighten my fingers around her scalp. "Answer the man, Lips. It's rude if ye don't." I bring my hand up and spank that bubbled arse, leaving my handprint behind.

"I ... I ... I'm going to come."

"Ye aren't allowed to until ye answer him, Lips."

"Oh God," she cries, clawing the bed to try to get away from me because the pleasure is too much. "It's so much. It's so much. Oh my God!" she cries to the ceiling. "I want your finger in my ass, Skirt. I want you to fill me in every way."

"Fuck me, you have the perfect woman, Skirt," Bullseye moans when he pinches the tip of his cock.

"Don't I know it." I plunge my finger deep in her arse, and Dawn buries her face in the mattress as another orgasm shakes her core, that beautiful tightness milking me, begging for my seed to hit her womb.

Before I can think better of it, Dawn pulls away from me, gets on her knees, and sucks my cock into her mouth. I try to yank away, knowing she doesn't like giving head. It's a trigger for her, but she laps at me, her fears gone for some reason. Maybe having another person in the room helps with her fear? I'm not sure, but I'm thankful.

I've never felt her mouth before, and it is heaven.

"She's sucking your cock good Skirt, and she's touching herself. You like finger fucking herself, Dawn?"

She shakes her head as she looks up at me, mouth stretched wide as she bobs that pretty head, sending jolts of pleasure to the core of my shaft.

"Fucking hell, Dawn. Ye look good with ye lips wrapped around me. Fuck, ye keep going. I'm going to come down that throat."

It urges her to go faster, and Bullseye groans. I can't tell if it's a sad groan because the session is nearly over, or one of pleasure.

"Ye like being watched, Lips?"

She nods, gagging on my dick, a string of spit leaving her sinful mouth. The inferno of her mouth resurrects me and shines the fucking glorious light in the void of my soul, bringing it back to life.

"Fuck," I snarl and pull out of her, flip her onto her back, lift her legs onto my shoulder, and ride. My balls slap against her arse, and my hips jackhammer into her as hard as I possibly can. She's shouting my name in a new alto, nearly singing.

She makes me feel like a god, and if she thinks for one minute I'm taking her body above the damn clouds, she has another thing coming; I'm going to take her to the sinner's playground.

A sheen of sweat allows our bodies to slide together, and Dawn turns her head to look at Bullseye, who's watching us fuck like his favorite porno, and then her eyes land on me, and instead of crying my name, she whispers it.

The explosion inside her has me almost going cross-eyed. Her cunt is so wet, so tight, a vice gripping me to the point of pain. I have no choice but to fall over the edge with her and fill her up.

"Dawn, fucking hell, yes! Fucking take it, Lips. Take every drop," I pound into her as my seed leaves my sack, surging out of me at a supersonic speed. "Shite." I collapse just as Bullseye grunts.

I bury my head in the crook of Dawn's neck, but I turn to watch him come.

So fucking dirty.

"Holy hell," Bullseye's voice trembles from his orgasm. "We can do that whenever you fucking want. Every day. For the rest of my life."

Dawn covers her face and giggles. "Oh my God. I can't believe I just did that."

"Do ye want to do it again?" I ask.

"Fuck yes, I do. That was hot."

We all sit there a minute and catch our breaths. Her body is trembling, and she's still hysterically giggling because she feels so good. Her fantasies might be different than other people's, but I'm the man who's always going to make them come true.

Until my last fucking breath, until the last beat of my heart, Dawn will own me.

Shucks, I'm one lucky bastard.

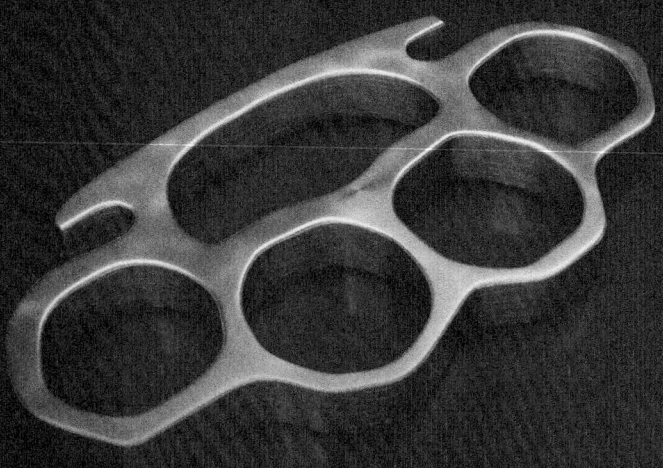

EPILOGUE

Skirl

Scotland. Six months later.

"**I**T'S GOING TO BE OKAY," DAWN SAYS AS WE WALK TOWARD my parents' house. I haven't seen them in almost six years, not since my brother's death. "It's beautiful here," she says, laying her hand on her pregnant belly.

Shucks, I'm going to be a father. Jesus. I'm terrified. I'm happy. I'm in love. Our relationship might have moved fast for others, but for me, I couldn't be happier that she's pregnant. I never took her with a condom, so I knew the consequence.

Part of me wanted her to get pregnant. I wanted to tie her to me in every single fucking way possible. I wanted to claim every single cell in her body that made her, her.

"Yeah, it's gorgeous." I'm not even looking at my

surroundings. I'm looking at the mailbox that says 'Blackwood' in big red letters and the cottage at the end of the dirt driveway. "I can't do this. My ma hates me, Dawn. She fucking hates me. I haven't talked to either of my parents in five years. We can go to a bed and breakfast in the city, and I'll treat ye to a nice day at the spa."

"You're going to do that anyway," she says, rubbing her lower back. She's been aching since she's carrying a damn watermelon in the front of her body. Blackwood babies are fucking big. I'm worried that she's going to get hurt during labor. She looks like she's about to pop, but she has three months left.

"I am." I kiss the side of her head, then look down at Aidan. "Ye ready to meet your grandparents?"

He doesn't even answer me. He runs down the driveway and jumps onto the porch, then rings the doorbell.

"I take that as a yes," I let out a nervous chuckle.

Dawn slips her hand in mine, and we walk down the driveway. I want to vomit when the door opens and my da steps out, smiling down at Aidan. He looks to see if an adult is close by when his eyes land on me.

"Hi, Da." I stop at the bottom of the porch steps, the salt in the air breezing over us unlike that day five years ago.

"Boyo," he says in disbelief. "Oh, son." My da breaks down in tears, and I get choked up when he slams into me, giving me a bear hug until I can't breathe.

And I fucking return it.

"I've missed ye. Oh, me boy. Let me look at ye." My da grabs my face and looks me up and down. "Ye look good. Ye look real good."

"Who is at the door, dear?" my ma comes to the door next, and I freeze. "Rohan?" Ma utters. "Rohan, is that ye?" She takes a step out of the house and holds a hand over her face. Mascara runs down her cheeks as she cries. "Yer back!" She runs down the steps and throws her arms around me, sobbing against my chest.

I'm shocked. I didn't think she ever wanted to see me again. With confusion, I wrap my arms around her small frame, and sigh in relief. I'm so glad to see them again.

"I'm so sorry, Rohan. I'm so sorry. I didn't mean what I said. I was so angry when your brother died. I had to go to therapy. I ... I was so sad, and I wasn't the mother you needed. I didn't know how to be. I love ye more than anything."

"Why didn't ye reach out then?"

"I was scared," she admits. "I thought ye hated me."

"No..." I shake my head, "I could never hate ye, Ma."

She pinches my cheeks until they hurt, but I relish it because she used to do that when I was a boy. "Yer so handsome. Just like yer brother." Ma and Da finally turn their attention to Dawn. "And who is this lovely lady and young man?"

"I'm Aidan." He holds out his hand for introduction.

"Oh, manners. How nice to meet you, Aidan."

"I'm Dawson, but everyone calls me Dawn."

"Dawn. That's beautiful," Ma says, then her eyes drop to Dawn's stomach, then to Aidan, and then to me.

She jumps as she stops breathing when realization hits her. "Yer children?"

I nod. "Well, Aidan is my nephew. Yer grandson. Seems Conor and Dawn knew each other before..." *he died.* "We had no idea until six months ago, when I pulled out Conor's picture."

Dawn blushes. "I know what it looks like." Because the night between her and Conor was a one-night stand.

Da and Ma fall into each other's embrace, both of them a sobbing mess at this point. "He has Conor's eyes."

"He does," I agree.

"Can I hug ye, Aidan?"

Aidan wraps his arms around Ma, and she sags, like a big fucking weight has been lifted off her shoulders. Her hand cups the back of Aidan's head, burying her face in the tiny nook of his neck.

"I can't believe it," she cries.

"Told you," Dawn nudges my shoulder.

"I owe ye, Lips."

"No, you've already given me everything, Skirt." She rubs her belly and looks at her son with his grandparents.

I've fought for love, and I've learned there's nothing more important to fight for. Everything means nothing if love isn't the center.

ALSO BY K.L. SAVAGE

PREQUEL - REAPER'S RISE
BOOK ONE - REAPER
BOOK TWO - BOOMER
BOOK THREE - TOOL
BOOK FOUR - POODLE
BOOK FIVE - SKIRT
BOOK SIX - PIRATE
BOOK SEVEN - DOC
BOOK EIGHT - TONGUE

OTHER BOOKS IN THE RUTHLESS KINGS SERIES
A RUTHLESS HALLOWEEN

RUTHLESS KINGS MC IS NOW ON AUDIBLE.

CLICK HERE TO JOIN RUTHLESS READERS AND GET
THE LATEST UPDATES BEFORE ANYONE ELSE. OR
VISIT AUTHORKLSAVAGE.COM OR STALK THEM AT
THE SITES BELOW.

FACEBOOK | INSTAGRAM |RUTHLESS READERS
AMAZON | TWITTER | BOOKBUB | GOODREADS |
PINTEREST | WEBSITE

FOR UPDATES FROM
K.L. SAVAGE TEXT:

KL SAVAGE

RUTHLESS ROMANCE THAT WILL *RIP* YOUR HEART OUT.

725-225-0825

Printed in Great Britain
by Amazon

33392406R00149